THE EXTRAORDINARY COLORS OF AUDEN DARE

THE EXTRAORDINARY COLORS OF AUDEN DARE

ZILLAH BETHELL

FEIWEL AND FRIENDS

NEW YORK

A FEIWEL AND FRIENDS BOOK
An imprint of Macmillan Publishing Group, LLC
175 Fifth Avenue, New York, NY 10010

THE EXTRAORDINARY COLORS OF AUDEN DARE. Copyright © 2018 by Zillah
Bethell. All rights reserved. Printed in the United States of America by LSC
Communications, Harrisonburg, Virginia.

Our books may be purchased in bulk for promotional, educational,
or business use. Please contact your local bookseller or the Macmillan
Corporate and Premium Sales Department at (800) 221-7945 ext. 5442 or by
e-mail at MacmillanSpecialMarkets@macmillan.com.

Library of Congress Cataloging-in-Publication Data is available.

ISBN 978-1-250-09404-9 (hardcover) / ISBN 978-1-250-09405-6 (ebook)

Book design by Rebecca Syracuse

Feiwel and Friends logo designed by Filomena Tuosto

First US edition, 2018

First published in Great Britain in 2017 by Piccadilly Press

1   3   5   7   9   10   8   6   4   2

mackids.com

To Simon

I asked the little boy who cannot see,

"And what is color like?"

"Why, green," said he,

"Is like the rustle when the wind blows through

The forest; running water, that is blue;

And red is like a trumpet sound; and pink

Is like the smell of roses; and I think

That purple must be like a thunderstorm;

And yellow is like something soft and warm;

And white is a pleasant stillness when you lie

And dream."

—*Anonymous*

PART ONE

GREEN

CHAPTER 1

A DIFFICULT WORD TO PRONOUNCE

Sometimes, after school, I stand and watch the traffic lights. I stand and wait for the red to turn to amber and then the amber to turn to green. Not that I understand what is meant by red, amber, or green. They are just words to me. Words to describe things, to tell one thing from another. To pick things apart. Only, that's something I just can't do. The top light is red, the middle one is amber, the bottom light is green. I know that much. Like a fact from history that means nothing nowadays. Like the names of Egyptian kings and queens, or the ancient tribes of Great Britain. But if somebody had gotten up early one morning and turned the lights upside down—switched them around—I never would have known. They all look exactly the same to me. They all look the same sort of gooey gray.

Green, blue, red, pink, purple, yellow.

I don't understand any of them. Not one.

I have a condition, you see. It's got a funny name—a long name—that I can barely pronounce or spell. It sounds impressive, I know. But having a condition with a long name that you can barely pronounce or spell isn't much of a comfort when you can't even tell which side in football you're on at school. (The number of times I've given the ball away to the opposing team . . . !)

Not that I notice my condition most of the time. I suppose everyone gets used to everything about themselves. I'm used to seeing everything look black and white and a washed-out gray. Everything.

I mean, it's not even like I was once okay. I've always had this condition. Right from my very first breath. It would be worse, I'm sure, if once upon a time I had been able to see color. Then I would know precisely what it was I had lost.

But the truth is I didn't lose anything.

I am how I've always been.

My name has always been Auden Dare.

I am eleven years old.

CHAPTER 2

THE BOT JOB

Over the years my mother developed lots of ways to avoid using color to describe things to me—she would try to use other means to single things out. She counts: "the second one along" sort of thing. She compares sizes: "the third smallest." She does both at the same time: "the fourth smallest in the fifth row." She even uses the alphabet to describe different shades of a color. (*A* is the very lightest and, theoretically, *Z* would be the darkest. However she only ever really gets up to a *D* or an *E*, as her feel for shades is a little too crude for an entire twenty-six letters.) When I was really young, she drew symbols to help me understand the colors of certain things. For green she would draw an apple. For blue she would draw two wavy lines. She would scribble them on stickers and go around putting the stickers on everything so that I got to understand which things were which color. I don't think she did it for my benefit, though. I mean, it didn't actually bother me to know if a particular sweater was red or yellow. But I think she did it so that I wouldn't struggle around other people and stand out too much from the crowd. She did it so that I wouldn't look too much of a freak.

However . . . having said all that . . . even though my mother had come up with some inventive ways of avoiding making reference to color, sometimes—just sometimes—it would slip her busy mind.

Like it did the day she bought the Bot Job.

"I've bought a car," she said, pulling her coat off and slamming the front door behind her.

"You've bought a car?" I replied. "Why?"

She hooked the coat over the hanger on the back of the door and ignored my question.

"Don't you want to know what sort of car it is?"

I put the pencil down on the pad of paper. I'd barely started the sketch of Sandwich curled up and purring on her cushion, her eyes squashed shut, contentedly dreaming of baby birds and tiny mice. All I'd drawn so far were her ears.

"Okay, then. What sort of a car is it?"

"Not sure. I don't know much about cars. All I know is it's a big one."

I sighed. "A big one?"

Mum nodded. "Have a look for yourself. I've parked it out front."

"How much did you pay for it?" I pulled the curtains aside and peered down to the road, ten flights down. A number of cars—all of them old—were lined up on the sides of the road, each of them waiting for their owners to return to spark them back to life.

"How much? Only a quarter of a million pounds."

"A quarter of a million?" I couldn't believe it. You couldn't get any car for a quarter of million nowadays. It must've been a real bot job. Perhaps it only had three wheels or something. Perhaps the passengers had to hold their legs up because of the holes in the floor. "That's cheap." I turned back to look at my mother, who was now kneeling in front of the chest of drawers and pulling out lots of pieces of paper. "I bet it doesn't even go," I added, hardly able to hide my suspicions. "If that's all it cost."

Mum did her scowl face at me. "Of course it goes. Drives very well. It got me back here all the way from Romford, didn't it?" She took the large pile of paper and shoved it roughly into a plastic bag, before opening up another drawer and doing exactly the same. "Honestly, Auden. You should have more faith."

I looked back down at the segmented snake of cars below. "Which one is it?"

And that was when she did it.

"The green one. The long green one."

Green!

"Mum!"

"Oh." She shoved the large bag aside, stood up, and came

over to the window. "Sorry, Auden. I didn't mean to do it." She snapped the elastic band she kept around her wrist for such occasions against her thin skin. A tiny punishment for a tiny crime. "You know what I'm like. Too much on my mind." She looked out the window and stabbed her finger downward. "That one there. This side. One, two, three along."

I could see it. It had a long bonnet and a long roof and looked as if some giant creature had picked it up at both ends and stretched it.

"It *is* big."

We stood there in silence for a while, watching the people down below coming and going like dust on the breeze. Behind us on the sofa, Sandwich gave a short squeak, and clawed the corner of her little fluff-covered cushion. She scratched it hard, pulling out threads.

"I don't understand why you've bought a car," I said. "We don't need one."

"You know why," she answered, not even bothering to turn to look at me. "We talked about this last week."

It was true. We had talked about it last week. Or should I say *she* talked about it while *I* tried my best not to listen.

"Yeah, but what about Dad?"

"What about him?"

"Well, when he comes back home, he's not going to know where we are."

She reached along the windowsill and tried her best

to give my hand a gentle squeeze. "It'll be all right. I'll write him a letter."

A letter? What good was writing a letter?

"But he's fighting. You can't just send him a letter. He won't get it. It'll just get lost or something. It'll get trampled into the mud in Paris or Rome or wherever he is. Then, when the war's over and he comes back here, he won't find us."

She leaned in close, trying to hug me and kiss me on the head. But I wasn't having any of it. I *am* eleven years old, after all.

"Silly," she said. "He'll know where we are. Don't worry."

Out the window a Scoot drone—one of the ones with reflectors for eyes and extended antennae—hovered its way along the street, its tiny camera head swinging left to right to left to right to left as it went. The sound of the buzzing wings dropped a semitone as it passed by, watching out for trouble on the streets below. Eventually, it disappeared from view.

"So . . ." It was no good fighting it. It was all going to go ahead anyway, regardless of what I said or thought. She obviously thought it was for the best. "When do we go?"

"I've given two days' notice on this place. I've notified the Water Allocation Board and the War Authority, so we'll have to pack up and be gone by Thursday."

It wasn't like there was a great deal to pack up anyway. We didn't own much stuff. A load of clothes; a stick or two of furniture; a handful of books; some documents and papers; Sandwich. That was about it. Two days was more than enough in which to pack all that away. We could probably do it three times over in that amount of time.

"When we get there," Mum added quickly, keen to stop me from changing my mind again, "we'll find a nice school for you. A good school this time. Somewhere you can make friends. Yes?"

I wandered over to where Sandwich was yawning and stroked her until she began to dribble.

....

It may well have been a bot job (the way the doors rattled every time you opened them seemed to suggest that it had never been exposed to a single human being during its construction, only robots) but the car was massive. Absolutely massive. It had more than enough room to fit all of our belongings, and by the time we had finished filling it, there was still space for a few more suitcases and crates. I propped Sandwich, who was in her wicker basket, on top of a box of books just behind my seat and, after we had said our goodbyes to the empty flat and the neighbors who couldn't have cared less about us anyway, we strapped ourselves into the car and headed off.

At the garage, Mum filled the Bot Job full of the cheap petrol—price at an all-time low, apparently—and then, reluctantly, added some of the much, *much* more expensive water to the water reservoir.

"It's a long trip, I'm afraid," she said, climbing back into the driver's seat. "Might take us a few hours. Make yourself comfortable."

The car rumbled unconvincingly along beneath us as my mother steered and braked and crunched gears in spectacular fashion, speeding up through the narrow, twisting streets of East London. There seemed to be very little traffic on the road. A couple of other cars. A few food lorries. Some war effort supply vans. A heavily protected water tanker. One or two refugees with heavy packs on their backs or pushing handcarts full of possessions. That was about it.

As we drove on—the Bot Job giving out the occasional backfiring bang—the buildings became smaller and fewer, and the roads longer and straighter. Eventually, the city faded into the countryside and the trees began to cluster together in dry-looking patches. There weren't many trees, not since the rains slowed and water got scarce. Field after field of ornamental cacti lined the roads while small towns and villages swept by.

"Let's play I Spy!" Mum suddenly sounded weirdly enthusiastic. If only Dad were here, I thought, so they could jabber on together while I sat in the back listening to music.

"I'm not four years old!"

"Go on. You go first."

I sighed. "Erm . . . I spy with my little eye something beginning with . . . er . . . R."

"Road!" she shouted triumphantly.

"You got it."

"That was easy. Do another one."

"Okay, then. I spy with my little eye something beginning with . . . *T*."

"Tree?"

"No."

"Truck?"

"No. No trucks here anyway."

"Er . . ." Her eyes scanned around, trying to find something. "Telegraph pole?"

"Nope."

"I give up. What is it?"

"Tarmac."

"Tarmac?"

"Yep."

"So you've had 'road' and you've had 'tarmac.' Hmm. I think I see a pattern emerging."

"It's pretty much all I've seen for the last two hours."

"Well, not to worry." Mum smiled. "We're nearly there."

Having consulted my wrist computer, called a QWERTY, ten minutes earlier, I knew this already. Cambridge was five miles away and at the speed we were traveling (fifty miles an hour, which, for my mother, is speedy, let me tell you) we would be there in six minutes. I also knew that the chance of precipitation was nil (as always), though the breeze was fair to moderate, that Cambridge was the epicenter of good taste and vending machines and that the vintage cinema on Collier Road was screening a black-and-white movie for the Old and Moldies, even distributing free popcorn to those who still possessed a set of their own teeth.

I eyed my mother sideways wondering whether to try the joke out on her but decided against it. She looked tired and strained and her hands were gripping the steering wheel like she was going a heck of a lot faster than fifty miles an hour.

"Yippidee-do-dey!" I said, trying to reach behind my seat to stroke Sandwich through the bars of her basket.

CHAPTER 3
UNICORN COTTAGE

You might imagine that a house called Unicorn Cottage would be a magical, enchanted place possibly made out of sweets, like in that story *Hansel and Gretel*. You know the one. The one with the two irritating kids who nearly get eaten by a witch and only escape due to her poor eyesight and a thin stick. Yeah, really believable! For a start, a stick doesn't even feel like someone's finger. It's all cold and stiff. A finger, on the other hand (Ha! On the other hand! Geddit?), is warm and a bit squashier. Also, why would anyone build a house out of sweets? You couldn't possibly live in a house made of sweets. In the summer it would get all sticky and bits of it would probably start to melt. After a while, it would also start to rot. What a load of ridiculous, childish rubbish. I'm glad I'm not such a kid anymore.

Anyway. As I was saying. You might imagine that a place called Unicorn Cottage would be hidden away deep in the wood, surrounded by trees that whispered to each other, next to a rickety wishing well with a little roof and a shiny bucket dangling down. With uneven walls that seemed to sway in and out, and a roof made of wiry thatch. Perhaps a small, fenced-off rose garden that was overlooked by shuttered windows and a creaky wooden door with a small heart cut out of its center.

That's what you might imagine.

Instead, the Unicorn Cottage that my mother parked the Bot Job next to looked as though it might once have been a public lavatory. Or an electricity substation. Something dull and practical with no charm or beauty whatsoever. As if the construction crew who built it couldn't be bothered to come back to finish it off.

It sat on a lane on the very edge of the town, backing onto a low, flat field that stretched into the distance. There were no houses on either side of it—not for a good few hundred meters, anyhow—and only a small crop of tall trees across the lane in front of it.

If the house were a person, I realized, it would have been a very sad and lonely one. There was even a trail of damp underneath one of the two wide windows, which made it look as if it had recently been crying.

Actually, to call it a house was wrong. It was one of those little bungalow thingies that had been converted so it had an upstairs. A "dormer bungalow," I think they're called.

Weird things. *A contradiction in terms*—that's how my mother puts it. *A contradiction in terms*. A bungalow, by its very definition, is a single-story construction. So to have an "upstairs" in a bungalow surely doesn't make it a bungalow anymore. Surely it becomes a house—yes? No? Yes? Don't worry about it. I'm always going off on a tangent like that. Sorry. You'll get used to it.

Anyway, Mum parked the car on the gravelly driveway at the side of the house and we both got out.

"Why did Uncle Jonah call it Unicorn Cottage?" I asked, shifting my seat forward so I could pull Sandwich out more easily.

Mum gave her shoulders an awkward shrug and fished about for the keys. "I don't know."

"I think . . ." I said, looking upward and shading my eyes from the sun. "I think it must have been because the chimney looks like a horn. Right? It looks a bit like a horn coming out from a unicorn's head."

She looked up, too, and squinted, trying to focus. "Not really."

I smiled. "No. It doesn't really, does it?"

"No." She gave the keys a shake and they tinkled against each other. "Shall we take a look at our new home, Auden?"

....

It was in a terrible state.

After Mum had managed to shove the front door open, pushing the weeks and months of old letters and political flyers out of the way, the first thing you noticed was the smell. The cold, stale smell of damp. Like somebody had given a particularly fat and pungent fungus a kick, sending spores flying all over the place.

It was obvious from that smell that no one had lived here in months.

The second thing you noticed was the mess.

All across the hallway were strewn papers and folders. Books bent back hard on their spines, with buckled pages and half-ripped corners. A side table had been toppled, the contents of a small drawer spilling out and trailing like a tongue toward the floor.

"Oh dear." Mum treaded carefully across the debris, the occasional worrying scrunch under her feet, and pushed open a door into a different room. I followed.

The curtains were still drawn in what, I assumed, was the sitting room. What little light there was struggled to reveal anything. Now, one of the few good things about my condition—my inability to see color—is that I can actually see pretty well in the dark. Everything is much clearer to me than to other people, so they reckon. The outlines of shapes are more defined. The detail more obvious. Call it a lucky side effect, if you like. So, to me, the mess in the sitting room was easy to see. However, my mother was finding it difficult, so I grabbed the nearest curtain and pulled it hard.

If there were a carpet, you would never have known.

The floor had more papers and folders and bits and bobs thrown all over it. An armchair had been rolled onto its side, and the cushions on a nearby sofa were all pulled out of place. On a table near another door sat a number of dirty plates and bowls, a small cloud of flies buzzing over them. A picture of a ship on the wall was hung at a very dodgy angle and it looked as though nothing had been dusted for a long, long time.

"There's been a robbery," I said. "Somebody's broken in and turned the place over."

Mum smiled and shook her head. "No. I doubt it."

"What do you mean?"

"Well, your uncle Jonah was a brilliant man. Absolutely brilliant. The cleverest man I ever knew. He could come up with the most incredible ideas, and find their solutions, like that." She clicked her fingers in front of my face. "He was a genius. No question." She looked about at the scruffy sitting room. "However, one of the things he always had difficulty with was taking good care of himself and his belongings. Sometimes, when he was in the middle of a brilliant idea, he would forget to eat—he ended up in hospital once due to not eating. Or he would neglect his appearance—his hair and beard would grow far too long and his clothes would start to look dirty. The other thing he didn't do very well was to clean up after himself. Remember, I grew up with him, and even as a child he never tidied his room. In fact"—she gave a wink—"he reminds me an awful lot of you."

"Ugh!" I moaned. "I couldn't live in a place like this. Just look at it."

"Well, this is your home now, Auden," she said, scraping a finger along a very dust-lined shelf and inspecting it. "So you need to get used to it. Come on. Let's grab some sacks and start filling them."

CHAPTER 4

TRINITY

You see, the house had once belonged to my uncle Jonah. Jonah Bloom. *Doctor* Jonah Bloom. A brilliant physicist and mathematician at the University of Cambridge. *Jonah Bloom, MA (Oxon), PhD (Cantab)*, to use his full and correct academic name. My mother's brother. He had spent years working in the areas of artificial intelligence and synchronicity. Apparently. Not that I had any sort of clue as to what that meant. We haven't done much of that in school recently!

He was only thirty-eight when he was discovered dead in a field close to Unicorn Cottage. Just six years older than my mother.

Heart attack, they said.

Stress from overwork, they said.

Unable to cope, they said.

When he died, he left all of his worldly possessions to his only living relative: Christabel Dare (née Bloom). Wife of Leo Dare. Mother of Auden.

My mum.

All his worldly possessions. And that included Unicorn Cottage.

....

The room that was to become my bedroom overlooked the garden and the lifeless beech tree. A large metal bed took up most of the space, and I think I'd once slept in it when we visited Uncle Jonah a few years before. Before the war started. Before my dad went off to fight.

I tried to make the room mine. I hung all my clothes in the flimsy wardrobe. I put some of my sketches on the wall— even the really bad one of my dad chowing down on ice cream. I kept my pencils and my pads on the tiny desk squished up next to the door. I put Sandwich's bed on the floor alongside my own.

Sandwich had made herself at home as soon as she had arrived. She skulked out first thing in the morning, popping back for food and the occasional tickle and sleep. In the evening, she would skulk back out again before bringing something dead into the kitchen and dropping it like a gift on the floor for us. Sometimes, though, it wasn't dead. If it was a mouse, it would skitter off under the tables and dressers until Mum would manage to drop a metal colander over it, slide a large piece of cardboard underneath—petrified squeaks as she did so (from the mouse, not my mother)—and carry the poor thing out to the bottom of the garden, freeing it near the ramshackle collection of sheds that Uncle Jonah had acquired and filled full of utter junk.

When not trying to catch mice, Mum spent those first few days busying herself, making the place nice and arranging our water rationing. She went off into the town and filled the cupboards with food from the shops and markets.

One day, I went with her. We both got into the Bot Job and, after the fourth or fifth attempt, the engine started and we trundled on our way. We drove up the long road to the roundabout with the big hospital and then farther on into town. The houses were large and long with big wrought-iron gates and everything looked clean and neat.

Eventually, we got to the shopping area and Mum parked the car, which seemed to just shudder itself to death when she turned off the ignition.

Most of the shops were open. Only a handful looked closed with big boarded-up windows and To RENT signs sticking out at right angles to the walls. Which surprised me, as most of the shops in Forest Gate had long been abandoned. In Forest Gate, you had to walk or catch the bus all the way in to Stratford to get to any real places to buy stuff. There was nothing in Forest Gate. Not even a sweetshop.

Here, people—mostly women and old men, of course— were working their way along the shopping precinct, nipping in and out of the hardware shops and paper shops and clothing stores, stumping about with their carrier bags.

We slipped into one of the electrical shops and Mum

bought a new toaster, which was on sale. Fifty percent off. Only fifteen thousand pounds. A bargain. She pushed it down into the bottom of her little hemp sack and carried on.

At the end of the pedestrianized area we turned the corner toward the food markets. And the world seemed to change.

The buildings suddenly seemed to leap back in time.

The pedestrianized area had been lined on each side by incredibly shiny and modern-looking buildings. Brand-spanking-new (or newish) and sterile and dull.

But these buildings . . .

Huge and impressive, with wide arched doors and slim-cut windows. Spires and battlements and straight-out-of-the-ground columns. Flat, even lawns lay stretched in front of the buildings, some of which looked like churches, some of which looked like castles. Even the roads had changed from spacious, level tarmac to narrow cobblestones.

"What are these?" I asked my mother, my head swiveling from one side of the road to the other as we walked.

"Colleges. The Cambridge Colleges. Part of the university."

Trapped in between the walls of the old buildings, however—sitting in the center of the old road—was a massive slice of modern life. The rectangular, shiny vending machine—perhaps a quarter of a mile long—looked completely out of place here. Row upon row and column upon column of metallic drawers, each of them with a small scrolling screen on the front revealing what was inside and the price.

King Edward Potatoes, it flashed on some of the drawers. *£5000 a bag.*

Carrots . . . fresh today . . . £1000.

Beef steak . . . £80000.

Naturally, very few people were buying any of the meat—hardly anyone could afford it, after all. So the chilled drawers of beef and chicken and lamb and pork mostly remained untouched.

The shoppers' chattering voices all blurred into one another and bounced off the stone walls in this strangely cramped street, while a couple of the squat, rather funny-looking Dodo drones were busy cleaning and refilling the empty drawers from a supply trolley, their short, shuffling feet making them waddle from side to side.

"The university? Where Uncle Jonah worked?" I asked eventually.

She nodded. "Yes. He was a fellow of Trinity College."

"A fellow?"

Mum shrugged. "I don't really know what it means," she said, and fed a thick handful of notes into the slot next to one of the drawers. The door lowered, there was a happy sort of bleep, and a small paper bag of potatoes was gently pushed out into her hands. "But I think it means he was very high up. Very clever." She took the potatoes and shoved them into the hemp sack alongside the toaster.

"Where's Trinity College?" I asked. "Which one's Trinity?"

"I don't know."

"Can we go and find it?"

"What? Now?"

"Why not?"

Mum sighed. "But there are things at the house that I need to do, Auden. Things that can't wait."

I put on one of my *puleeeeease* faces—she can never resist one of my *puleeeeease* faces—and she shook her head, giving herself up to the idea.

She asked one of the other shoppers and he pointed us in the right direction. We made our way along the street and turned off down an even narrower and much quieter cobblestone road.

A couple of signposts later and we were standing outside the main entrance to Trinity College. Set back slightly from the main lane, it was one of the ones that looked like a castle with towers either side of the main door, each with funny stunted turrets.

To the right of the main portcullis-style door was a smaller entrance, and we watched as two young men—clearly not conscripted—both dressed like that old comic book hero Batman with capes and funny hats, slipped in through this second door.

"Shall we have a look?" I asked.

"I don't think we're allowed, are we?"

"We could try. See what happens."

"Well . . ."

"Come on."

We both walked in through the small door, Mum a few steps behind me.

The room we entered felt a little bit like a tunnel. To the rear of us was the door through which we had just come, and ahead of us was a larger, open door leading out onto a green square. But the room itself was dark.

Along one of the walls I could make out row upon row of boxes, each of them with tiny names written on them.

"What is it?" Mum couldn't see as clearly as I could see in this half-light.

"Boxes. Pigeonholes. For mail."

The boxes were in alphabetical order and in some of them, envelopes and sheets of paper curved or slumped to one side.

I went in closer and ran my fingers over the names. When I got to Jonah Bloom, I froze. The pigeonhole was empty, that was to be expected. But the fact that the university authorities hadn't removed his name, despite the fact that it had been a good six or seven months since Uncle Jonah had died, gave me a chill. Perhaps it was just because if they removed his name then—because it was all alphabetical—they would have to move everybody else (with a surname that came after Bloom), too. Shift them all along one place. Perhaps they just didn't want to have to bother with all that.

Mum came alongside me, saw the name and ran her fingers over the lettering.

"You all right, Mum?" I asked.

"Yes," she said unconvincingly. "I'm okay."

We walked out through the other door into the brightness of the morning once again. Some of the young students flapping about in their weird costumes gave us a quick glance but otherwise nobody paid us any attention. The square into which we stepped was unlike anything I'd ever seen before. Surrounded on all four sides by lots of different tall windowed walls, it felt a little like a really old prison—though there were loads of doors leading onto other places. The grass was neatly trimmed but dull, and a weird domed fountain thing sat oddly off-center, looking like it needed a good shove to put it into its correct position—like an accident nobody ever repaired.

Mum and I stared up at all the windows, neither of us saying—but both of us wondering—which one belonged to Uncle Jonah. Our feet tapped lightly on the flagstones as we worked our way across the quad.

In the far corner, we found ourselves drifting through another small door into a passageway with cold stone steps—like those from a dungeon—leading upward.

"Shall we go up?" I asked, pointing up the stairs.

"No," Mum answered quickly. "No. Let's not. I don't think I want to get farther into this place. It's cold. Let's get out of here. Knowing he used to work here . . . I don't think I like it."

"Okay, Mum."

Instead of taking the stairs we found another door coming out onto a small pebbly path to the side of the college.

We followed the path around a corner until the skyline opened up a bit and the remnants of a river flickered in the sun.

"Sorry. It was silly of me to make you go into the college. I just thought that . . . I thought that perhaps that was one of the reasons for moving to Cambridge in the first place. To . . . sort of . . . find him."

Mum tried that squeezing-the-shoulder thing with me again, and this time I thought I'd better allow her to have it.

"There're a load of reasons for moving here, Auden. Loads. That might be one of them, I suppose. But it's not one of the main ones." She smiled. "We were paying a lot of rent in London. With Dad away, we were really starting to struggle. And then poor Jonah passed away, leaving us with a tiny bit of money and his house. A house we could live in free of rent. And what with the situation in London—I just thought we could live a better life here. Start again. Wipe the window clean and start from the beginning."

"Yeah." I nodded, not saying anything else.

CHAPTER 5
SNOWFLAKE 843A

Uncle Jonah's death had come as a surprise to everyone—particularly Mum. She took it hard.

Now, I suppose that's the thing with having older brothers or sisters—they start off bigger and braver than you, so you imagine they'll *always* be bigger and braver than you. You imagine them going on and on and that they'll be there forever. (Not that I've any experience of that myself. Being an only child means I've missed out on that particular perspective of existence—yet another thing to add to the list!)

Of course, older brothers and sisters *don't* go on forever, and they aren't *always* bigger and braver than you. Only, most people have an entire lifetime to come to realize that. But Mum had to discover it a little too early.

What with Dad being away and the whole war thing going on, I suppose it was inevitable that, as soon as the keys to Unicorn Cottage had been handed over by the solicitor, Mum was going to want to try to get closer to her late brother. There was nothing really holding either of us in London anymore, so why not? Why not move into Uncle Jonah's old house? The whole "moving" thing was, in a way, a sort of therapy for her. Perhaps, over time, when this stupid war had run itself into the earth and Dad had returned, she would come to terms with her own brother's death, and life would just move on as it should.

But for now . . .

For now, she was surrounding herself with Uncle Jonah's things, seeing sights that Uncle Jonah would see every day. It was a sort of grieving process, I guess.

Of course, she wasn't the only one who was sad about Jonah Bloom's death. I'd lost an uncle—a bonkers, fluttering genius of an uncle who would send me pictures of the phases of the moon and old, unsolvable cryptic crosswords and yellowing books on European amphibians. A man who once told me that everything in life goes around in a circle—the planets, the universe, the days, evolution, molecules, blood . . . even water. All of it on a long-winded journey back to where it all began. I've no idea what he meant, but it sounded impressive. Most things he said sounded impressive.

Once, he had visited us in London and taken me out for a walk. We made our way to where the old canal had once flowed—me with my coat pulled tight across my shoulders, him with his wild, flailing arms pointing and drawing figures in the sky. Always talking. Always explaining.

Dilapidated houseboats, sucked down by the mud, lolled unevenly down in the wide groove that had once been filled to the top with water.

Uncle Jonah gesticulated all about.

"Tell me, Auden. . . . Tell me, what do you see?"

I twisted this way and that. "Er . . . some buildings. An old bin. A couple of smashed-up boats. A bit of rope. A man over there with a limp."

Jonah smiled.

"Why?" I asked. "What do *you* see?"

"Well"—he straightened himself up and looked around—"obviously I see everything that you see—you missed that half-ripped-up bench over there, by the way." He pointed and I nodded. "But the thing you must always remember is that what you see—whatever images pass themselves across the retinas of your eyes—is not what will *always* be."

"Eh?" He sometimes did that. Talked like what he was saying was obvious even though it wasn't.

"What I mean is, that image," he said, sweeping his arm out toward the canal, "is not the end of the story. It is not fixed. It is not how it will be for the rest of time. For example, those 'smashed-up boats,' as you put it, may one day soon be stripped apart and the wood reclaimed for another purpose. Something useful. They may be rebuilt, or even disintegrate, rotting into the mud. We simply can't assume that the broken boats are broken boats and that is that. Broken boats forever. Everything evolves in some way or another—either with or without our help. The old bin may be put right and serve its purpose once more. The limping man may simply have a blister on his foot and recover in a day or two. On the other hand, it may be the onset of bone cancer, and he will die soon."

"Nice," I groaned. "Cheery."

Jonah ignored me. "In fact, who knows, the whole canal may one day be filled with water again. You see, things evolve—they turn themselves completely around and upside down—and all you can really say about anything is that that is how it is *right now*. In a year or two's time . . . in a minute or two's time, even . . . who knows?"

I watched the man on the opposite bank hobbling up the steps and hoped for his sake it was just that his boots didn't fit him properly, or that one of his socks had a big hole in it.

"What about color?" I asked after the man had stumbled away completely. "Color is fixed. Red is always red and blue is always blue and I can never see either of them. What about color?"

"But color, itself, is unimportant." Uncle Jonah seemed to wrinkle up his forehead to squeeze some extra thoughts out of his brain. "Color is just a label. A way of comparing things." I quickly thought back to the way my mother always tried to skirt around the concept of color. "Admittedly it is true that color *does* occur in nature . . . but the color itself is often unimportant. It is what the color *represents* that is important."

I didn't have a clue what he was talking about.

We stood there in silence for a while, listening to the buzz of the city above us.

"Uncle Jonah?" I eventually asked. "You're a scientist. Do you think you might be able to invent something that could help me to see color?"

He stared into the distance like the other side of the canal was about a mile away. Then he smiled. "Maybe, Auden. One day. When my current work is complete, I shall give it some thought."

....

When the solicitor brought the keys over to our flat in Forest Gate, he brought a few other things, too. Most of them were boring legal things—the deeds to Unicorn Cottage; Uncle Jonah's bank details; his Water Allocation Board usage record. Stuff like that.

But there was also a little cardboard box.

With my name on it.

"Your uncle left this. For you," the small, sweating solicitor had whined as he handed it over to me. I gave him fifteen years, tops. If you're a sweater, you're a goner—on the way to being extinct. Losing all that fluid puts too much of a strain on the kidneys, you see.

Inside the box was a rock. Well, half a rock. It was egg-shaped—or had been egg-shaped once upon a time, before whatever had caused it to break in half had occurred—and was smooth along its curved surface, but all jaggedy and rough in the middle. I picked it out and held it up to the light. It wasn't particularly beautiful or exciting and I twisted it around to see if there were any secret diamonds hiding inside it.

"There's a letter, too." The solicitor held the envelope out to me before wiping his brow with his handkerchief.

I took it off him and ripped it open. Unfolding the paper I could see line after line of Uncle Jonah's spidery hand-writing, slightly curling down as it made its way across the page from left to right.

I read what it said to myself.

Auden, it said. *If you are reading this then I suppose I am no longer alive. Which is a bit of a shame as I rather enjoyed our friendly chats and walks whenever you came to visit me in Cambridge, or I you in London. Hopefully you got a degree of enjoyment out of them, too. Perhaps a little knowledge, even?*

Anyway, I have left all of my possessions to your mother—I'm sure you know this by now—but there is a small something that I have deliberately kept aside for you.

In the box that accompanies this letter is what appears to be half a small rock. A funny thing to be left by your uncle, you may think. Only, this rock is a rather special rock. In fact, it is not a rock at all. It is a meteorite. Its official name is Snowflake 843A, after having fallen just outside of the small town of Snowflake (yes, there is such a place) in Arizona in 1957. An appropriate name, I'm sure you will agree.

Imagine. For millions of years this ball of chrondrite was hurtling around the deepest parts of space, minding its own business, before eventually straying into our tiny, insignificant little universe and finding itself pulled into the Earth's atmosphere where it finally slammed into the soft sands of Arizona, coming to rest, and splitting in two.

Now, given the practically immeasurable, infinite nature of space, the chances of any meteor getting close enough to crash into this speck of a planet is undoubtedly somewhere in the region of a trillion to the power of a trillion to one, I am certain. The probability of it coming into contact with us is—essentially—negligible.

So do not be put off by the fact that it looks like any other lump of stone or rock that you can find on any hillside or in any quarry or even in the garden at the rear of Unicorn Cottage.

What it appears to be is irrelevant.

What it is is something of a miracle.

I picked up the chunk of meteorite and turned it around in my hand.

By the way, I continued reading, its sister—Snowflake 843B—I have left to someone I know at Trinity College—my dear friend Six Six. Six Six is one of the brightest, cleverest, kindest people I've ever met in my life and, if you should ever find yourself needing to . . . I don't know, say, find out about space, stars, constellations, etc., then do pay a visit to Six Six.

Six Six? I thought. What sort of a name is Six Six?

Anyway, Auden . . . look after your mother and remember that your condition may sometimes actually be a strength and not a weakness.

Dig deep, my boy. Dig deep.

Always remember to dig deep.

Yours,

Jonah

Nowadays Snowflake 843A resides in the right-hand pocket of my jacket, so that whenever I am outside and I find my condition getting me down, I can reach inside and run my fingers over it, scratching the tips across the sharp, jagged ridges in the middle, or even give it a little squeeze to try to remind myself of Uncle Jonah's words.

Sometimes it helps, I find.

But sometimes, I'm afraid, it doesn't.

⋯⋯⋯⋯

A few weeks after moving in, I found myself standing in the tiny attic at Unicorn Cottage. Uncle Jonah had put a sort of retractable ladder thing into the hatch and, after lowering it, you could easily climb up into the damp-smelling loft.

It was dark up there, but my eyes could cope easily with such dinginess. Nevertheless I used the torch function on my QWERTY so that I could see as far as I could into the farthest corners and crannies.

Spiderwebs filled the spaces between the buckled rafters, and tiny specks of dust floated aimlessly in the beam of the torch. I waved them away with my hand and looked around.

A number of packing boxes—big wooden crates without lids—were dumped randomly across the uneven floor. I peered into one only to find a ton of old clothes neatly folded into ten or twelve seagrass bags. I pulled something out of one bag and held it up. It was probably the busiest and most horrible waistcoat I'd ever seen in my life. I dropped it back into the crate before fishing out a long tie with a zigzaggy pattern that seemed even more nasty and headache-inducing than the waistcoat, and for once I was actually quite glad that I couldn't see color. Uncle Jonah might well have been a genius, but he had no taste in clothing.

I looked into another of the packing cases. It was filled with books. Dull, pictureless scientific books, mostly. The damp had somehow managed to ease its way inside, and the pages of most of them looked curled and soggy and almost unreadable.

The other crates were just as dull. Just piles and piles of junk that Uncle Jonah probably intended to get rid of at some point, but in the end never got around to. It was like a sort-of waiting room for garbage.

I turned to go back down the ladder but, as I did so, something caught my eye and I stopped. In a small stony alcove—probably nothing more than an imperfection in the brickwork—sat a long manila envelope. I came around one of the packing cases and picked it up, blowing thick lumps of dust from its glossy surface. It had not been sealed up, so I lifted its end and let the contents slide out into my other hand.

Photographs.

Lots of photographs.

Mostly pictures of a young family. A mother, a father, a son, and a younger sister. There were photos taken in a wide, tree-filled garden. There were photos of the family washing an old-fashioned-looking car—yes, actually using water to wash a car! A dog . . . no, a *number* of different dogs jumping up and licking the faces of the boy and the girl. A picture of the boy standing proudly next to what looked to me like a homemade rocket. A picture of the girl standing on a chair in a kitchen, making cookies with the mother. A picture of both children leaping around in the pouring rain.

Photographs. Dozens and dozens of them.

I recognized them all straightaway, of course. The girl was my mother. The boy, Uncle Jonah. The mother and the father, my long-dead grandparents.

I leveled the photos in my hand and was about to just throw the envelope down onto the floor when I realized there was something else inside. Something a bit heavier than some photos. I gave the envelope a quick shake and a short, fat lump of metal landed on top of the pictures.

It was a key.

Looped around it with short lengths of string were two labels. The first—a newish-looking label—had the words OFFICE SPARE scrawled in the unmistakably bulbous capitals that Uncle Jonah liked to use when he thought something was important. The second—smaller and much older than the other—had neat, tiny handwriting that certainly didn't belong to Jonah Bloom. PROPERTY OF TRINITY COLLEGE, CAMBRIDGE, it said, like it was ever so slightly ashamed of the fact.

I slipped the key into my pocket and took the photographs downstairs, where Mum proceeded to spend the next two hours laughing and crying over the images in about equal amounts.

·············

I didn't tell my mum about the key. You see, I don't think I really wanted her to know. The fact that it was me who found it hidden away in the attic made it—sort of—my property in a way. I gave her the photos—they belonged to her. But the key was mine.

Anyway, I wanted to do some investigating of my own. You see, I was starting to have my own doubts about Uncle Jonah's death.

He was very young to just die. Heart attack or no heart attack. And I started to think the worst. What if there was something more to his death than just a bad heart? What if there was something that triggered his previously undiscovered heart condition? I might just be scrabbling up the wrong tree but I wasn't completely sure.

I wanted to check.

Thinking back, it was weird the way Unicorn Cottage had been all messed up when we arrived. I mean, I know Uncle Jonah was not the tidiest of men, but there was something about it that made me worry. It was too . . . all over the place. Mum didn't question it at first, so I went along with her. After all, she knew him better than anyone.

But, after a while, I found myself wondering, what if the mess wasn't made by him? What if the mess was made by someone else?

It didn't make sense to me at all. It was just an idea. A nagging, if you like.

But I was determined to find out.

··········

Late one afternoon, I hopped on the bus into town. I'd told Mum that I was going for a walk to get some fresh air—after all, the stink of cleaning products in the cottage was getting a bit overwhelming. She smiled and nodded before going back to polishing Uncle Jonah's framed degree certificates on the wall.

I got off the bus as near to Trinity College as I could and walked the rest of the way. Perhaps it was just my suspicious mind, but there seemed to be a surprising number of Water Allocation Board men patrolling the city center that afternoon. Armed with their machine guns and equipped with bulletproof vests and helmets—every single one of them with ice for eyes—they cast a fear across your chest that made you feel automatically guilty. In a way, I suppose they were there to protect us all, but you couldn't help feeling that it was *you* they were watching. Of course, the people who had most to fear were the black marketers—the men and women who tried to sell contaminated or corrupted water. "Cat's Pee," as everyone referred to it. Thirst and dirt and desperation drove many people to extremes and for a couple thousand pounds they could buy a liter of water that wasn't fit for consumption. I'd heard stories of entire families going mad after drinking just a cupful of the stuff. Old and Moldies would curl up and die in their beds just hours after sipping it. And the teeth of toddlers would just drop out if they were washed in the terrible radioactive liquid. That's what people said, anyway, and even if some of the stories weren't true or badly exaggerated, Cat's Pee was definitely best avoided.

I kept my head down and hurried past a pair of particularly vicious-looking WAB men.

A couple of corners later and I found myself standing outside the entrance to Trinity College once again. I stopped to look up and admire the wide-open arch and the turrets on each side. It really did look like it had come from another planet, or at least another time. There was nothing in East London that I could compare it to.

Suddenly feeling nervous, I tugged up the collar on my coat and walked in.

In the dark alcove, the rows of pigeonholes clung to the wall, some of them stuffed full with envelopes and packages. Making sure there was nobody around, I reached up and pushed my hand into the slot marked *Dr. Jonah Bloom*. I swept it around, left and right, and pushed to the very back of the pigeonhole, but there was still nothing inside.

I stood back a little and looked at all the names. Was there a Six Six? My eyes read along to the *S* level . . . but, no. There was no Six Six. Not that I was expecting one. Six Six was not exactly your average common-or-garden surname, after all. No. Six Six must be a nickname for somebody. Or a code name, even!

I carried on through the second arch and stepped out into

the large open space surrounded on all four sides by the old, crumbly walls of the college. The windows all stared down like a ring of ancient professors closely observing the comings and goings, and that strange, domed fountain thingy was still sitting in what seemed to me like quite the wrong place.

A couple of students with their daft-looking cloaks were lounging on the dull lawn to the right of me, so I quickly turned left and headed toward another wide arch, my feet scrunching over the gravel. I went inside and made my way up some stony stairs, not knowing where I was going.

As the stairs turned and curled back on themselves, I came out onto a corridor. Along the corridor were doors, each of them with a name displayed in ornate carvings. The doors were all heavy and wooden and even though I put my ear to some of them and tried to quiet my breathing, I couldn't hear a single noise coming from inside. Were these people even there, or were they so clever and obsessed with their work that they all sat silently at their desks, scribbling their genius little ideas into notebooks? Perhaps some of them were even away fighting. After all, I suppose not all professors are old and crumpled-looking. Some might be quite young.

I pushed on around the corner and up another smaller flight of stairs. More doors lined the long, cold corridor. Suddenly the corridor opened up into a wide room where a number of fat, comfy-looking armchairs and coffee tables sat in front of a growling fire burning away in a huge granite hearth. As I wandered through the room toward the doorway opposite, I realized that two wispy-haired old men reading newspapers were snuggled down into a pair of the chairs. They were so engrossed with the news stories that they appeared to be ignoring each other and hadn't even spotted me coming into the room. I moved slightly lighter and quicker and passed through into the next corridor.

The place was enormous, and after about twenty minutes of getting myself lost in the maze that was Trinity College, I was about to give up.

It was then that I found it.

Tucked down a tiny dead end with an almost microscopic window looking out over the rooftops was the door I'd been looking for.

Dr. Jonah Bloom (Dept. of Physics)

My hand dug about in my jacket pocket. Nudging Snowflake 843A aside, my fingers picked out the short, stumpy metal key that I'd found in the attic. Looking around to make sure no one was watching, I slipped it into the keyhole and tried turning.

It wouldn't budge.

I grabbed it with both hands and twisted hard, but still the lock wouldn't turn.

Frustrated, I gave the door a kick. The loud thud reverberated down the long, echoey corridor and I swore at myself for being so stupid.

Desperate, I pulled the large ring handle with all my strength and tried the key once more. It was hard to move it but . . .

Click.

It unlocked. Just.

I smiled.

The door was slightly buckled. That had been the problem. The door curved ever so slightly inward and the mechanism had been grinding against the other part of the lock inside the door frame.

I looked closer at the part of the door near the lock. Was that damage? Chunks of the wood were missing and a couple of small splinters were sticking right out. I brushed them away so they fell onto the floor, before pushing open the heavy oak door.

Inside sat a huge wooden desk in front of an ornately designed fireplace. A shiny leather chair—one of those ones you could lie down on if you wanted to—was against the wall under the window, and on the opposite wall were row upon row of shelves.

They were all empty.

Because all the files and books that had once been stored on them were now tossed and crumpled all over the floor. My heart bounced in my chest and my mind jumped back to the first time Mum and I went into the cottage and saw the mess that it was in.

I was right. This wasn't normal, not even for untidy, easily distracted Uncle Jonah.

Something was definitely wrong.

Somebody else had made this mess. Somebody had damaged the door somehow and got into the office and turned it all upside down.

But why?

What were they looking for?

I walked into the room and around to the desk before sitting myself in the soft swivel chair behind it. So, this was where Uncle Jonah spent his working days, I thought. His thinking days. Sat in this chair, staring out the window across the Trinity quad. Directly ahead, on the wall alongside the door, was stuck an enormous poster. It was glossy and currently catching the light from the window on one side.

It was a photograph of some clouds. Large, thick black ones rolling across the sky with—what I assumed to be—hints of blue beyond.

I twisted around in the chair a few times before standing up and turning to the fireplace. Nobody had cleaned it out recently and it was bulging with ash. Lots of the ash had spilled out onto the grate and the floor in front of it, and I found myself unavoidably treading it into the carpet. The ash was light and thin and I realized that it had once been paper. Tiny slivers of paper that had managed to avoid the flames stuck out of the mass of black, and I reached for the poker and began prodding it into the mountain of ash.

I scattered some of the ash left and right until, underneath, I found almost half a sheet that had escaped being burned. I knelt down and picked it out, dusting the dirty black bits from it. On it were typed the words "PROJECT RAINBOW."

"What are you doing?"

I jumped and looked over to the door. A tall, broad, dark-haired woman was standing just inside the door, her arms crossed and her face scrunched into a scowl.

"I said, what are you doing here?"

"I . . . er . . ."

Suddenly, her eyes spotted all the files and books that had been ripped from the shelves and thrown to the floor. She looked horrified.

"Why . . . you little vandal . . ." Her arms unfolded and she started marching around the desk to where I was standing by the fireplace. "Disrespecting the dead. When I get hold of—"

I didn't wait around. I quickly jumped onto the desk and down the other side. The woman spun on her heels and watched me as I walked quickly to the door.

"Come back! Don't you just run away. . . ."

I threw the door open and stepped out into the corridor.

"STOP!" the woman shouted.

I started running, my feet slapping hard on the stone flooring, and I jumped down a staircase and out into the daylight.

Up above me, a window opened and the woman shouted from it.

"STOP THAT BOY!"

I raced across the quad, past the domed fountain thing toward the arch.

"STOP HIM!" I could hear her voice coming from somewhere far behind me.

To my left, one of the cloaked students on the grass seemed to be struggling up to his feet, his eyes on me.

Realizing he was going to try to catch me before I reached the doorway, I sprinted even harder and faster, my eyes fixed on that archway.

Thankfully the student was slowed down by his flapping cloak, and I bolted through the room with the pigeonholes and out the other side into the street with the quarter-of-a-mile-long vending machine. Without thinking, I turned right before quickly turning right again—shoppers and passersby all lurching out of my way—and then slipped left down a tiny alleyway.

After a minute, I slowed down, and then—when I was certain that no one was following me—came to a complete stop. I wiped the sweat from my face and tried to catch my breath. My chest ached and I felt even more thirsty than usual.

I also felt stupid and foolish. It was probably the noise of me kicking the door that attracted the attention of the woman in the first place. If I hadn't been interrupted I would still be in Uncle Jonah's office now. Who knows what I might have found. I swore to myself.

It was then that I remembered I was holding something. I lifted it up and looked at it once again.

The half-charred piece of paper.
PROJECT RAINBOW.

....

Along the bank of the river, a large truck was being unloaded and a second was being filled with plastic crates. On the side of the trucks it read: BARLOW'S INDUSTRIAL WASHING SERVICE.

It was the day after my little visit to Trinity and Mum had insisted we both take a trip into town. I wasn't exactly delighted by the prospect, as I didn't want to be recognized by anyone from the previous day. We stopped off in a small cake shop and Mum treated us both to a wholemeal scone. But later, as Mum steered me away from the shopping precinct toward the backs of the colleges, I'm sure my heart thudded even louder than it usually did.

"What are we doing here, Mum?" I asked, my eyes flashing from side to side in the hope of not seeing that woman again.

"You'll see," she replied cryptically. "We can't live off your uncle's money forever, you know."

As we neared the pitiful stream that trickled its way past the tree-lined gardens, I could make out row upon row of washing lines strung across the river from one bank to the other. In the middle of the stream stood—wearing Wellington boots—a whole crowd of women, many of them old, some of them young. Each of them was pulling clothing out of a large basket that sat on the mudbanks beside them and was dipping and squeezing it and rubbing it in the pathetic flow at their feet before reaching up and pegging it to the line. The lines were pulleyed at both ends, so that once something had been pegged, the washer simply had to give the line a gentle tug and the washing would move along, giving them a free stretch of line directly overhead.

"A very good morning to you!"

We turned to see a man with a little goatee beard and a walking stick approaching us.

"Hello."

"Good morning. Are you looking to have some washing undertaken?" He spoke in a strange clipped way, like he could only really manage a syllable at a time. "Best service on this stretch of the Cam, we are. No second-rate, over-charged robot jobs here—all washing lovingly done by human hand. Like in the old days. Twice winners of the Cambridgeshire Utility Service Award (hygiene section). Clothes guaranteed clean and intact or your money back. Cheap rates. Availability today."

He looked at us like a living, breathing ad, deliberately showing off his perfectly white teeth.

"Not at the moment, thank you."

"Oh." The teeth disappeared.

"But . . ." Mum was looking out at the long, busy row of women in the middle of the river. "But I *was* wondering . . . I've done some washing in my time—not on such an industrial scale, I'll admit—but I was wondering if you were taking people on?"

I looked at her and raised my eyebrows.

"Taking people on?" The man stroked his goatee and looked like some sort of villain in one of those silent movies—you know, the ones who were always tying damsels in distress to railway lines. Big waxy mustaches. "I'm always looking for new people. How strong are your arms?"

Mum put her sack down and rolled her sleeves up, holding them out to him.

"Yes. Not bad. Not bad. Might be good for a few dozen kilos in the mornings. I don't pay much, mind you. Twenty K for a half day's work. That's all I can offer."

"That's all I need," said Mum, covering her forearms again. "When can I start?"

The man was stunned at how quickly this had all taken place. "Er . . . what about tomorrow?"

"Perfect."

....

"What are you thinking, Mum?" I asked as we made our way back toward the Bot Job. "You can't go washing. You've no idea about washing."

"I can manage, don't worry about me. Anyway, we're going to need a bit of money coming in. We might not be paying any rent now, but Uncle Jonah's cash won't last that long. Besides—" She opened the boot to the car and lowered the sack into it. "I'm going to need something to do while you're at school."

CHAPTER 6
VIVI ROOKMINI

The following morning found us both sitting in the head-master's office at Hill's Road Primary. My mother kept glancing at her QWERTY, aware that she needed to arrive on time for her first day in her new job, and Mr. Belsey—who was a big, Father Christmassy sort of man with a big Father Christmassy sort of nose—eventually waved her away and led me down the corridor to my classroom.

"Must be very difficult." He seemed to have a stiff neck, and half swung his entire body around to talk to me as we walked. "Being unable to see color, I mean. Must make life very, very difficult. I can't imagine it, myself. I just can't imagine it."

And that's the thing. It is impossible for someone who has always been able to see colors—who has always known of their qualities and their differences from day one—it is impossible to understand what it might be like to *not* see them. No amount of explanation can get that idea through. People can squint and squash their eyes together and try to cut out the color. They can detune their televisions so that everything is in black-and-white. But nothing can really make them see the world as I—and others, there must be others, I'm sure—see it.

Then again, you can flip that argument. You could, of course, say that there was no way on earth that *I* could understand how *they* see the world. No clever device or tool to help me understand the—apparently—beautiful world of color.

We are in two distinct camps. Two separate Venn diagrams.

Definitely no overlap.

Mr. Belsey stopped outside a room, tapped on the glass window in the door, and let himself in.

Inside, the teacher—an older woman with curly hair—turned back from the whiteboard as Mr. Belsey entered.

"Ah," the headmaster started. "Miss Holbrook, this is our new pupil, Auden Dare." He tipped her the wink. "The one we talked about earlier."

"Hello, Auden." She came around the front of her desk, narrowly missing the large potted cactus that sat on the edge of it, and beckoned me to her. "Class!" The children sitting around the square tables stopped whatever it was they were doing and looked up at their teacher. "We have a new student joining us today. His name is Auden Dare. Please join me in wishing him a good morning."

"Good morn-ing, Au-den," the entire class said as one in a bored, singsong way. I gave an awkward little wave and as I did so the magnifying glass that I keep on a chain around my neck peeped out from under my jacket. I noticed one or two of the children look at it, so I lifted it and tucked it inside my shirt.

"Excellent!" Mr. Belsey pulled his far-too-tight jacket even tighter around his large frame. "I'll leave you in the capable hands of Miss Holbrook, then, Auden." Without a further look at me, he yanked open the door and left.

"Vivi?" The teacher caught the attention of a girl sitting on her own at the back of the class. "Perhaps Auden can sit with you? Perhaps you can be his New School Buddy for the next few days? Hmm?"

"Yes, Miss Holbrook."

I made my way through the classroom to the table and sat alongside the girl.

"Hello," she said, her questioning eyes almost burning into my face as she shifted her chair a couple of inches away from me. "I'm Vivi."

"Hi, Vivi." A notebook and a pen suddenly slapped onto the table in front of me and I nodded a sort of thank-you to the teacher.

"So . . ." She seemed slightly nervous. "You're new."

"Yes. Tell me"—I kept my voice down to a whisper, as the teacher had found her way back to the whiteboard and was continuing where she had left off with the frightening-looking fraction question—"what's a 'New School Buddy'?"

Her long black hair was pulled back into a wavy pony-tail. Sparkly umbrella earrings shone in her ears, and her eyes were big and round and bright with cleverness. "A 'New School Buddy' is someone who helps a new person at the school settle in. So, for example, I will show you where your classes are, where the bathrooms are, where the dining hall is, and so on and so forth. I will tell you the running order of the day, the start times, the end times. I will tell you who the pupils are and who the staff are. I will tell you what days to bring in your PE kit and also which days you will require a specially prepared packed lunch." She gave an enormously wide grin. "Basically, I'm your best friend until you find a new one."

"Vivi. Shh." Miss Holbrook glared at the girl before turning back to the problem on adding two improper fractions.

Vivi went into a whisper just like me. "I'm also the person who'll get told off for trying to answer your questions."

....

We both sat on the edge of a small wall and watched some Year Fives kicking a ball about. None of the other kids had introduced themselves to me yet, so I stuck to Vivi like a snail on a stone.

"Have you always been at this school?" I asked as one of the bigger boys fouled one of the smaller ones.

"Yes. Always," she answered. "I've never been anywhere

else. What about you? I mean, you're new, but what school did you go to before coming here?"

I scraped my nail against some earth that was wedged between a couple of the bricks.

"I went to a school in London. Nothing much more to tell, really. The other children weren't very nice." I tried to deflect the questioning away from me. "So, what sort of jobs do your parents do?"

"My mother is the seamstress for the colleges," she said. "She fixes all of the fellows' robes. Makes them, too. She also adjusts some of the students' ballgowns—the bot-made ones are really very inferior, you see. They go to her to have them altered." She looked proud. "She's well known all across the university as the best sewer and stitcher there is."

"What about your father? Is he away fighting?"

She shook her head and her ponytail gave a tiny wobble. "No. He's dead."

"Oh."

"Don't worry. He died before I was born. I never knew him. It's only me and my mum now. And Migishoo."

"Migishoo?" I asked.

"My parrot. He's a Senegal parrot, actually. He lives with us. Do you have any pets?"

I told her about Sandwich and the way she likes to stretch herself across the bottom of my bed when I'm sleeping in it, and the way she licks all the juice off her food but leaves the meat itself.

"She sounds sweet." Her eyes dipped to my neck for a

second. "Er . . . I couldn't help noticing . . . you've got a magnifying glass around your neck."

"Yeah." I dug it out and waggled it about before tucking it back into my shirt.

"Why?"

I stared down at my feet. "I don't have very good eyesight."

"You don't? Really? You would never know. You look at me okay. You've been watching the football okay. It can't be very bad, can it?"

"Well . . . I can't see color."

"What do you mean? You have red-green deficiency? Lots of people have that."

"Red-green . . . what?"

"They confuse the colors red and green. It's quite common."

I shook my head. "No. It's worse than that. I can't see any color at all."

"What, nothing?"

"No."

She stared away into the distance, her eyes not focusing at all on the football match. "So everything's black and white?"

I nodded.

"What's the name of your condition? What's it called? I love words. What's the word for it?"

"I never remember. It's a long word. Too many letters."

She stood up and pushed her hand deep into her trouser pocket before pulling out a tiny notebook with an even tinier pen stuck into the spirally wire spine. She took the pen, flipped the book open, and scribbled something in it.

"There! Made a note to look it up." She put the pad back into her pocket and sat down again. "Doesn't really explain why you have a magnifying glass around your neck, though, does it?"

"No."

"So?"

"So, what?"

"Why *do* you have a magnifying glass? Are you keen on ants or spiders? Do you collect stamps?"

"No, I'm not. I don't." I fished the glass out from under my shirt again and held it in front of my right eye, scrunching up the left one. "Sometimes, in certain lights, I find it difficult to make out small details. When it's really sunny or when it's really cloudy. Tiny print looks blurred. So I have to use this." I wriggled it around on the end of the chain before tucking it back inside my shirt.

Suddenly, a loud, fluttering buzz filled the air. The football game stopped, and everybody looked upward. Two Ariel drones eased themselves over the playground and landed on the electricity cable that passed overhead, connecting to the supply to recharge themselves. Their activity sensors looked like the curved beaks of a hawk, their two inactive light sources like a hawk's dilated eyes.

"I quite like the Ariels. They remind me of Migishoo," Vivi said, shading her eyes from the dull sun. "What's your favorite sort of drone?"

"I don't know. I don't think I've ever thought about it. Er . . . I suppose I quite like the Scoots. They're cool. They fly really high."

"The Dodos are just stupid, I think."

"Yeah. The way they bounce along the pavement. And they bump into lampposts all the time."

"I know." She laughed, a high-pitched rat-a-tat of a laugh. "They fall over, too. Have you ever seen one fall over?"

I remembered seeing one topple over just outside our block of flats and snorted at the memory. "Yeah. I have."

"Believe it or not," Vivi said, grinning, "Cambridge is full of Dodos."

"Hey!"

I jumped. Suddenly standing next to me was one of the footballers—the big one who'd just fouled the little one. He was tall and slim with black, spiky hair that stuck up above his sulky face.

"Hey!" he shouted again—slightly louder than before—despite only standing a few feet from me. "What's that around your neck?"

"What?"

He seemed to go all flushed in the face. "I said, what's that around your neck? You deaf or something?" Two slightly shorter boys came alongside, their faces fixed with uncertain smirks.

"Go on, Boyle. Punch him."

"Yeah. Go on."

I looked at Vivi and smiled, but her eyes had a sort of scared look.

The big boy leaned in closer to me. "What is it? I wanna see."

The stench from his breath nearly knocked me out, so I shuffled a little farther along the wall before pulling the magnifying glass out again.

The boy stared at it. "A magnifying glass? What do you want a magnifying glass for?"

I sighed. "It's a long story," I muttered.

"Go on, hit him," the kid on the left with the fat nose repeated.

"Yeah. Go on," the kid on the right with the swollen lips said again. "He's asking for it."

"Leave him alone," Vivi blurted out before looking scared again.

The big kid leaned across me and glared at her.

"You shut yer face, Rookmini. Or I'll throw you halfway to those Ariel drones up there."

I shook my head. I'd had enough. "Look," I said. "I don't know who you are but we've done nothing to you, so why don't you just leave us alone?"

The big kid's face screwed up into a ball of confusion and

flushed even more. "What did you just say?" he almost whispered in anger.

"I said—"

"No one talks to me like that." His hand seemed to curl up into a fist. "No one EVER talks to me like that. Least of all some magnifying-glass-wearing weirdo like you. I'm going to teach you—"

"Belsey, seven o'clock!" the one with the nose squawked before turning on his heel and walking away, closely followed by the swollen-lipped one.

The big kid straightened up and looked behind him to see the headmaster on playground duty. He turned back to me and pointed at my face.

"Soon. I'll get you soon. I'll find out who you are and I'll get you. No one EVER talks to me like that. Freak!"

And with that, he twisted away and strolled back toward the football game.

....

"Who was—"

"That was Boyle," Vivi interrupted me. The bell had sounded and we were making our way back to the classroom. "Fabius Boyle. He thinks he rules the school. He doesn't, of course. But that doesn't stop him from trying."

"And what about the other two?"

"Oh, just Putter and Keane. They're probably the two people most scared of him, so they hang around and pretend to be his friends. They're just hopeless." She gave the side of her head a little tap. "Not exactly geniuses."

"Boyle didn't sound too bright, either," I said as we both sat back down at our table. "Did the football hit him hard in the head or something? Dislodge a few brain cells?"

Vivi smiled.

"No. He's always been like that." She looked serious again. "You want to keep away from him, though. He's trouble. Just beats people up if he doesn't like them. That sort of thing."

Well, one thing was for certain—Boyle didn't like *me*.

....

PROJECT RAINBOW.

I pinched the piece of paper between my fingers and held it up to the light, turning it over and over in the hope that some missing secret might just drop out of it.

But it didn't.

Project Rainbow?

Did it mean what I hoped it meant?

Sandwich jumped up onto the bed and started one of her dribbly purrs, trying to edge her way into my lap. I let her and gave her a rough tickle around the chin—which she *looooves*. She pushed harder against my nails and rolled onto her side, her eyes all half-closed and dreamy. Then she began the terrible dribbling.

I lowered the burned sheet of paper to the bed and tickled her with both hands—my mind a hundred miles away.

Was Project Rainbow what I imagined it was?

Was Uncle Jonah working on a way of helping me see color?

The first week of school shot past like a Scoot drone. Miss Holbrook was nice. Vivi was nicer. But nobody else seemed to even approach me. It was as if the incident with Boyle had already obliterated my reputation. He'd obviously been putting word around that I was a magnifying-glass-wearing oddball, and everyone else seemed determined to stay away from me. To be honest, it didn't bother me. Well, not much, anyway. I'd had similar experiences in my old schools. I'd grown used to it.

It probably didn't help that I was friends with Vivi. She seemed a bit on her own, too. There was nobody I could really call her friend. Okay, she might pass the occasional word or two with a couple of the other girls, but nothing much more. In a way, she was almost as isolated as I was.

One lunchtime, I decided to show off. Life's too short not to show off sometimes; now and again you just have to do it. You see, it may surprise you to find out that I was the East London Under-Tens Gymnastics Club champion for three years in a row. I bet you thought I'd be a thin, pale, sport-hating boy who'd avoid all activity like some sort of disease, preferring to sit in a room playing computer games and feeling sorry for myself. But no. I'm not. I was the blond-haired king of the straddle jumps and double-front somersaults. My box splits were better than anyone's and my work on the vault was usually spotless. For three years I was pretty much top dog in my category.

But then I hit eleven and the competition suddenly got

harder. Along with the fact that I was getting taller, and tall people don't do very well in gymnastics. So a few months before moving to Cambridge, I gave it all up. It's true, I miss it a bit. All the evenings spent stretching and jumping and spinning around.

But in the end, it wasn't for me.

Also, you go through an awful lot of your weekly allowance of water when you're training, and Mum and I couldn't afford that. We had to hold back.

However, I'm still as fit as a fireman, and a game of football would be a total *breeze*. So if anyone had asked me to join in with their lunchtime game, they would have quickly realized that I was pretty good with a football.

But nobody did.

So that lunchtime, I thought I'd show off.

I got off the wall where Vivi and I usually sat, ran onto the pitch, and launched into a quadruple roundoff flip followed by a backward somersault. Landing perfectly securely on my feet, barely out of breath, I looked around.

People stood still, mouths and eyes wide open. I even saw appreciative nods coming from Putter and Keane.

"Whoa!" said a particularly short Year Four boy. "Whoa!"

"Dat's cool," a thin Year Three girl with a runny nose said, and grinned.

But everybody else just stood and stared.

"Hey! Freak Show!" Boyle pushed his way onto the pitch and pointed his finger at me. Again. "Freak Show! Didya grow up in a circus, eh? Is that what it is?" Putter and Keane snorted unconvincingly. "Half man, half monkey, are you? Have to lock you up in a cage at night, did they? People pay to see you perform, eh?" He looked so bitter.

Meanwhile, the looks of awe faded away.

"Wanna keep that sort of behavior under control," Boyle mumbled into my face. "Nobody likes a show-off. Speshally freaky ones that wear magnifying glasses. Ha!"

He turned and walked off the pitch, Putter and Keane fawning close behind. Everybody else tried their best to ignore me.

Not that I minded. Not at all. If that was the way they operated, then I wouldn't want to play with them, anyway. They could carry on being scared of Boyle, keeping to themselves and casting the odd, untrusting, sideways look at me. Let them.

I didn't need them.

I had Vivi.

You see, Vivi Rookmini was funny, smart—and I mean *really* smart—and honest. She knew almost everything, and the things she didn't know, she enjoyed finding out about. Knowledge was almost as important to her as water, and not a day would go by when she wouldn't spill out a dozen newly learned facts like they were the most important things ever.

Besides, Vivi Rookmini was my friend—not just a New School Buddy.

And I liked her a lot.

CHAPTER 7
HISTORY

Miss Holbrook was a decent enough teacher. Not particularly exciting or inspiring—she fed us facts like they were vitamin pills—but her head was jam-crammed full of knowledge. And the sort of knowledge that seemed to take up most of the space had to do with history.

She knew all there was to know about the Romans, the Vikings, the ancient Egyptians. There was no one to touch her on the Tudors and Stuarts, the Georgians and the Windsors. And as for the First and Second World Wars . . .

"Please, select a monitor and turn on your QWERTYs," she would say, and we would all swivel around and position ourselves in front of one of the screens placed along the edge of the classroom. Then we would tap on our wrist computers—our QWERTYs—and get them to project the image of a keyboard in front of us, before awaiting further instruction.

We all had QWERTYs. They were standard school equipment. If you ever went to school without your QWERTY you would be sent home to get it. Some people had newer, better-quality QWERTYs than others (mine was a few years out of date, Vivi's was almost obsolete) but every single pupil in all the schools I've ever been to had a QWERTY strapped around their wrist. You could use them to access the etherweb, to phone, to send messages, to project images, to tell you your energy requirements for the next twenty-four hours, to read your blood pressure, to tell you where you were, to tell you where you should be, to stream your favorite music, to play games, to watch the news. Oh, and it could also tell you the time.

Everybody loved their QWERTY.

Anyway, Miss Holbrook would wait for us all to settle down before continuing, "Today, class, I would like you to research the battle of Agincourt," or something like that. "Find out as much as you can and then write a seven-hundred-word essay on what happened and the effect it had on the world and its development."

We used our QWERTYs to piece everything together and type away on our virtual keyboards until we'd hit the golden figure of seven hundred words—very few people would have as many as 701.

This was something Miss Holbrook regularly made us do.

And I hated it.

You see, I'm not the greatest fan of history. I really do not see the point. I mean, what can some old war or some old battle from hundreds and thousands of years ago matter? I'm sure that, while it was going on, the battle of Agincourt was an extremely important thing. For the people who were there it was probably the most important thing in the world. No question.

But nowadays?

Time moves on. It always does. That's the point of it. It never stops.

And history is all around us. It is here and now. Everything that happens now is a part of history. Every little thing. It all contributes. It all rolls together and becomes something bigger.

So why waste our time on things long dead when we can discuss the world as it is now?

Why do we hide behind the past?

....

We are at war.

Over water.

The whole world is at war over water. That simple life-giving substance that everybody once took for granted. That beautiful, silvery, fragile stuff.

You see, there's not enough of it to go round. Since the rains started to dry up more than twenty years ago, the only major source of water has been from the sea. And you can't drink seawater. Nobody can. It has to have all its salt removed first. That's why the government and the Water Allocation Board took control of the coastline all those years ago. The whole entire edge of Britain is now a protected area (I've never even seen the sea—not many kids my age have) and huge desalting units are busy sucking up the undrinkable seawater and turning it into something more pure. Something we can use.

We're lucky in this country. The sea is all around us. Because we're an island, we are surrounded by it. However, there are lots of countries that aren't. Landlocked countries stuck between others. Countries that are completely dependent on the tiny drizzles of rain that happen once or twice a year.

Some countries have water. Others don't. Some need to get it. Others are unwilling to give it up. Some countries want to share. Others just want to take it all.

BOOM!

War.

That is why so many parents and siblings are away fighting right now.

So, excuse me if I don't get overexcited at the prospect of writing a seven-hundred-word essay on the Hundred Years' War or the Battle of Hastings or something, because *this* war is more important. To me. To the rest of the class.

This is *our* war.

After all, not many members of the class have been unaffected by the war. Sofia Meacham's father had only recently come back home in a coffin draped with a flag. Kai Everitt had had to move in with his aunt because both his father and his mother were killed fighting in Romania. Naomi Blackwell's older brother had lost both legs after straying onto a minefield in Barcelona. And everybody else had at least one close member of the family who was away fighting.

Everybody except Vivi, that is.

CHAPTER 8
THE SEAMSTRESS

One day after school, Vivi invited me back to her house for tea.

"Don't expect too much," she said as we put on our coats and made our way out through the school gates. "Mum's not exactly a brilliant cook. Whatever she gives you, just try your best to nibble it and don't make a face. If you can manage to swallow it as well, that would be a bonus."

We walked all the way into town, past the big hospital, past the big shops with the big Closed Down windows, past the big vending machines, and into the big area with the big old college buildings.

It was only when we turned onto the small road leading toward Trinity that I started to wonder where it was she was taking me.

"Er . . . Vivi," I asked. "Where exactly do you live?"

We stopped and Vivi pointed up ahead. "Here. Just here."

She was pointing to Trinity College.

"Wait. Hold on. You live at Trinity?"

She smiled at me. "Yes."

"But . . . but you're not a student. And you're definitely not a . . ." I struggled to pick out the right word. "A fellow. So you can't live in the college."

"Oh, yes I can," she said, before turning around and continuing. I watched her for a second before rushing to catch up.

"But I don't understand."

She explained. "Because my mother is the university seamstress, we are allowed to live in some of the rooms on the top floor. It's part of the job. She fixes all the robes and we get to live there. Come on."

It had been a couple of weeks since my little visit to Uncle Jonah's rooms and I suddenly found myself getting all nervous, and I started worrying about someone recognizing me. I pulled the collar up on my coat, bent my head downward a bit, and marched on.

We passed through the pigeonhole area and stepped out into the quad. We tapped our shoes across the flagstones in the courtyard and went in through a tiny door in the opposite wall.

The cold stone steps spiraled upward and we came out onto a long, narrow corridor with windows on the right overlooking the quad. It wasn't that far away from Uncle Jonah's rooms, I realized, and a horrible thought hit me.

What if—

"Come on." Vivi waved me on before I could think any further. "This is it here."

At the far end of the corridor, Vivi pushed open a door and we stepped into her rooms.

The word *busy* leaped to mind. If I could see colors, I'm sure I would have been hit in the face with an incredible rainbow of the things. For a start, small, even patches of cloth—each of them about a foot square—had been sewn together and pinned in lots of places to the long ceiling, so it looked like the ceiling itself was made of soft cushions.

A beaded curtain split the room into two, hiding away whatever was beyond it from the front door. A scruffy, threadbare sofa sat in front of an old fireplace on each side of which was a large cactus, and a really old black-and-white television set was positioned on top of what looked like a cardboard box covered in crepe paper.

Near one of the dirty arched windows, a parrot sat on a swinging perch, its head twisting this way and that as it watched me enter the room. Next to that was a table across which were spilled hundreds of cotton reels and pieces of silky cloths and materials, and, dominating the far end of the table, a sewing machine looking more like an instrument of torture than something used to join things together.

A dressmaker's dummy—headless and limbless with an

adjustable waist, draped with something unfinished—stood alongside a cluttered bookcase overspilling with books.

And in an armchair, quietly stitching the brim of a hat, was Vivi's mother. Her skin was darker than Vivi's, but the shape of the face and the long flowing hair with the slight curl would give the game away in a matter of seconds.

My mouth went even drier than usual.

She was also the woman who'd found me in the middle of Uncle Jonah's rooms just the other week.

As we came in, Vivi's mum barely looked up. Her eyes focused on the job literally in hand.

"Mum," Vivi said, dumping her schoolbag down on the sofa. "Mum. This is Auden."

"Ah." She still didn't look up. "Auden. I've heard so much about you."

Finally she stood up and propped the hat on top of the headless dummy before turning to me and shaking my hand.

"I'm Immaculata." Her voice had an accent to it, I now noticed. Something European. "It's lovely to meet you."

Her eyes squinted momentarily as if she recognized me from somewhere.

"Hello," I replied, trying not to let my voice crack too much. "Good to meet you."

Behind the beaded curtain was a small kitchen and dining area where Immaculata had prepared some things for tea. Small triangular cheese sandwiches, quinoa biscuits, whole-wheat muffins. Vivi was wrong about her mother being an awful cook. The food was amazing. We drank milk from plastic cups as we ate and Immaculata watched me with her big dark eyes and asked questions. It made me nervous.

"Vivi tells me that you cannot see color. Is that right?"

I nodded, spilling a few scone crumbs over the table.

"Achromatopsia," Vivi said.

"Hmm?"

"Achromatopsia. I looked it up. An inability to see color. Achromatopsia."

I nodded again. "That's it. That's the word. I always forget. Too many letters."

Immaculata continued. "Can the doctors do anything about it? Can they operate or put you on medication? Something that will help you see color?"

"No. There's nothing they can do. I am going to see everything in black and white for the rest of my life."

"That's terrible."

"Is it?" I gratefully accepted one of the muffins as Immaculata held out the plate to me. "It is what it is, I suppose. It's not important."

Immaculata's eyes seemed to question my last statement and I quickly tucked into the muffin to avoid having to look at them again.

"Actually," I said eventually, "my uncle once promised that he would try to help me to see. He was a scientist." I stole another quick look at Immaculata. "He said he would try to work on something."

"Is he still trying?"

I put the remains of the muffin back onto my small plate. It was quite dry and was making me thirsty and I didn't want to drink more of their milk than I had to.

"No. He died."

"Oh, I am sorry."

I shrugged. "It's okay. Just one of those things."

After tea, we went back into the main room and Vivi introduced me to Migishoo.

"He loves to fly out over the quad at night. His favorite food is sunflower seeds." She smiled at the bird. "He'll repeat anything you say. 'Pretty parrot. I . . . am . . . a . . . pretty . . . parrot.'"

Migishoo tilted his head as if he was wondering what the girl in front of him was on about. Then, after a few seconds, he squawked.

"Priddy parod. I yamma priddy parod."

We laughed.

"Go on. You try," said Vivi.

"Okay. Erm . . . 'Auden Dare is clever and handsome.'"

It looked at me as if I was mad. And then . . .

"Or town tare is clerer ant ansum."

"Ha!"

I sort of fell backward, laughing, and as I did so my eye jumped onto something tucked away on a shelf. I suddenly stopped laughing.

"Auden?" Vivi asked. "What is it?"

I walked across to the shelf and reached up. I grabbed hold of the thing I'd seen and pulled it down. It was cold and hard, smooth along its curved surface but jagged in the middle. And about a hundred different things slotted into place in my mind.

"What's wrong?" she asked again.

I turned it over in my hands, not able to believe my eyes.

"Snowflake," I said mostly to myself. "Snowflake 843B."

Vivi jumped up off the chair. "How do you know . . ."

Before she could finish, I went over to where my coat was lying over the back of an armchair and reached into the right-hand pocket. I pulled out the small half of meteorite that Uncle Jonah had left me in his will and slotted it onto this new discovery.

They were a perfect fit.

Vivi stopped where she was.

"Vivi?" I said, amazed. "Six Six? *You* are Six Six?"

She looked stunned. "And *you* must be the Golden Boy."

....

Of course, it made perfect sense.

Vivi. Six Six. Break up her name into the roman numerals *VI VI*. Six six. It was exactly the sort of cryptic crosswordy-type thing that Uncle Jonah loved doing. Stripping words back to their basic elements and toying with them, piecing them back together—back to front; down, then up.

"It's what Dr. Bloom always called me. Six Six. I used to like Dr. Bloom. He was really nice to me. Always used to give me lollipops whenever I had to run errands to his rooms. Always asked me how school was going. Things like that."

"And what was that you called me?" I asked. "The Golden Boy?"

Vivi nodded and got up from her chair. "I suppose it must come from Auden. The chemical symbol for gold is Au. *Au* Den. *Gold* Den. Golden. That must be it." She dragged a folded sheet of paper down from the same shelf on which had been sitting Snowflake 843B. "He mentions you in the letter that went with the meteorite." She opened the paper and handed it to me.

I recognized the spidery, slanting scrawl. It was just like the letter Uncle Jonah had left me. In fact, it said lots of the same things. A description of Snowflake 843B and of where it had come from. A small paragraph explaining just how tiny the chances of it hitting Earth actually were. A mention of the fact that the meteorite looked just like a rock that could be found in the garden of Unicorn Cottage.

And then another paragraph.

By the way, it said, *its sister—Snowflake 843A—I have left to an extraordinary young man that I know. I like to think of him as the Golden Boy. The Golden Boy is one of the strongest and bravest people that I have ever met—he has had an awful lot to contend with in his life. I also have a feeling that after my death, he might well move to Cambridge. If you should ever come across him then, do, please, make him feel at home. He will need a good friend, and I know for a fact you are one of the best.*

Anyway, Six Six . . . take very good care of yourself and your dear mother, and remember that your mind is bigger and sharper than any number of universes squared.

Dig deep, my girl. Dig deep.

Always remember to dig deep.

Yours,

Jonah (Dr. Bloom)

I didn't know how to feel. Uncle Jonah was referring to me as the Golden Boy—which I think I kind of liked.

But then again . . .

Uncle Jonah—my uncle—had written a letter, just like the one he'd written me, to someone else. Someone he wasn't even related to. Vivi was just somebody who happened to live in the same college as him. That's all. What right did she have to the other part of the meteorite?

"That's weird," Vivi said, taking the letter from me. "Don't you think?"

"What?"

"Well, the fact that you were put next to me in school and then weeks later we find out that—without either of us knowing—we both have a connection. Dr. Bloom."

"*Uncle* Jonah," I churlishly added. "I didn't know him as Dr. Bloom. I knew him as *Uncle* Jonah."

Vivi fell quiet and I suddenly felt guilty. She was my friend. A good friend. The best friend—as Jonah said in his letter. And as my best friend, I had a duty to take care of her. Not upset her.

"He must have thought very highly of you," I said. "To leave you the other half of Snowflake."

Vivi smiled. "He was nice. A very clever man. I liked him a lot."

Suddenly, the bead curtain between the sitting room and the kitchen flew open and Immaculata marched in, pointing her finger straight at me.

"It just came to me! *You* are the boy who ransacked poor Dr. Bloom's rooms! You!"

....

Don't worry. It was all okay. Vivi quickly explained everything to her mother, who calmed down almost immediately.

"Oh, goodness." Immaculata fell back into a chair, her hand clasping her chest. "Dr. Bloom was your uncle? Dr. Bloom was a gentleman. A real gentleman. The number of times I patched up his subfusc . . . Goodness! To think you're his nephew. Well, well." Her eyebrows suddenly got closer together. "It was a terrible thing—him dying like that. Out of the blue. There he was, perfectly fit, and then . . . Terrible. Nobody saw that coming, I can tell you."

"Yes." I thought I'd better explain. "You see, I went to his rooms to see if I could find something."

"Well, did you? Find it, I mean?"

I shook my head. "I don't know."

"Only you seemed to make an awful mess in his office, throwing all the books and files down on the floor like that."

"No. That wasn't me."

Immaculata squinted closely at me. "Wasn't it?"

"No. I think somebody else had been in his rooms before me. I think they might have been looking for something, too."

We all sat in silence for a few seconds, weighing this information.

"Well, perhaps we'd better inform someone about it." Immaculata shifted in the chair. "The police or the Water Allocation Board or somebody. Let them know—"

"No!" I realized I had spoken too loudly. "No," I said, calmer now. "I don't think we should."

"Why not?"

"Because if somebody's taken something, then chances are it will be gone for good. The police won't be able to help now. They're far too busy as it is. Anyway, Uncle Jonah died months ago. Who knows how long his rooms have been like that."

Immaculata nodded, realizing that what I'd said was all true.

"It is true. After I found you in his rooms I had them cleaned up. I couldn't just leave them like that. It seemed disrespectful somehow. So even if there were fingerprints or anything like that, they'd all be swept away now. Oh dear." She shook her head. "Why would anyone want to break into his rooms? What were they looking for? He wasn't a spy, was he? Trinity has a great tradition of employing spies as lecturers."

"Mum!" Vivi protested. "Dr. Bloom wasn't a spy."

"How do you know?" Immaculata snapped back. "You've never met a spy before, have you? How would you know what one looks like? That's the point of spies, isn't it, to be able to look normal? Fit in?"

Vivi tutted and sighed.

"I'm certain Uncle Jonah wasn't a spy, Mrs. Rookmini," I said. "But whatever they were looking for must have had something to do with his work. I'm sure."

....

Vivi's room was small but as busily packed as the main room just beyond her door. Her bed was stuffed against a wall, and above it a large, open umbrella dangled from the ceiling.

"It holds all of my old toys," she said. "All the ones I can't bear to throw away."

Looking up I noticed a couple of teddy bears and dolls peering over the edge of the umbrella.

"You can't *bear* to throw them away, can you? Geddit? Bear. Yes?"

Vivi shook her head and didn't bother to give my joke the loud laugh it so clearly deserved.

Next to the window, a huge telescope was pointing upward to the sky, and all over the room were posters and pictures of planets, moons, and constellations. Books on space and space exploration were stacked up neatly on the floor and a weird device looking like it was made of balls and wire seemed to have pride of place on top of a small table.

"It's an orrery."

"A what-ery?"

"An orrery." She went up to it and started winding up a key. "It's a model of the universe. It shows how the planets rotate around the sun." She let the key go and the thing started to whir. The smaller balls all turned about the larger ball at the center—the sun. Some of them revolved faster than others. After a few seconds it started to slow until it came to a complete stop.

"This particular orrery dates from when Pluto was still considered to be a proper planet—before it was reclassified as a dwarf." Vivi gave the key an extra turn and watched the what-ery with fascination. "Back then there were thought to be nine planets in our solar system. Nowadays there are only the eight."

"Right." I pointed to the ceiling. "You've got a hole. In your roof."

"That's not a hole, silly. That's a skyspace."

"What's a skyspace?"

"A skyspace is a window that looks out onto the sky. One of the old professors had it built when these were his rooms."

"What's it do?"

Vivi stared at me like I was some sort of irritating kid who kept asking questions just to wind the teacher up. Either that or she thought I was just stupid.

"You're meant to stare up as the clouds roll by. The sky always changes. It never stops moving. People do it when they are thinking—it helps them concentrate. Focusing on the sky helps you relax and order your thoughts."

"Sounds like a load of rubbish."

She ignored me. "I sometimes watch the stars at night. As the world rotates, the stars do, too. Changing position. Within an hour you can have a completely different view. The whole sky changes." She looked at me. "Come on. Give it a go."

"What?"

"I'll lie on my bed. You lie on the floor—you can have one of my pillows, if you like." She picked one of her pillows off the bed and dropped it onto the floor next to the bed. "Try it. Just lie there and stare at the sky." She hopped onto her bed and stretched out.

I sighed and got down onto the floor, resting my head on the pillow.

"I feel stupid."

"Now just watch. Relax and watch the sky."

I sighed again but did as I was told. I stared up through the strange, perfect square of window that had been cut out of Vivi's ceiling. The clouds were thin and wispy and there was obviously a bit of a breeze outside, as they appeared to be moving quite fast.

"They're moving fast," I said.

"Scudding," replied Vivi.

"Eh?"

"Shh."

We both lay there in silence as we gazed at the movement in the little pane of glass. After a few minutes, it started to feel like I wasn't watching the sky at all. It was as though the square sheet of glass was a picture—a painting—pinned to the ceiling. And the picture was always evolving. Shut your eyes for a few seconds and, when you opened them again, you had a brand-new picture to look at. Your eyes honed in on the detail. The tiny bumps and ridges and puffs that made up the clouds. The way some clouds overrode others—barging past—or crept out from behind another, slower one. It was oddly . . . hypnotic. Soothing. Comforting.

So much so that I nearly fell asleep.

Thankfully, Vivi spoke before I found myself snoring.

"Do you know the names for the different types of clouds?"

"Er, no."

"Well, there's stratus—those are the low-looking patchy ones you sometimes see. Like cotton wool that's been pulled apart. The big fluffy ones are called cumulus. The ones that look really high up and wispy are called cirrus."

"Which sort are they?" I asked, pointing upward.

"Probably cirrus," she said. "Yes. Definitely cirrus."

We fell silent again and watched the sky above.

"You know," Vivi whispered eventually—the silence had clearly lasted long enough for her to feel like it would be wrong to begin to speak with anything other than a whisper. "You know, it was your uncle who originally got me interested in the stars. He gave me a star map for my birthday a few years ago, and showed me all the different constellations. Kept testing me on my knowledge of them. He was the person who said I should get a telescope. Mum saved for ages to get it."

I watched as a slightly thicker, bleaker cloud forced its way onto the canvas. It appeared to be shoving the other, lighter clouds out of the frame. I thought back to the poster in Uncle Jonah's office. I thought back to the ashes. I thought back to the piece of paper with PROJECT RAINBOW printed on it.

"When I was in Uncle Jonah's office," I said quietly, "I found a piece of burned paper in the grate."

"Oh?"

My eyes relaxed watching the clouds.

"Yes. There were only two words on it. 'Project Rainbow.'"

"Project Rainbow?" Vivi asked, her head peering over the side of her bed.

"Hmm."

"What is Project Rainbow?"

"I don't know. But . . ." I turned my head to look at Vivi. "Well, what's the first thing you think of when you think of a rainbow?"

"Atmospheric moisture content. Diffraction."

"Okay," I corrected myself, "what do *normal* people think of when they think of a rainbow?"

She thought. "Colors?"

"Yes, colors."

"Ah . . ."

"I think Uncle Jonah had finally started working on a way to help me see color."

"Project Rainbow."

"Yes. Only . . ."

"What?" She rested her chin on her elbows.

"Why did he burn all the papers? Why did he destroy all the work he'd put into helping me?"

Vivi didn't say anything.

"Perhaps . . . ," I started. "He'd given up. Couldn't do it. Found it wasn't possible."

Vivi still didn't say anything.

"Perhaps . . . ," I continued. "Perhaps that was what the people in his office were searching for. Yes. I think that's what they were after. I think they were trying to find his work on curing achromatopsia."

PART TWO

BLUE

CHAPTER 9
TRAMPOLINE

Pretty soon, the summer came along and school wound itself up, stumbling to its inevitable end. I've always loved summer vacation. Six weeks of doing not very much whenever you didn't want to do it. Bliss! The only problem was that Mum's work didn't stop, and for most of the time off I was going to be alone in the house. So it was agreed that Mum would drop me off outside Trinity most mornings and I would spend the day with Vivi.

One of the best things about visiting Vivi was her parrot, Migishoo. Once or twice I tried to get him to say something rude, but Immaculata caught me and gave me one of her looks. So I apologized nicely and promised not to do it again.

Vivi and I spent most of the days exploring the town and

the area of countryside that hovered just outside Cambridge. It was quite a flat land with not many hills but lots of lanes that twisted around on themselves through villages and small woods.

One of our favorite places to visit was the Sunny Vale Caravan Park.

The Sunny Vale Caravan Park had been badly named. For a start, it was hardly ever sunny in this part of the world. Second, it wasn't positioned in any sort of vale or valley—it stood perfectly on display in the middle of a couple of fields two miles outside the city center.

It had also seen better times. The digital, flashing sign-post under which visitors would drive into the camp was actually rotting and buckled, with one of the posts supporting the sign having been knocked some way out of the ground. In the wind the whole thing swayed and squeaked like it was about to topple, and the lettering faltered and flickered until you couldn't read what it was trying to say anyway.

The camp consisted of about two dozen trailers, or caravans, all of them desperately needing a fresh coat of paint. If you peered through a window into one of the empty ones, you could see that the furnishings were old and beaten up, and spiderwebs were starting to take over. Some of the windows were cracked and quite a few of them were screaming out for a good wipe-over with a damp rag.

However, even though the place was run-down, Sunny Vale still had its fair share of customers. Holidaymakers from

London and other cities who'd saved their hard-earned cash for a short break in the countryside. Three or four caravans at a time appeared to be occupied—some with young families, others with old people—but nobody ever looked especially pleased to be there.

Some days, Vivi and I would walk out to Sunny Vale and spy on its current inhabitants. The way the caravans were placed across the fields made it easy to hide from view. We could skip along behind one and then dash across the overgrown path to another. It also became clear quite early on that the owners only ever put people in the same few caravans. Obviously they could just about manage the upkeep of four or five caravans, and everything else was left untouched.

It was great fun sneaking about and hiding from everyone. In fact, sometimes, when the camp was particularly quiet, we would run and hide from each other. We would play an elaborate game of hide-and-seek across the whole park, with the extra rule that nobody else was to ever see us. Both Vivi and I found ourselves to be experts at keeping out of sight, and we never even once saw the owners in their own battered little house on the edge of the site.

Another place we liked to visit was the old junkyard south of the city. All the thrown-out nonsense that people didn't want anymore ended up here. Enormous hills of busted-up metal and crunched-down plastic littered the wide yard like an upside-down egg carton. A type of drone I'd never seen before—Sifters, I think they are called—were working their laborious way through the piles, sorting out the salvageable from the useless and dropping anything that could be saved into large buckets on their backs. They were slightly larger than the Dodos, with wheels instead of legs that propelled them easily across the bumpy, rubbish-strewn ground.

It was at the junkyard that we found the trampoline.

"There's nothing wrong with it." I rolled it out and prodded the springs and netting with my hand. "Why would anyone want to get rid of this? There's absolutely nothing the matter with it." A Sifter approached and, sensing our presence, wheeled itself around us.

Vivi shook her head and looked me up and down. "You're not thinking of taking that, are you? Please tell me you're not."

"But it's okay. Be a shame to waste it."

"I just don't see the point of it. It's a bit childish, if you ask me. Bouncing up and down on a mat."

"You don't see the point because you've never been sporty. Apart from during PE at school, I don't think I've ever seen you running."

"But a trampoline? Isn't it a bit like a bouncy castle? For kids."

I pushed it even farther away from the pile. "No. When I was doing gymnastics I got really good at the trampoline—and I mean *really* good. If we can get this back home I'll show you."

Vivi folded her arms and huffed. "Home? You think

you're going to take this back to your house? But you live about a mile and a half away. You can't carry it—in fact, you can't even pick it up. It's too big. Even with the two of us, it's too big."

"Ah," I said. "But we can try rolling it." The trampoline was one of those round ones with the safety netting all around the side. "There aren't many steep hills between here and home. It'll be easy." As if to make the point, I gave it a big shove and it rolled about four feet ahead of me. "See?"

As it turned out, it wasn't easy. Far from it. The first problem we found was that trying to make it go in the direction you wanted was difficult. You had to stop it from rolling, then give it a bit of a push on one end to make it turn slightly, before shoving it onward again. Soon enough you'd have to stop it once more and push it on the opposite end to readjust it. Left, then right, then left, then right again. Zigzagging along the road. It was slow going.

Another problem was actually getting the thing to stop moving whenever it was going down a small hill. Vivi nearly got crushed on a couple of occasions as she jumped in front of it and tried thrusting it back. Being so light and thin, she had to lean all her weight into it to make any difference at all.

Unfortunately, I'd badly underestimated just how uneven the road between the dump and Unicorn Cottage would be. There were significantly more ups and downs than I'd imagined. And the ups were the worst. It took both of us all our strength to get the trampoline to roll up even the slightest of inclines, giving it bursts of energy in the hope that momentum would carry it farther.

By the time we got it onto the drive at Unicorn Cottage, both Vivi and I were exhausted. I unlocked the door with my key, went into the kitchen, and turned on the tap, filling two large glasses of water and—according to the flashing light attached to the tap—using up my personal allocation for the next two days. We sat on the drive, sipping our drinks and staring at the trampoline.

"Hope you're happy now," said Vivi. "Now that you've nearly killed me for a bouncy castle."

I tutted. "It's not a bouncy castle. It's a much more technical piece of equipment than that. It takes great skill and judgment to use it properly."

"Okay. Show me, then."

The problem was that neither of us had an ounce of strength left after pushing the trampoline all the way home, so we left it lolling on its side for the evening like a beached whale.

The next day, Vivi came back to the house and we lifted the trampoline onto its feet and positioned it so that it was level. I tore all the safety netting off—I didn't need any of *that*, thank you very much—and dusted it all over before climbing on and testing it for spring.

"Not bad. Not bad," I said, finding a rhythm as I gently bounced. "Pretty responsive."

Vivi stood before me, not looking particularly impressed.

"Now watch this," I blurted, before bouncing harder and launching into a series of tuck jumps, straddle jumps, pikes, and levers.

Still not very impressed.

So I went for it.

Forward somersault. Straight back. Double som.

As my body twisted and twirled in the air, I could see the look on her face change.

"Wow," she said, her mouth wide. "Wow."

"You want a go?" I asked breathlessly as I brought myself to a stop and jumped off the trampoline onto the grass. "I'll show you some moves."

"No. No. I don't think so." She looked embarrassed. "I'm not very good at that sort of thing."

"Go on. It's easy enough."

"No. It's all right." She turned away and went over to stroke Sandwich, who was curled up on the kitchen doorstep.

"Suit yourself."

I caught my breath and looked around the garden. I looked at the tree with its tall branches overhanging the roof of the house. It was so close to my window that it blocked the sun every morning, and if my curtains suddenly disappeared I probably wouldn't notice any difference.

There was one branch—a really solid-looking thing—that hung about a foot or so higher than my window. As I stared at it, I had an idea.

I grabbed the trampoline by one of its legs and started to drag it toward the tree. As I pulled, it seemed to dig itself into the earth.

"What are you up to now?" Vivi sounded fed up. Sandwich was purring and dribbling under her fingers.

"Come on. Help me."

She sighed and walked slowly over to the trampoline. She pushed an end up and I pulled. Within a minute or two we had positioned it directly under the long branch near my window.

I climbed on and started to bounce, slowly building up height. Reaching upward, my hands were soon just below the branch. A little extra oomph and—

Got it!

I held on to the branch, dangling like laundry from a line.

"Wow!" I could see directly into my bedroom.

Vivi just stood there, shaking her head. "I don't know why you always have to do all this physical stuff. It's all so dumb, if you ask me."

I let go and bent my knees to absorb some of the bounce.

"Wait here!" I ran excitedly into the house and up the stairs to my room, where I opened the window as wide as I possibly could and pushed the bed so that it lay directly under the window. I then fished about in a small bag and managed to find some of the gymnastics chalk that I used to use at the gym.

Down in the garden, Vivi had gone back to stroking

Sandwich. I rubbed some of the chalk onto the palms of my hands and dusted off the excess.

I jumped back onto the trampoline and got going again. In a few seconds I had hold of the branch.

Now for the tricky bit.

I slowly rocked my legs back and forth, back and forth. Building up momentum.

"Be careful!" Vivi called.

I ignored her. I needed to focus fully to get this right. My hands slipped easily around the rough branch as I rocked and my legs swung increasingly upward. The window was only a few feet below me. The power in my body slowly grew, until, feeling the moment to be perfect . . . I let go.

My body arced through the air and my legs slipped in through the window, closely followed by the rest of me. As my feet came into contact with the bed, my body bounced slightly and the back of my head caught the very edge of the windowsill, smacking it hard.

"Ow!"

I lay on the bed for a few seconds, recovering. My scalp felt bruised and my arms ached a little, but otherwise I was fine. I'd done it!

I got off the bed, ran downstairs, and did it again. This time I made myself increase the height of the swing before releasing my hands. This meant my head had time to get through the window before my feet hit the bed. It was perfect.

After the fourth attempt—by which time I could have done it with my eyes closed—Vivi got up and walked toward the lane. "Perhaps I'll just go home."

"No, don't. Please don't go," I called out from my bedroom window. "Let me try just one more thing and we'll find something else to do."

"One more thing?"

"Yes." I climbed out my window and sat on the ledge.

I placed my feet flat against the outside wall and pushed, my arms reaching out for the branch. I grabbed it and held on tight as my body rocked itself to a stop. I hung there for a few seconds just looking around, taking everything in. The fields that swept away into the distance looked strangely regular and square. They reminded me of the pieces of cloth pinned to Vivi and Immaculata's ceiling. Across the fields, you could see the irrigation pylons dotted here and there like tall, thin pyramids. For a few minutes every day the farmers would be allowed to blast the crops with water, spraying the fields with a fine mist. Once or twice—when the farmer wasn't looking—I had crawled in and stood beneath one of the pylons, allowing myself to get soaked and licking up the drips that ran down my face. I could probably be in big trouble for it—I'd seen the Water Allocation Board violently arrest people in the street for less—but it was nice to wipe the grime from my face and hair, and anyway, an allowance of four minutes per week in the real shower was never enough. Not for anyone.

I looked down across the garden of Unicorn Cottage.

Like most of the things that had belonged to Uncle Jonah, it was messy and uncared for, the lawn hopelessly patchy. In fact the lawn seemed to sort of bubble up in parts, like it wasn't sitting properly.

Then suddenly . . . *Click!*

It was at that moment that a number of things shot through my head.

When I think back on it now it almost seems like I was meant to be hanging from the tree facing that particular direction at that particular time having those particular thoughts.

Not that I believe in fate or anything like that. I mean, how can you believe in fate when so many random things seem to happen in the world? Try telling the millions of people whose relatives have died or lost limbs in a war over water that it must all have been fate. People who believe in fate just don't want to accept responsibility for anything. They'd rather see the world in black-and-white with no gray in between. You're alive, you're dead, end of story, in their opinion. People who believe in fate have already given up.

Had Uncle Jonah given up?

So, no. It wasn't fate. It wasn't *meant* to happen. It just did. A lucky chance that my thoughts all came together at that moment.

It was the letters that I found myself thinking of.

The letters that Uncle Jonah had written to both Vivi and me.

Do not be put off by the fact that it looks like any other lump of stone or rock that you can find on any hillside or in any quarry or even in the garden at the rear of Unicorn Cottage.

That's what he'd written in both the letters. About the two parts of the Snowflake meteorite.

. . . or even in the garden at the rear of Unicorn Cottage.

And later in the letters . . .

Dig deep, my boy. Dig deep.

Always remember to dig deep.

I remembered how, when I first read the note that came with Snowflake 843A how strange and odd that sounded. *Dig deep.* I had assumed that Uncle Jonah was telling me to be brave, to try to stay true to the sort of person I was. Same thing with Vivi.

But what if it was something more than that?

What if it was a code? A clue?

I scanned across the lawn and my eyes were drawn to a spot in front of one of Uncle Jonah's rubbish-stuffed sheds. And for the first time I noticed that the grass seemed especially bumpy there.

I let myself drop from the branch and climbed back down onto the ground.

"Finished now?" Vivi asked, turning back from the lane and following me.

I picked my way across the dead grass toward the shed.

"What is it?"

I knelt down just before the shed. The lawn felt oddly buckled and it slightly shifted under my knees. I dug a couple of fingers into the earth and tried ripping up a clod. To my surprise, it came up incredibly easily. I threw it behind me and did it again.

Vivi laughed. "What *are* you doing, Auden?"

I ignored her and pulled up a few more lumps of the knotted, rooty turf.

Suddenly, something shone back at me from beneath the lawn.

"There's something metal in the ground," I blurted. I brushed some of the black grit out from the hole I'd just made.

"What's that?" Vivi stood over me.

"I don't know."

I tried grabbing another part of the turf and pulling it up, but this area was tightly packed after years of knotty roots had tied it all together. If Uncle Jonah had been a little bit negligent with the house, then he had completely ignored the garden. The lawn hadn't seen a rake or a hoe in many long years. The discarded boxes and bins that littered it were almost deliberately placed to make the whole area look (and smell) as awful as possible.

"Is there a shovel? Or a fork? Can you see one?"

Vivi looked around. "No."

"Have a look in one of the sheds."

She went to the shed farthest away, opening the door and springing backward as a ton of rubbish seemed to spew out. She poked about for a bit and then came back with something in her hand.

"I found this." She held it out to me. It was a small gardening trowel. "That's all there was."

"Okay." I took it from her and started hacking away at the roots and earth, digging at them until they loosened. After a couple of minutes of hard work, I dropped the trowel and grabbed at the turf with my hands again. I pulled clumps away and threw them over my shoulder behind me.

Whatever the metal thing was, it was long. And wide. Over the next ten minutes, I managed to expose a good four feet by two feet.

I tapped on the metal. It clanged, the sound almost bouncing back at me. I looked up at Vivi, who was frowning. She was clearly thinking the same as me.

"It's hollow," she said.

"What do you think it is?"

She shook her head. "I don't know. An old pipe?"

"But pipes are curved. This is flat on the top."

Vivi dropped to the ground and joined in, clawing away at the earth and roots surrounding the thing. At one point, we changed direction. Instead of working our way along the garden toward the house, we dug back toward the second shed. I loosened the turf with the trowel before we both ripped it away with our bare hands. Soon we'd removed all the earth up to the base of the shed, and the metal thing still hadn't come to an end.

"It goes under the shed," I realized.

"What does that mean?"

"I'm not sure." I sat there for a second, thinking. If it

went under the shed, then it must have been put there before the shed was built. It wasn't that deeply buried, so whoever put the shed on top *must* have known the metal thing was there. The shed wasn't that old—the bitumen didn't look at all faded—so, presumably, Uncle Jonah must have put it there. "We need to empty the shed," I said, suddenly jumping up and wiping the earth from my trousers. "Come on."

This shed was as full of junk as the other. Lots of discarded cardboard and technical-looking metal things seemed to fall out as we opened the door wide, and the stuff that didn't fall out remained utterly jammed to the roof, the little plastic windows of the shed barely detectable in the mess.

"You want to get all of this out?" Vivi asked.

"We need to see what happens under the shed."

"There's an awful lot of it. And I don't think your mum's going to be too happy when she sees it all spread out on the lawn."

I gave her a wink. "Don't worry about my mum. I can handle her." Although, to be honest, I was a bit concerned myself. Still . . .

I reached in and pulled something large and wooden out and dumped it on the lawn. Vivi grabbed something smaller—a black bin liner full of rubbery bits and pieces—and put it down next to the wooden thing. Some of the stuff was large and heavy enough for us both to have to carry it from either end, and within an hour we had almost emptied the shed.

There was one last item that needed to be removed: a

large, shopping-cart-size rectangular thing against the far wall that was covered in a tight-fitting tarpaulin. The tarpaulin didn't reach all the way to the floor, and at the bottom you could see that whatever it was it had wheels. Four big, fat wheels.

"What is that?" Vivi asked.

"Not sure. Let's get it out first and look at it outside."

The thing was heavy but rolled easily enough. I turned it around in the tight confines of the shed before pushing it out over the lip of the door and onto the grass.

The sheet of tarpaulin was tied around whatever it was, so we got on our knees again and started easing the knots open with our fingers. Eventually, the knots were undone and we yanked the tarpaulin off with some difficulty.

It was some sort of machine. Like a huge black box on wheels. On the top of the box, toward what I assumed to be the front, was a wide hole that seemed to funnel downward into its center. Slightly farther back on the top was a kind of flap. Vivi unclicked the latch and opened it up. We both leaned over and peered inside. There was nothing. Just an empty cube-shaped space about the size of a football.

On one of the sides sat two huge square plastic buttons. I punched one of them. Then I punched the other. Nothing happened.

"Is there a cord? Do we need to plug it in?"

Vivi pointed back at the cube-shaped space under the

flap. "I've a feeling that this is where the battery is meant to go."

"What sort of battery is that?" I said. The space was much bigger than ordinary batteries, but not as big as a car battery.

"Perhaps Dr. Bloom hadn't got around to inventing the battery for it when he died," Vivi answered.

"No. That doesn't make any sense. You build something around a battery. Not the other way around." I inspected the junk we'd spread out over the garden. There was nothing that looked as though it would fit the space. "It must be here somewhere."

"Perhaps it's in the other shed."

"Could be."

I went back to the black box on wheels and punched uselessly at the buttons again. Walking around to the other side I noticed something written on it. In chalk. Some of the chalk had rubbed off—possibly when we removed the tarpaulin—and some of the letters had just smudged themselves into a blur. I squatted so that I was level with the writing and dug out my magnifying glass to focus. I could just about make out, in Uncle Jonah's scratchy handwriting, the words:

Ra
Machi

"Rainbow machine!"

"What?"

"This is his rainbow machine. The one I think he was building. For me."

....

Instead of being annoyed, Mum was delighted when she saw that we'd cleared out the two sheds at the bottom of the garden.

"That was a job desperately in need of doing," she said when she saw all the rubbish covering the lawn. "Thank you both. Now"—she looked all over the garden—"if you could pack it all away in black bin bags and put it out front for the rubbish drones, I would be exceptionally grateful."

We both groaned but got to work, carrying all the awkwardly shaped bits and pieces between us and leaving them out on the scrappy patch of grass in the lane until the garden was cleaner than it had been even before we began.

There was no sign of the battery in the second shed. We had picked through everything but couldn't find it. Not a sign.

"Perhaps it was only a prototype," Vivi said as we pulled the tarpaulin back over the machine and wheeled it to the back fence, tucking it away under the overhanging branches of a tree in the field behind the house. "Perhaps he used the battery for something else because the rainbow machine wasn't going to work. After all, he burned all his notes on it, didn't he? Why would he do that if it was something that was going to work?"

"I don't know," I answered, getting a bit irritated with her. "I don't understand any of it. But if we can find that battery, we can *see* if it works or not."

Vivi gave her head a little shake.

"What?" I asked.

"Well . . . the thing is . . . I don't really understand what it could do to help you see color. Does it make a rainbow? If you turn on the machine, does it make a rainbow in the sky? Because, if that's all it does, you're still not going to be able to see any colors, are you?"

"Perhaps the rainbows are more vivid . . . stronger or something, so that I can see them."

"You can't make rainbows stronger than they are. That doesn't make sense. Rainbows are just rainbows. You can't just turn up the volume on them."

"How do *you* know?"

"I just do. It's obvious."

"Well, perhaps it doesn't make a rainbow," I spat. "Perhaps I have to put my face in the funnel part and it will cure me."

Vivi smiled.

"Anyway, what do you care?" I ducked, avoiding the branches. "It doesn't matter to you. You can see every color there is. You don't care about whether or not I can see colors. It doesn't bother you. You can just go through your life admiring the sky and the sun and the flowers. I can't."

"That's not fair!" she said, her eyes beginning to fill with tears. "Of course I care."

"No, you don't! You sit up there in your room, watching the sky flying past, poking your telescope into the stars and talking to no one but your bloody parrot."

Vivi marched quickly off into the lane, her shoulders high and tight. As she went around the corner, she didn't even bother to look at me.

CHAPTER 10

INVISIBLE INK

I hardly slept that night. I felt so guilty, the pillow seemed to become shapeless and lumpy and impossible to rest my head on. I wondered about going down into the garden and investigating the pipe that seemed to run under it, but I realized that I would probably wake Mum and then I'd have to own up about the rainbow machine. So in the early hours—having finally given up on sleep altogether—I grabbed my QWERTY and swiped it out of standby mode. I sat up and projected recent news bulletins onto the wall. The scrolling headlines didn't do anything to cheer me up.

ONE HUNDRED AND TWENTY BRITISH
SOLDIERS KILLED DURING SKIRMISHES
IN NORTHERN HUNGARY

BRITISH TANK REGIMENT ALMOST COMPLETELY
WIPED OUT AFTER AMBUSH BY ENEMY
TROOPS IN MAASTRICHT

DESALTING UNIT IN EASTBOURNE RAIDED
AND DESTROYED

UK WATER PRODUCTION DOWN
BY 12% SINCE LAST YEAR

....

I kept the sound low and watched footage of soldiers under attack in the center of Turin. Huge smoky explosions followed by lots of shouting and running. Guns and helmets. Armored vehicles scrunching over rubble. Women huddling young children in corners of derelict buildings.

I turned my QWERTY off.

Miserable stuff.

As usual.

....

I hadn't heard from my dad in nearly three months. The last time I talked to him, he was on three-day leave in Zurich. He buzzed me on my QWERTY and kept telling me how much he missed Mum and me. I couldn't see his face clearly— the signal kept being interrupted due to the army's encryption software—but he looked okay. A bit sadder around the eyes than normal and with more stubble around his chin than he usually had—which is understandable when you think he's been off fighting for nearly two years now—but otherwise he looked okay. I asked him what it was like, fighting in places he'd never even heard of before. He said that it was weird but that you got used to it. I asked him what food and water they were giving him and he said that the army fed and watered its troops well and that Mum and I didn't have anything to worry about. I wanted to ask him loads of things, but I didn't get the chance because the encryption software cut us off and wouldn't allow us to reconnect.

That was three months ago, and I haven't heard from him since.

....

I must have eventually dropped off because, before I knew it, I was waking up with a terrible, horrible thirst.

Of course, everybody wakes up thirsty. Well, everybody's *always* thirsty. All day long. Twenty-four seven, three sixty-five. Everybody talks with a click in their voice because of the dryness of their mouth and lips that look as if they are jigsaws. Tongues are always darting in and out, trying to spread around what little moisture there is. And everyone's dirty. Don't forget dirty. Nothing and nobody is ever truly, properly clean nowadays. Restricted water supplies do that to you, you know. Make you thirsty and dirty. Thirsty, dirty, and desperate.

But on this particular morning, my throat was even drier than usual. Perhaps I'd sweat during the night. Yes, that must have been it. In fact, my pillow seemed especially damp with sweat.

Downstairs, Mum had to let me have some of her allocation since I'd used up so much of mine just the day before, and I stuffed down my breakfast of eggs and potato fritters before jumping in the car and driving up to the city center with her.

At Trinity, Vivi was perched on the weird fountain thing reading a book that looked way too complicated for someone our age. She glanced up when she saw me approaching, then her eyes seemed to quickly jump back into the book.

"I'm sorry," I said. I don't like apologizing, but sometimes you just have to, don't you? Especially when you've said things that you know you shouldn't have. It's better for the other people and it's better for yourself. "I'm *really* sorry. I was an idiot yesterday. I didn't mean any of it."

Slowly, she closed her book and put it down on the crumbling wall beside her. "I know," she said, sounding the same as she always did. "You were just frustrated because we couldn't find the battery. I realize that." She hopped off the wall and took the book down. "Anyway, I was thinking . . ."

"What?" I was amazed. I thought I was going to have to do some serious begging to win her round. But she'd appeared to be over it all. Was she pretending? I wasn't sure. I watched her closely.

"I was thinking that you were right. There must be a power source for that machine somewhere. Must be. Anything else just doesn't add up." We walked across the courtyard. "And I think I know where it might be."

"Where?" I asked. Looking at her face I could see that she had spent a good while last night thinking this all through.

"Under the ground," she replied. "In that pipe thing under your garden."

....

We stood in the empty shed, looking at the floor. It wasn't flimsy—it was actual planks of wood secured in place with screws.

The pipe seemed to run under the far end of the shed, so I grabbed a screwdriver and started there. The first screw came loose quite easily. A couple of minutes later I'd removed all of the screws in the first plank, so I wedged the end of the tool into a crack and levered it out of position.

A hole. A gap. Beneath the shed. A deep, dark hole into which I could put my extended arm and still not touch the ground below.

"What is it?" Vivi asked somewhere behind me.

"It's a sort of . . . a sort of chamber."

I quickly unscrewed the next plank and the next one. Now I could push my head down into the hole. The air beneath felt cold on my face and I looked around. Most people would have needed a torch to see into that black pit. Not me. Even in dim light. I can make out shapes and detail that not many people can.

The small room had a brick floor and brick walls to which moss was clinging. It was about four feet wide by five feet long and the floor was about seven feet below the floor of the shed. I peered down into each of the corners (having to almost twist over onto myself to see into the corners still under the floor of the shed) and saw nothing at all. It was completely empty.

Then there was a flicker in my left eye. I turned to see where it had come from and I could just about make out a box shape on the wall. Only a few inches long and a few inches wide. The battery? I tried to focus on it and then—flash—another flicker came from the box.

I pulled my head out of the hole and hurriedly started removing the next few planks of wood.

"What's down there?" Vivi asked impatiently.

I dumped another plank near her feet and ignored the question. "Go round the side of the house," I said. "Against the wall is a rusty stepladder. Bring it here."

She ran out of the shed.

The boards came up easily and, eventually, I lifted the last one that covered the pit.

Vivi bashed the stepladder into the shed. There was very little space in which to maneuver, so when she brought it in the wrong way around we had to take it back out into the garden and turn it so that we could lower it into the hole properly. I wedged the bottom end of the ladder into the far corner and wobbled it to make sure it was secure. It was, so I went down first and Vivi followed.

"It's dark. I can't see."

It was definitely dark. The roof of the shed above blocked

out most of the light and only a little light got through the grubby windows.

"Use your QWERTY," I told her.

Vivi tapped the screen. Then she tapped it again.

"It's not working," she said.

"The torch function?"

"No. All of it."

I tutted. "You need to get a new one. Here, use mine." I unstrapped my QWERTY from my wrist and handed it to her.

"Yours isn't working, either."

"What?"

"Look." She handed it back to me and I swiped my finger across it. Nothing. It was utterly dead.

"I don't understand. It was fine last night."

"Well, it's not now."

"Weird." I slipped it back onto my wrist.

The little light on the box flickered again. Vivi noticed it, too, so I leaned forward and touched it. Suddenly the whole box seemed to glow, filling the chamber with light.

The box was a numerical keypad and above the keypad was a small screen with a flashing cursor. It was then that I noticed that most of the fourth wall was not a wall at all. It was made of the same shiny metal that we'd discovered just below the lawn, but with a slight, almost infinitesimal, gap straight down the middle.

"It's a door," I spat. "It's a door into the pipe. . . . No, wait. It's not a pipe. It's a tunnel."

Vivi's mouth had fallen wide open but her eyes were bright with excitement.

"We need the code," she said. "What's the code?"

I tapped some random numbers into the pad just to see what would happen. After the sixth digit the pad gave a long, critical beep like it was telling me off.

TWO ATTEMPTS LEFT. . . . scrolled across the screen.

"Oh no."

"If we don't get the right code it will shut itself down, won't it?" Vivi asked. "And then we'll never open the door." She gave me a glare. "Why did you have to go and waste one of the attempts?"

"Er, possibly because I didn't *know* I was wasting one of them!" I replied sarcastically. "Possibly because the rules aren't exactly scribbled on the wall."

"No need to be like that," she said sulkily.

I tried to think. What would it be? Assuming Uncle Jonah had put the door here, what code would he have programmed it with? It could have been anything. I didn't exactly know how Uncle Jonah's mind worked—I didn't know him that well. The random numbers I'd just punched in were as likely as anything else. Surely he must have left a clue of what they were somewhere.

In desperation I looked around the walls in the hope that I might find a small strip of paper with the numbers on it.

There was nothing. No clue. Nothing to point you in the right direction.

"Don't put any more numbers in until we know what it is," Vivi said, coming in closer and looking at the blinking box herself. "We can't waste any more chances."

I turned to go back up the ladder.

"Where are you going?"

"Outside. Standing around down here isn't going to help us, is it?"

In the garden, I walked along the length of the metal strip just under the grass.

"How far back do you think this tunnel goes?" asked Vivi as she came alongside me. "Do you think it goes all the way under the house? Or even farther?"

"I don't know," I mumbled. The last couple of days had started off like an adventure, but had just become frustrating. Everything seemed to just fall apart the more you looked at it. "Perhaps it's all just a complete waste of time. I mean, is there even anything under there?"

"Of course there is!" She almost screamed. "Why would Dr. Bloom go to the bother of hiding that tunnel away? There must be something incredibly important on the other side of the door. Can't you see?"

I kicked at some of the loose edges of grass with the tip of my shoe.

"Come on." She softened her voice. "Let's go back down and look at it again. There must be a way of working it out."

I sighed and walked over to the shed. As I got closer to the door I looked up. On the strip of thin wood at the top of the door frame somebody had written something.

"What's that?"

"What's what?"

"That." I pointed to the beam. "Something's written there."

"I can't see anything."

"Look. Just there." I got on tiptoe and tried to see. Struggling, I fished the magnifying glass out from inside my shirt and held it up. The word *ADDOBUS*—all capitals—was scrawled in a thin, wiry hand over the rough-cut wood. "See?"

"There's nothing there." Vivi held her hand up to shield her eyes from the light.

"Look." I spelled it out for her. "A.D.D.O.B.U.S."

She looked at me like I was mad. "Auden, there's nothing there."

"You can't see that?"

"No. Honestly, I think you're seeing things."

My mind suddenly jumped back to something that happened a couple of years before. A kid at school brought in a spy kit. Just lots of stupid plastic junk designed to occupy an eight-year-old for about half an hour. See-behind-you shades; an earpiece that helped you listen in on conversations the other side of the yard; sheets of codes to decipher. That sort of thing.

And a pen of invisible ink. Ink that could only be seen after being exposed to a blast of hot air.

I remember everyone gathering around as he scribbled something down on a sheet of paper and then held it up for everyone to see. Of course, nobody could see what he'd written. Except me. I could see it. Yet another of the peculiar benefits of my condition. Stupidly, I told them all what it said. If I'd had any sense at all I'd've kept my mouth shut and pretended to be normal like everyone else. But I didn't. The kid who'd written it looked at me like I was some sort of cheat and then, when everyone else had found out that I was right, they all looked at me like I was some sort of freak. Which is a bit odd because if you saw that happen in a comic or in a film, it would be obvious that the person was a superhero. But in real life, nobody believes in superheroes. Only weirdos. Weirdos like me are easy to believe in.

"It's invisible ink," I said.

"You mean there *is* something written there?"

I smiled, remembering telling Uncle Jonah about the incident at school, and him finding it incredibly funny. "Uncle Jonah put it there because he knew I'd be able to read it."

"What does it say again?" I could see the spark in Vivi's eyes flaring up.

"ADDOBUS."

"What does that mean? It's a pity our QWERTYs aren't—oh. It's working again."

I looked at mine. The screen was glowing away. "Mine's working, too. Strange."

Vivi tapped on her QWERTY. "ADDOBUS doesn't mean anything. Not according to this."

We stood there in silence for a minute.

"There must be a way of figuring out what it means," Vivi said. "Do you think it might be an anagram?" She used her QWERTY to run the letters through an etherweb anagram checker. "No. Nothing. Gah! This is annoying!"

We both stood at the door to the shed and stared up at the strip of wood with the invisible letters on it. "Hold on." It was Vivi again. "You said it was written in capitals, yes?"

"Mmm."

"Well . . . that might mean the letters stand for something."

"Yes, but what?"

"I don't know. . . . Wait . . . DOB. You see that all the time, don't you?"

"Do you?"

"Yes. D.O.B. Date of birth. You always see it on forms." She was right. "So what do the other let—"

A lightbulb moment.

"What?"

"A.D. Auden Dare," I said. "Auden Dare's date of birth. My date of birth!" I rushed into the shed and practically jumped down the ladder.

"Wait, Auden . . ."

I punched my date of birth into the keypad. The pad

gave another long, critical beep and *ONE ATTEMPT LEFT* . . . scrolled across the screen.

"No!"

Vivi came down the ladder beside me. "Wait! We need to think it all through." At the bottom of the ladder she dusted some rust off her hands. "ADDOBUS. Auden Dare. Date of birth. What about the *U* and the *S*? You rushed in too quickly and forgot about the *U* and the *S*?"

I thought. "The only thing I can think of is the US. The United States."

"That's it!" Vivi cried.

"What is?"

"In the USA they write their dates all awkwardly. In this country we always write the day, then the month, and then the year. Over there they swap the day and the month over."

"Why'd they do that?" I asked.

"No idea. But surely that's what it means. Auden Dare's date of birth in the US format. Go on, try it."

"It's our last attempt. Are you sure?"

Vivi looked doubtful for a second.

Before she had time to answer I tapped it in, swapping the month and the date around.

A beep. A much nicer beep, almost like it was congratulating me.

OPEN . . . filled the screen and—

The doors separated, withdrawing into the walls on either side.

"You did it!" Vivi squealed.

"*We* did it," I corrected her.

However, our joy didn't last very long. Beyond the doors was a squarish metal tunnel and we stepped into it, the clanging sound of our feet echoing around the room. The tunnel was only about eight feet long and ended . . . at another door! Another *closed* door. With another pad positioned on the wall next to it.

"Oh no."

"Not again!"

The pad was slightly different from the one just outside the tunnel. There were no numbers or letters to press. It was just a screen. And on the screen were sixteen glowing dots. The dots were not in any sort of order, they seemed to just be randomly thrown all over the place, and some of the dots were slightly bigger than the others.

"What's all this about now?" I asked, barely managing to hide the fed-up tone in my voice.

But Vivi didn't answer. She was staring hard at the arrangement of dots on the screen.

"Don't tell me you can see a pattern in them!" I laughed. "They're just random, aren't they?"

Still she didn't answer. After about a minute she grinned.

"In the letters that Doctor Bloom wrote to us . . ."

"Yes?"

"Well, he gave us the clue for finding this tunnel, didn't he?"

"So?"

"Well, he also told you that if you needed to find out anything about stars and space to ask Six Six, yes?"

"Uh-huh." I nodded.

"When did you say your birthday was?" Vivi asked me.

"March second."

"March second . . . That makes you a Pisces." She squinted at the screen again. "Pisces. Yes!"

She moved closer to the screen and put a finger on one of the dots, then dragged it across to another. A line appeared on the screen, tracing her movements. "This is the constellation of Pisces." She dragged her finger across the screen to another of the dots then another like some sort of connect-the-dots puzzle. "You know what a constellation is, don't you?"

"Of course I do. It's all about the stars, isn't it?"

"It's a collection of stars. This one—the one connected to your birthday—is Pisces. It's supposed to look like two fish jumping out of water."

The shape she was drawing on the screen looked nothing whatsoever like two fish jumping out of water to me. If anything, it looked like a bent stick. With a leaf still attached to one end.

Vivi did a sort of loop on the bottom right-hand side of the screen, linking up the last of the dots and then stood back. The image remained fixed on the screen before . . .

Beep.

OPEN . . .

The doors pulled apart.

"You, Vivi Rookmini," I laughed, "are a genius!"

"Oh, I don't know about that. It was obvious, really."

Beyond this door was another small room. There were still no lights and Vivi tried to access the torch function on her QWERTY but it wasn't working again. I looked at mine—nothing.

We stepped into the room and I suddenly froze.

"What? What is it?" Vivi couldn't see a thing.

But I could.

Something was sitting on the floor at the far end of the room.

"Tell me," Vivi said again. "What is it?"

I turned to look at her and found myself whispering a reply.

"It's a man."

PART THREE

RED

CHAPTER 11
PARAGON

Vivi shone the torch that she'd found in the utility room over the figure slumped against the metal wall.

"What is it? Is it alive?"

I knelt down beside whatever it was and looked it up and down.

"Is it a drone?" Vivi asked.

"Funny-looking drone," I said. "I've never seen a drone shaped like a human before, have you?"

"No. Perhaps he's a new sort of drone. One they haven't released yet."

"Perhaps."

After the shock of seeing a man lying in the small chamber, I had edged myself forward carefully and seen that it was, in fact, not a man at all. It was man-shaped—that was true—but it was made of metal and wires and lights. Its "back" was resting against the wall, and its "head" was nodding forward onto its "chest" like it was asleep. Vivi had run off to get a torch and returned waving it around like a sword fighter.

"What's it doing here?" The day seemed to be filled to the top with questions.

"I don't know," I answered, poking my finger toward the thing.

"Why hide it away down here? Why keep it under the ground in a secret tunnel with two sets of security doors to protect it? Come to think of it, there's obviously something creating an electromagnetic disturbance down here that's making our QWERTYs stop working. That can't be a coincidence. Why? Why go to all this trouble to hide a drone?"

"I don't think it's a drone. I think it's more than that. I think it's a robot."

"A bot? But bots build cars and boats and planes. They stitch clothes together—very badly. They're machines bolted to the floors of factories. They don't move. They're unthinking things with a single job that they're designed to do. And they certainly don't look like humans."

I poked its arm again. Nothing happened. The metal was bright and cold and I could see my face in it.

"Is it . . ." Vivi struggled to find the right word. "Dead?"

It was then I noticed the button. Big and round and positioned somewhere you might describe as being just under the collarbone. I imagined it to be green—whatever green is. Green for go.

"Should you be doing that?" Vivi watched as my finger headed toward the button. "Shouldn't we tell someone about this? An adult?"

I was excited. This whole situation was set up for *me*. Not anyone else. Uncle Jonah knew that when he died Mum would inherit the house and that I would be with her. He used *my* birthday as the code on the first door and *my* star sign on the second. It was all set up for *me* to find. Me. Not some random adult.

I looked up at Vivi. "Er . . . no!"

I hit the button.

The robot started to whir—a high-pitched whir a bit like when etherweb boxes at school are turned on. It whirred and then it hissed slightly. Lights flickered on the front of its chest and along its arms.

"I think I found the on switch." I grinned at Vivi, who had taken a step backward.

Suddenly, lights where its eyes would be flashed into existence and its "head" turned to look at me. It felt weird to have this thing with its bright, inhuman eyes staring at me and, for a brief moment, I was scared.

What had I done?

The head swiveled slowly and took in Vivi, who gave a tiny whimper, her trembling hands making the torch vibrate—the light twitching in the tiny room.

Then the robot's body shifted, easing its weight forward

until the legs bent back before straightening again, pushing it upright. All accompanied by hisses and whirs and tiny internal bleeps that bounced loudly around the walls.

Soon, it was standing up. And—*whoa*—was it tall. The top of its head was only a couple of inches below the ceiling, making it six foot five at the very least.

I got up from the floor and stood next to Vivi.

"Perhaps you'd better . . . turn it off now . . . don't you think?" Vivi's anxious eyes seemed to be begging me. "Perhaps we'd better stop . . . now. Yes?"

"Not yet," I whispered.

The robot's head twisted and tilted as it took in its surroundings.

"Hello!" I said, and its head jerked back to look at me. "Er . . . hello." I don't know why—I'd never even done it with a real human being before—but I extended my hand toward the bot to shake its hand. "Hello."

Its glowing eyes stared at me for a few seconds before . . .

The pneumatic or hydraulic pistons or whatever they were in its arm lifted the hand up toward mine, and the fingers curled around me. For a moment I was worried that they were going to crush my hand, but the fingers stopped moving and the hand felt gentle wrapped around my own.

"Hello," I repeated, and tried shifting my arm up and down—shaking hands. To my surprise the robot's forearm moved along with mine. Easily. Softly.

"Hi," the robot said.

I don't know what I was expecting. I suppose I was expecting it to be a bit like Migishoo—copying, repeating back whatever I said and not properly understanding. The fact that it didn't—it said hi, not hello—surprised me. Unnerved me.

Vivi came forward a little.

"My name is Auden Dare. And this is Vivi Rookmini."

The robot lifted its hand and stared at it, twisting it around in front of its face like it was trying to understand what it was.

"Hi, Audendare," it said, still inspecting its hand. "Hi, Vivirookmini." The robot said our names like there was no gap in between them.

"What is *your* name?" Vivi asked, trying to be brave but allowing the shiver in her voice to come through.

The robot dropped its hand to its side and looked straight at us.

"My name?" it asked. It seemed to be thinking, like it wasn't sure. Perhaps it didn't have a name. I mean, why would you give a bot a name? I could see Vivi was thinking exactly the same thing and clearly felt a bit foolish for asking, her eyes dancing between the robot and the floor.

"My name," said the robot, "is Paragon."

"Paragon?"

"Yes. My name is Paragon."

It spoke (if that is the right word to use for a mechanical, automated lump of metal) with an American accent, like it had just walked out of a movie. It took a small step forward and twisted its torso around to take in the room in which it had been sitting.

"Good to meet you, Audendare and Vivirookmini."

Vivi gave a small laugh. It wasn't the sort of voice you would imagine coming out of a robot. You would think that a machine would talk with a stuttering monotone. Some-thing-a-Lit-tle-Like-This. But it didn't. Its voice was smooth and clear and kind of . . . normal.

"Paragon," Vivi said. "What a lovely name."

"Is it?" I looked at her.

"Yes. A paragon is a perfect thing. A shining example. A model for others to follow."

"Thanks, Miss Dictionary." I turned to the machine. "Who made you? Was it Jonah Bloom? Did he put you here?"

A couple of lights flickered on the face.

"I," Paragon started, "do not know. I do not have that information. Sorry, Audendare."

"That's all right." For some reason—even though I knew that this thing in front of me was nothing more than wires and circuit boards—I found myself not wanting him—sorry, *it*—to feel as if it had anything to apologize for. Doesn't make much sense, I know, but if something looks and acts like a human being, you find yourself feeling as if you should treat it like a human being. I tried to shake the silly idea out of me. This was, after all, something man-made. A machine. That's all. A machine with pretend arms and pretend legs.

"What job were you built to do?" I asked. "What is your purpose?"

It paused like it was thinking again. "I do not have that information, Audendare. I do not know my purpose."

"But you must. You must know why my uncle built you. There must be something in your computer brain that tells you what it is you are meant to do. Every bot has some kind of role."

The machine in front of me seemed to straighten up slightly. "A *bot* is a device created by humans to undertake simple construction tasks. I don't believe I am *that*." It sounded as if it was offended. "I do not know for what reason I was created . . . but I am certainly not a bot."

Vivi smiled at me.

"What about a drone, then?" I said. "Are you a drone?"

It tilted its head like it was thinking the idea over.

"Nope."

Nope? What sort of a word was *nope* for a robot? *Negative* or something would be more appropriate, wouldn't it?

"Well, what *are* you, then?"

"I don't know." It looked around again. "Tell me, Audendare and Vivirookmini . . . where am I?"

....

The thing climbed the ladder with ease and had to duck as it made its way out of the shed into the bright light of late morning. It scanned around, taking everything in—the house, the garden, the sky.

" 'There is another sky,' " Paragon started.

"Ever serene and fair,

"And there is another sunshine,

"Though it be darkness there.'"

"What?" I asked.

"It's poetry," Vivi said, her eyes staring up at the strange creature revealed in all its metallic wonder before us. I didn't know the first thing about engineering, but you could see that it was lovingly and precisely crafted. "He's reciting poetry. Aren't you?"

"Emily Dickinson," Paragon answered.

Poetry? Why bother programming a machine with poetry? What's the point of poetry? Poetry doesn't take out the garbage. Poetry doesn't fix your TV. Poetry doesn't pump up the tires on your car. A machine that recites poetry is a waste of vital electronic equipment, surely? A waste of valuable resources.

I didn't say anything. There were things I wanted that I thought Paragon might be able to give me.

"Do you recognize this place?" I asked it.

"Er . . ." It seemed to doubt itself. "Er . . . nope."

"You sure?"

"I . . . don't . . . think so. Nope. Definitely not."

Again, I was confused. A true machine would instantly know and would be able to instantly tell you. That's how computers work. There's a "Yes." There's a "No." And nothing in between. Definitely no "Er." . . . So why the element of doubt in its "voice"? Paragon wandered away from us, peering about at some of the rubbish still left in the grass, picking it up and dropping it with its "hands." I turned to Vivi, who was clearly thinking the same things.

"There's a thing called 'fuzzy logic,'" she said. "I read about it once. It's where you give a computer a chance of getting things wrong. It's a way of making a computer's brain more like a human brain."

"What's the point in that?" I asked. It didn't make much sense to me.

She shrugged.

"So even though it's acting like it's human . . . it's still just a robot."

She shrugged again.

I led Paragon into the house. I took it into the sitting room and the kitchen and the utility room.

"You're certain you've never been here before?" Perhaps—at some point—the fuzzy logic might turn in my favor and reveal the truth.

"Nope. I do not recall ever having been here before. In fact . . . I do not recall ever having been *anywhere* before." He stressed the "anywhere" perfectly. "This is the first place I have ever been."

"What do you mean?"

"He's been reprogrammed," Vivi said somewhere behind me. "Your uncle must have wiped his memory before putting him down below the shed."

"And you've never heard of Jonah Bloom?" I asked again.

"Nope. No idea. I know the tale of Jonah and the whale. Do you know it?"

I sighed. "No. I don't know it and, to be honest, I don't care. What about the rainbow machine? Have you any idea where the battery for the rainbow machine is hidden?"

"Sorry, Audendare . . . I don't know anything about a rainbow machine. I can tell you how rainbows are made—"

"No."

Paragon straightened again, as if it was slightly taken aback. "O-kay." It turned to look at Vivi and, even though it didn't have eyebrows, it appeared to raise them.

I marched over to Paragon and punched the button that started it up in the first place. The electric hum died along with the flashing lights, and the machine stopped dead still where it stood.

"What did you do that for?" Vivi frowned.

"Look. It doesn't know anything. It hasn't got a clue. I don't know why Uncle Jonah even bothered to build it. I mean, it doesn't serve any purpose."

"Just because he doesn't know what his purpose is doesn't mean he hasn't got one."

"And will you *please* stop referring to it as 'he.' It's a thing. Not a person. It's a load of wire and metal acting like it's human. That's all. Just a slightly more advanced lawn mower or something. Stop calling it a 'he.'"

Vivi went quiet. We both stood there staring at the robot, stuck there completely still, halfway through a movement.

"Anyway," Vivi spoke quietly. "Why does it have to have a purpose? Is that the reason why everything exists? Because it's useful? And if it's just a machine, why did you shake its hand?"

"I was confused for a second. I wasn't thinking properly."

"Well, what are you going to do about him? You can't just leave him here in the middle of your utility room. Your mother will be back from work later and I don't think she'll be all that pleased to see a robot blocking the back door."

Mum. I thought for a second. Should I tell her about Paragon? What would she say? She would probably say that we should let the authorities know. Then it would be taken away. And even though it said that it knew nothing about a rainbow machine or its power source, I wasn't so sure. Perhaps it had orders from my uncle to hold back on certain pieces of information and not to reveal them for some reason. Perhaps, even though it had—according to Vivi—been reprogrammed, it might have the information still deeply scratched somewhere into its memory bank. All I knew was that if the authorities took this . . . thing . . . away, I would never find the battery and I would never get the rainbow machine to work.

"We'd better take it back underground. For now," I said. "I don't think we should tell anyone about this."

"No," Vivi agreed. "But I was thinking . . ."

"What?"

"Perhaps it's true that he has never been here—to this house—before. I mean, it's unlikely that Dr. Bloom actually built him here."

"*It*," I corrected her. "It's a *thing*."

She ignored me. "But perhaps he might remember *another* place. If we were to take him places he might have a memory of, then it's not impossible he might have some idea of why he was built. Yes?"

"Yes. I suppose." I stopped and thought. "Hold on, you're not suggesting we take it to Uncle Jonah's rooms in Trinity, are you?"

"Well . . . ideally, yes."

"But . . . look at it. It's massive. How are we meant to get it there?"

She thought for a minute. "Well, okay. You're right. Perhaps instead we could show him Cambridge from a distance. If we go up one of the hills not far from here, we might be able to show him the city, and hopefully he'll remember why he was built."

"Yes. But tomorrow. Not now. Now I think it'd better go back into its room under the shed." I hit the on switch and the robot seemed to immediately continue the movement it had started before I'd turned it off.

"Hi again, Audendare and Vivirookmini. How are you both?"

"You're going back underground," I said.

"Hmm?"

"You heard."

Vivi stepped toward Paragon. "We'll come back and see you tomorrow. We're going to take you out and see if we can work out what your purpose is."

" 'Tomorrow, and tomorrow, and tomorrow,

"Creeps in this petty pace from day to day.' "

"Poetry?" asked Vivi.

"Shakespeare," replied Paragon.

"Will you please pack it in with the poetry!" I sighed. "And get yourself back into the shed. Now."

The machine made its way without complaint back to the hidden room under the garden.

"You promise you will return tomorrow?" it said in the gloom of the chamber, and it almost sounded pitiful. "I think I would like it if you were to help me find what it was I was built for. That sounds good. And in exchange perhaps I could—"

"Yes, yes," I said dismissively, and punched the button one more time.

CHAPTER 12
PURPOSE

"Good morning, Audendare."

"Look . . . er . . ."

"Paragon."

"Yes. Paragon." Giving a thing a name felt funny. "Look, my name isn't Audendare."

"Isn't it?"

"No. It's Auden."

"Oh, I see." It nodded its head like it understood. "Your first name is Auden and your last name is Dare. Am I right?"

"Yes. That's right."

"That makes sense." It moved its head closer as if it was sharing a secret with me. "To be honest . . . I did think that Audendare was quite an unusual name. And I suppose

Vivirookmimi's name is really Vivi. . . ." It paused for a second. "Rookmini. Yes? Two separate names again?"

"Yes." I was having a conversation with a tin can.

Paragon crawled up the ladder and stepped back out onto the patchy lawn, where Vivi greeted it like it was a long-lost uncle or something.

"So?" it said. "What's the plan?"

"Well," Vivi began, "I think that it might be a good idea to just see if it becomes obvious what you were constructed for."

"And to try to see if you really do know anything about the rainbow machine and how to work it," I added quickly. That, to me, was much more important than finding out what this glorified wheelbarrow was made for. If Uncle Jonah had *really* found a way of fixing my problem, then obviously I was keen to try it out. After all, Paragon was probably just a little side project for Jonah—a hobby— like the way some people rebuild old cars or weave willow baskets or something. No, Paragon itself wasn't important in my eyes (so to speak!). It was what it might know or what it might be able to do that was exciting to me.

You see, I know I rather go on about how it doesn't matter not being able to see color, and how it makes me special in a way. Like I'm a superhero. And sometimes I really believe that. When I'm happy and things are going right, I feel like it's kind of a good thing not to be able to know the difference between red and green. I can persuade myself that everything is simplified and, in a sense, color is just another complication. Those are the good days.

But there are many other times when I don't feel like that at all. When all I can think is how incomplete I actually am. Those are the bad days. The days I feel depressed or angry. Sometimes the anger slips out and I might punch my pillow or kick a wall. And sometimes the anger goes in—and that's a lot worse.

I don't like those days.

"And how are we going to do that?" Paragon replied, its "head" tilted a bit.

"Vivi thinks we should go for a walk," I moaned.

"A walk?"

"I know. Ridiculous, isn't it?"

Vivi stuck her tongue out at me. "Yes. Just to see if it gets you thinking. Try to tease out what it is you were designed for."

"And if you know about the rainbow machine," I repeated quickly.

"O-kay! Let's get going!" It started to walk.

"Hang on, hang on." I stuck my hand up in front of its "chest" and it stopped. "We can't exactly take you out looking like that."

"Like what?"

"Like *that*. Like a robot. Everyone will be staring at you. Then the authorities will probably take you away from us."

"Yes. We can't risk some of the Scoot drones or the Ariel drones spotting you, too," added Vivi.

"Oh, I wouldn't be too worried about any drones," said Paragon. "I can take care of them."

"You can take care of them?"

"Yep."

"How?"

"Whoever it was that built me gave me an EMD—that's an electromagnetic disabler. I can block any electronic device within two hundred meters. Any drones that pass by will simply stop functioning correctly. So don't you worry about drones."

Both Vivi and I glanced down at our QWERTYs at exactly the same time. I don't know about Vivi's, but mine certainly wasn't working properly.

"Yes, well, that's good news about the drones," Vivi said, "but we also have to worry about any people seeing you."

"So? What do you suggest, Vivi . . ." He paused. "Rookmini?"

"Ta-da!" She pulled the long dirty-looking trench coat with the big buckled belt from behind her back. "This used to belong to one of the professors at Trinity. He didn't want it anymore so he gave it to my mother to use. That and . . ." She pulled her other hand from behind her back. "This!" It was a hat. A large, wide-brimmed thing that would shade your eyes from even the sunniest of suns. "I thought you could wear them."

I shook my head. I couldn't believe we were about to put clothes on a walking tumble dryer.

"I . . . don't think I'm designed to wear clothes," Paragon said, looking from Vivi to me then back again. "Am I?"

"No. You're not," I answered. "You're just a machine. You're not human."

"Oh."

Was it just me or did it sound hurt?

And was it just me or did I feel a bit guilty?

"Anyway." Vivi came forward and held the coat and the hat out to Paragon. "We can't go out without you wearing something, so . . ."

Paragon took the clothes from her. It dropped the hat on the floor and seemed to throw the coat around itself. Considering it had never once before put a coat on, it did so slickly with not even a single struggle around the shoulders. I was impressed.

Then it bent to the ground and kind of flicked the hat, letting it roll itself along the length of its outstretched right arm, bouncing it up off the shoulder and onto the head, where it fell softly and securely.

"Wow." Vivi was openmouthed.

"Cool," I found myself saying with a smile on my face.

Paragon pulled the hat down gently. "Any good? How's it look?"

"Suits you," Vivi said, before popping together the buttons on the coat and pulling the belt tightly around Paragon's torso. "You look good."

We walked across the patchy fields of wheat that bent in the slight, warm breeze, past the tall pyramid-shaped irrigation pylons, and along the unkempt, unused tarmac roads. Both Vivi and I thought it best to avoid people if we could—even dressed in clothes, Paragon looked a bit odd and we were sure to get the occasional funny glance. So we headed out away from the city and into the countryside.

"Perhaps you were designed to fix the roads," I said after almost twisting an ankle in one of the many potholes that littered the lane along which we were walking. "And even if you weren't, they need to design *something* to fix the roads."

"Nope," Paragon answered. "Definitely not fixing roads. That's not me. I feel I have a greater purpose than that."

"You don't *feel* anything," I said, slightly irritated once again by the way this machine was pretending to be human. "You just *think* you feel. Well, actually, you don't even think. You just turn switches on and off in your computer brain. That's all. It's just combinations of switches and pistons and stuff."

Paragon stopped walking and turned to face me. "I have to say, Auden, you really are horribly analytical."

"What?"

"Well," it continued, "you seem intent on reducing everything to its basic, unimaginative, constituent parts."

"Hold on, are you—"

"Don't listen to him," Vivi interrupted, grabbing Paragon by its sleeve. "He's just a miseryguts. Come on."

They both walked off, leaving me standing alone in the middle of my pothole.

....

The countryside around Cambridge is mostly flat and even—a bit like somebody has taken a massive rolling pin to it, or stamped their huge boot across it—with only the occasional hill or valley, and as the morning eased on, we slowly made our way toward one of the hills topped with a spiky crown of trees.

At one point, a pair of Ariel drones drifted by above us, their usually blinking eyes dull and dead, before carrying on into the distance.

"Did they see us?" said Vivi.

"Nope. They didn't see a thing," Paragon replied. "Trust me."

The hill looked quite gentle from the lane and we climbed over the rotten stile into the field of lifeless grass and made our way toward the gritty path that wound its way upward.

Halfway up, we stopped and turned around to look at the spread of the land below.

"Okay." Vivi struggled to catch her breath. "So . . . in the distance there . . . you can see Cambridge. Some of those spires belong to the colleges of the university. Which was where Dr. Jonah Bloom worked—the man who built you. He was a fellow at Trinity College . . . ?" She looked at the machine in the hope something might click. But no. There was nothing. "Okay, then. All around us you can see the fields. Some growing the corn and wheat to make food with—those are the ones with the irrigation pylons. Other fields are growing succulents and cactuses . . . cacti . . . er . . ."

"Cacti. Cactuses. Either one's fine," confirmed Paragon.

"Okay. So some of the fields are growing succulents and cacti because they don't require much water and people can buy them to have in their houses. Nobody buys real flowers anymore." She shielded her eyes against the sun and pointed into the distance. I didn't even bother looking. When it's particularly sunny everything just seems to blur.

"Over there you can see transportable water storage units. Next to them you can see the recycling plant. Just in the distance on that side there are grain distribution centers—those warehouse buildings just there—can you see? And if you really squint, you can just about make out the thin line of where the river Cam used to flow. It's not much now, of course." She looked up at Paragon, who was scanning the whole of the horizon. "Now, does any of that mean anything to you?"

"Nope." It turned its head and looked slightly farther up the hill. "Although . . ." It stumped up the hill toward a large patch of weeds and grabbed one of the stalky plants, yanking it out of the ground so that its roots dangled uselessly and clods of earth dropped onto the dry path. Paragon came back down and held the plant up toward us.

"What?" I asked.

"Do you know what this is?" it asked back.

"Er, no," I replied as sarcastically as I could manage. "I don't *think* so."

"Hmm. Sarcasm. Nice." Paragon gave the long stem with the pointy flower at the top a bit of a shake. "This is *verbascum thapsus*. Also known as Aaron's Rod. Comes from the family *scrophulariaceae*. Biennial. Native to Britain although quite uncommon in both Scotland and Ireland. Generally grows on wasteland—like this. Was once used to treat bronchial difficulties. People would crush it up and put it in a pipe to smoke. Herbal medicine."

It stood there like it was waiting for one of us to comment. It was me who broke the silence.

"So?"

"So, what?"

"What's the point in knowing that?"

It looked slightly flustered.

Vivi went alongside Paragon and took the long stem from it. "Medicine. Perhaps that is why you were made. To treat people. Like a doctor."

Paragon gave its head a shake. "I don't think so. I know an awful lot about plants. Not all of them are used for medical purposes."

"If you know about plants," I started, "then you might have been designed for farming."

Its head carried on shaking. "No. I know lots of things. Not just about plants."

"What other things do you know?" Vivi said.

"There are too many to list right now. Far too many."

"Name some," I ordered.

"Some?"

I sighed. "Yes. *Some.*"

It gave the impression of thinking for a moment or two. "Okay. I can tell you the Latin and common names of every bird native to Britain and mainland Europe. I can tell you the Latin and common names of every *tree* native to Britain and Europe."

"You can recite poetry," Vivi added.

"Yes. I can recall every poem written by all the major world poets from approximately 3000 BC onward. I can identify and comfortably discuss every single significant piece of art—in all its forms—created over the last two thousand years. I can provide you with a list of constituent gases that make up the atmosphere of every planet in our solar system. I can tell you the quickest route between two places. I can list the members of every single government that held power in every single country of the world over the last three hundred years. I can also tell you the best way to make Welsh rarebit." It paused. "That sort of thing."

"So, you can tell us lots of stuff that we can just look up on the etherweb?" I sniffed. "Things that I can just find out from messing about on my QWERTY."

"Ah yes," Paragon replied. "But can your QWERTY do it with a smile on its face?" Paragon pointed comically with both hands to its shiny, metal, unmovable mouth.

"Is that meant to be a joke?" I found myself grinning.

"Of course. As well as being extraordinarily clever I have also been blessed with a tremendously advanced sense of humor!"

"Advanced, ha!" I spun around and stared up at the rest of the hill above us.

"Yes." Paragon came alongside me and leaned in close. "A sense of humor that doesn't rely as heavily on sarcasm as *other* people I could mention."

I ignored it and continued up the hill.

At the top, I pushed into the thick, dark wood, picking my feet over the fallen, rotting timber and slippery moss until I stepped out into a small clearing where brambles seemed to be taking over, snatching at the bottom of my trouser legs like the fingers of a Flute drone. A minute or so later Vivi and Paragon came into the gap, Paragon turning aside and tapping the bark of an ancient-looking tree.

"Engish oak. *Quercus robur.*"

I tutted and Vivi frowned at me.

"What?" I perched myself on the edge of a half-toppled log.

"It's all right, Vivi." Paragon picked its way over to where I was sitting. "I'm getting used to him now. I don't think he's particularly impressed by all the things I know."

"Yes, well—"

But Paragon cut me off—a rude thing for a robot to do, in my opinion. "I don't think Auden Dare has any time for flowers or trees or poetry, do you? I think he finds it all a little . . ." It pretended to struggle for the right word.

". . . useless. Yes. He finds all my knowledge a tad too impractical."

"It's not that—"

But it cut me off again. This time with an enormous flourish and a flick of the trench coat. Within a second, the coat was on the floor at the machine's feet.

"Excuse me," it said, "but I really feel I need to get this off my chest—if you'll pardon the pun. I've tried to put it off but I just can't any longer." It jabbed a finger toward the point a little below the on/off button. "There is a light—just here—that appears not to work. I've a feeling it should be red. Every other light on my body works, but this one does not. I've run diagnostics to try to isolate the problem, to no apparent avail. I initially assumed it was merely a faulty LED, but alas, no. I can't even work out what it is connected to. And I'm starting to feel a touch frustrated with it, to be honest." It turned and took both Vivi and me in before whispering, "I'm a bit worried about it."

"It's probably not important." Vivi talked in the sort of smooth, soothing voice that I sometimes used on Sandwich whenever she got a thorn or a piece of glass caught in her paw. "It's probably something that doesn't *need* to work, or something small that just wasn't finished."

Paragon seemed weirdly reassured. "You think so, Vivi? Yes, perhaps you're right. It might be just nothing, don't you think?"

A small light that didn't work? A tiny, almost insignificant thing that didn't seem to stop it from functioning correctly! I found myself virtually hissing in anger. Perhaps it was going to be one of the bad days after all. Paragon noticed.

"Auden? Are you okay?"

"No. I'm not okay. There you are worried about some silly little light not flashing, but you still seem to be working properly. Other people—*real* people—have more to struggle with than just a faulty light, you know? They have real problems. Real difficulties. Not just a stupid section of faulty wiring."

The machine's head tilted to one side and its eyes lowered their glow. "Are we"—its voice was quiet and soft—"talking about *you*, Auden?"

"What do you mean?"

"Is there something that troubles *you*, Auden Dare?"

Vivi answered instead of me. "Auden can't see color."

I sneered toward her. "Yeah. She's right. I can't see any color. Never have done. I suffer from . . . what is it? Aachrom . . . achromatopsia. So when you—"

But I stopped.

Upon hearing the word *achromatopsia*, Paragon did something strange. Something it hadn't done before. It suddenly jerked to attention. Not with the smooth humanlike movements that it had always used so far, but with stiff, quick, and regular movements. Like a robot. Like a *proper* robot, designed for building warships or something. It locked its arms at its sides, pulled its legs straight together, and fixed its head level and stared into the distance.

"Paragon?" I found myself asking.

Then it spoke. Not with the easy fake-human voice that it had been fooling Vivi with since we found it, but with a dull, monotonous robot voice.

"My . . . name . . . is . . . Paragon. . . . I . . . was . . . created . . . by . . . Dr. . . . Jonah . . . Bloom . . . fellow . . . in . . . physics . . . and . . . mathematics . . . at . . . Trinity . . . College . . . Cambridge . . . and . . . of . . . Unicorn . . . Cottage . . . Cambridge. . . . Dr. . . . Jonah . . . Bloom . . . has . . . no . . . children . . . of . . . his . . . own. . . . His . . . nearest . . . living . . . relatives . . . are . . . his . . . sister . . . Christabel . . . Dare . . . and . . . her . . . son . . . Auden . . . Dare . . . of . . . Forest . . . Gate . . . London. . . . Auden . . . Dare . . . suffers . . . from . . . achromatopsia . . . a . . . rare . . . inability . . . to . . . see . . . color."

It suddenly stopped its chant and remained completely still. Vivi and I just stared at Paragon as the breeze battled its way through the trees and into the clearing.

Then Paragon moved again with the free-flowing, almost natural movements that it normally made. It was a bit like it had been holding its breath and had suddenly exhaled, relieved to do so.

"The word unlocked him," Vivi said. "The word *achromatopsia* actually unlocked him."

"Huh?" I asked.

Vivi shook her impatient head at me. "That word was obviously used as a key by your uncle. By saying the word, it triggered some information." Vivi stood in front of Paragon—ridiculous now with the hat half-dangling off the side of its head—and stared straight up into the face. "Did it release any other information? Did you find out anything else?"

Paragon seemed to stumble before adjusting the hat. "No. I don't think so. Perhaps a little of the nature of Dr. Bloom's work, but nothing much." Vivi picked the trench coat up from the musty ground and held it out to the machine. Paragon took it and, this time, slowly swung it onto its shoulders, less enthusiastic than before—maybe even a little shaken up. "A bizarre sensation," it rather mumbled to itself. "Very, very odd."

I got up from the log. "So you *did* know my uncle," I said. "Did you know him well? Can you remember him?"

"I remember . . . a little."

"Like?"

"Like the way he hummed to himself as he fitted my central flange cooling system. Or the time he was adjusting my lower carotid piston and he nearly lost one of the primary T-junction valves. Things like that.

"I only knew him whenever he switched me on, I suppose."

"How many times was that?" Vivi asked.

"Seventeen times. Fifteen if you ignore the two accidental bumps from his elbow."

Fifteen times? And each of them just a few minutes long?

"What about the rainbow machine? Project Rainbow?"

I asked. "Do you know where the battery for the machine is? Do you know how to operate it?"

Paragon shook its head and I could barely contain my frustration. I punched the air in anger.

"But don't you see, Auden?" Vivi said. "If he was triggered with a word, he might be triggered again. By another word. Or by many different words." She stopped directing her speech at me and aimed it at Paragon instead. "Who knows what information you've got hidden away inside you? I think we can still find out your purpose. I think we can still find out about the rainbow machine. In fact, I'm certain we can."

············

"What are we doing here?" Vivi stepped softly into the room behind me and I pushed the door shut.

The room was much neater than the last time I was here—Immaculata was right about that. After she'd discovered me in Uncle Jonah's rooms, she had arranged for college cleaners to straighten the place up. So now, all the papers and books and folders and files were neatly stacked in no particular order on the desk and on a couple of the shelves. Even the hearth where I'd found the Project Rainbow sheet had been emptied and brushed clean.

"There must be something here. Something that will tell us . . . something. Anything."

Vivi positioned herself behind a teetering pile of folders.

"Do you think Dr. Bloom left information on Paragon in one of these files?"

I shrugged. In all honesty, I wasn't that bothered about Paragon. My mind was still on the rainbow machine. That was the ultimate prize as far as I was concerned. We'd left Paragon switched off in his room beneath the shed that morning and hopped on a bus to Trinity. For some reason, I felt drawn back to Uncle Jonah's rooms.

We stood side by side, working our way through tons of scientific waffle that meant absolutely nothing to me. Once or twice Vivi gave a little appreciative noise as if she'd just read something that impressed her—her massive brain obviously understanding a lot more of this stuff than mine ever could.

After dismissing a file, we would dump it heavily onto the floor before picking up another and flicking our way through the pages in that. It was in file number seven that I came across something.

Tucked into a plastic pocket on the cover was a sheet of looseleaf paper folded in half. I eased it out and opened it up.

It was a letter—a copy of a letter, at least. A handwritten note to Uncle Jonah. I flattened it on the desk and started reading to myself.

Dear Dr. Bloom, it began.

Thank you for your letter dated 2 November. I need you to understand that failure to complete the allotted work will result in your prosecution at the very least. These are dangerous times, Dr. Bloom, and we must all do our very best to keep our country safe and our citizens protected.

And then, a slightly menacing last line.

I do hope you take very good care of yourself.

At the bottom was a signature I couldn't fully decipher. The first word clearly started with an *H* before becoming illegible, and the second initial was either an *M* or a *W*—it was difficult to tell.

I showed Vivi.

"What does that mean?" she asked, frowning. "You don't really think he *was* a spy, do you?"

I shook my head and looked around the room.

"There's no QWERTY screen," I said, suddenly noticing. "He didn't have a QWERTY screen? Where is his QWERTY screen?"

Vivi looked. "That's strange. I'm certain he did have one. Perhaps the university authorities took it away. Gave it to another lecturer. They do that sort of thing sometimes."

But I wasn't so sure.

....

Walking back home from Trinity that afternoon, I couldn't help feeling that someone was following me.

As I turned a corner and passed one of the enormous and scary Water Allocation Board posters that warned everyone to Be on the Lookout for Black Marketeers. The Water They Sell You Will Kill You!, I glanced over my shoulder to check.

A man—a youngish man in his twenties—wearing a long coat and one of those tweedy flat caps was about thirty feet behind me. As soon as he saw me looking, he stopped and tried to pretend to stare in at a shoe shop window. There was something about him—the way he walked, the way he held himself, the cold eyes—that said soldier to me.

I suddenly felt sick. Why was he following me? Rounding the corner, I started to sprint, quickly diving down a small side street and then another.

Looking back, I couldn't see the man so I slowed down and took a shortcut through one of the cobbled lanes.

Bam!

I walked straight into someone, my shoulder knocking solidly into the arm of another boy who twisted and half fell into the road.

"Aaargh!" the boy barked.

One of the two companions with him—the one with the fat nose—lurched forward to try to catch him.

"Careful!" cried the other companion—the one with swollen lips. "Watch where you're going."

"You okay, Fabius?" said the one clutching on to the fallen boy's arm. "You ain't hurt, are you?"

"Gerroff me!" He jerked his arm away from Fat Nose and straightened up. "I don't need yer help."

It was Fabius Boyle.

Boyle looked angrily at me and then, as recognition slowly squeezed its way into his thick skull, he smirked.

"Oh, look who it is! The kid with the magnifying glass! Whatsis name again? Dare. That's it. Dare."

"Whaddya think you're playing at, Dare?" said Putter, positioning himself a little behind Boyle.

"Yeah. Running into Fabius like that," said Keane, shuffling alongside Putter. "Could've caused an accident."

"Shut up, Keane," Boyle growled. "I'll deal with this."

I looked past the three boys. There was nobody else in the lane.

"Look, Boyle," I started. "I'm sorry I nearly ran you over but—"

"Sorry?" Boyle frowned. "Oh yeah. You'll be sorry all right." He reached out and grabbed me by the collar before lifting me up and pinning me against a wall. He glanced around and started whispering. "See, I don't like little freaks like you. Little freaky fellas who think they're better than everyone else. Weirdos who have . . . magnifying glasses around their necks." Holding me in position with one hand, he ripped my magnifying glass away with the other. He looked briefly at it before tossing it away to Putter. "You see, I think you need to be taught a lesson. See anyone, boys?" he asked Putter and Keane.

"No one around, Fabius," one of them said.

"Go on. Hit him," said the other.

"Yeah! He deserves it, the little freak."

Boyle pulled his arm back into position and clenched his fist.

But not before I reached into my jacket pocket.

"You're gonna be sorry for coming to Cambridge, Freak Show," Boyle hissed smugly through his rotten teeth. "This is gonna be the worst beating you ever had."

"I doubt it." I smiled.

"Wha?" He looked confused.

And that was my moment to strike. My hand whipped out of my pocket and—slam!—Snowflake 843A smacked down hard on the side of his head. He staggered backward, dropping me back onto my feet.

Putter and Keane, as slow-witted as their leader, both stood there stunned as Boyle stumbled out into the middle of the lane, dazed.

So I took my opportunity and leaped over Boyle's hobbling body (see, my gymnastics training does sometimes come in useful), before shooting off past the two henchmen—snatching my magnifying glass out of Putter's weak hands—and running as fast as my quivering legs would allow. Halfway along the lane I heard a loud voice booming behind me.

"I'LL GET YOU, DARE! I'LL GET YOU AND I'LL GET THAT STUCK-UP GIRLFRIEND OF YOURS! JUST YOU WAIT AND SEE!"

I didn't even bother to look back.

....

I took a slightly different and roundabout route home after that. I kept checking over my shoulder to see if anyone was following me—Boyle or the soldier. But there was nobody.

Arriving back at Unicorn Cottage, I immediately closed the curtains and curled up on the sofa with Sandwich, who launched into one of her dribbly tickle episodes.

Just after half past six, Mum arrived home from work.

"What have you got the curtains closed for?" she asked, opening them up again. "It's summer. It's still light out."

"I . . . er . . . had a headache," I lied. "Mum. Can I ask you a question?" I said, getting up from the sofa and dropping Sandwich onto the floor. "When they found Uncle Jonah . . . in the field . . . did he have his QWERTY on him?"

She turned and looked straight at me.

"No. That was the strange part of it all. He wasn't wearing his QWERTY. Unusual for Jonah because he loved his QWERTY—always had the latest model." She put her hemp bag on the table. "I assumed someone at the hospital must have taken it. Either by accident or deliberately. I was going to report it but . . . well . . . in the end, I was too upset to. It doesn't really matter after all, does it? It was just a . . . thing."

"No."

I thought back to the letter—the horrible, menacing sneer of the words. I thought back to the soldier following me. I thought of the missing QWERTY and the missing QWERTY screen. They'd been taken, all right. Taken to see what information Uncle Jonah had stored on them. Or taken so that nobody else could *find* the secret information. Whatever the reason, it didn't really matter.

Now I was certain.

Uncle Jonah didn't just die.

He was murdered.

PART FOUR

PINK

CHAPTER 13

BOYLE

"Brunch. Brunette. Brunt. Bruschetta. Brush. Brushed. Brushstroke. Brushwood. Brushwork. Brusque. Brussels sprout. . . ."

"Vivi."

Vivi looked up at Paragon from her dictionary. "Yes?"

"I hope you don't mind me saying this. . . ."

"Yes?"

Paragon looked like it was shuffling uncomfortably on its deckchair in the middle of the garden.

"But the thing is . . . you see . . . well . . . all this . . . 'word' stuff you're doing with me . . ."

"Go on."

"Well, it's a bit . . . boring."

"Ha!" I couldn't stop myself from laughing out loud, as I dropped from the branch onto the trampoline below.

"Boring?"

"Yes. Just saying the words out loud like that. It feels a bit . . . tedious. Three days you've been at it now and . . . well . . ." It stabbed a finger at the dictionary. "We're only on B."

Vivi looked a bit hurt, but I still couldn't stop myself from laughing. It was annoying me as much as Paragon.

In fact, there were a number of things eating at me. You see, I hadn't told anyone my suspicions about Uncle Jonah. Not Mum. Not Vivi. I had swallowed it all down and it was slowly eating away at me, turning me into a nervous mess. At night I lay awake thinking up all the possibilities. Who would have killed him? Who would have wanted him killed? Over a few nights I had mentally accused everyone from other lecturers at Trinity to Mr. Belsey, the headmaster. Whenever I went out of the house I always looked around to make sure I wasn't being followed. I had even started to peer under my bed at night to check that there was nobody there.

I was worried.

And all the while, at the back of my mind, was the thought of the rainbow machine and the battery that was still missing.

"I mean," Paragon continued to a horrified Vivi, "I know all those words anyway. If you asked me to give you a definition for each of them . . . well . . . that's something I could easily do."

"But that's not the point," Vivi said with a slight croak in her voice. "I'll bet you knew the word *achromatopsia* before Auden said it the other day."

"Yes. Yes, I did."

"But it was the actual word being *said* that made you remember that it was Dr. Bloom who built you."

"True. True. It's just—"

"Just what?"

If Paragon could have sighed, it would have sighed. "It's just a bit boring."

Vivi put the book down on her lap. "But you're a robot. How can you find anything boring?"

"Coming around to my way of thinking now are you, Vivi?" I called over, and Vivi gave me another of her glares. "You'll be referring to Paragon as 'it' next."

Suddenly Paragon stood up. "How about a bit of poetry? Lighten the mood."

"Oh no," I groaned. But before I could say anything else, it was off.

" 'I think that I shall never see

"A billboard lovely as a tree.

"Indeed, unless the billboards fall,

"I'll never see a tree at all.' "

Vivi laughed. I laughed.

"Ogden Nash," Paragon finished.

"I don't mind that sort of poetry," I said, jumping down onto the ground, feeling slightly cheerier than I had in days. "Funny poems. I prefer them to all that 'aren't daffodils lovely' sort of thing."

"What about some Edward Lear, then?" Paragon asked, its eyes drilling straight into mine.

"Who?"

"Edward Lear. Nonsense poet. Wrote limericks."

"*Nonsense* poet!?"

"Yep." Paragon brought its clenched fist up to its mouth and pretended to clear its throat. "*Ahem.*

" 'There was an Old Person whose habits

"Induced him to feed upon rabbits;

"When he'd eaten eighteen

"He turned perfectly green

"Upon which he relinquished those habits.' "

Neither Vivi nor I laughed.

"That's just stupid," I said.

"Well, it *is* a nonsense poem," Paragon said. "It's meant to be stupid."

"Do another one, Paragon?" Vivi asked. "Please."

"No. Please, don't!" I shouted. "I don't think I can stand it!"

But Paragon ignored me again.

" 'There was an Old Man who supposed

"That the street door was partially closed;

"But some very large rats

"Ate his coats and his hats

"While that futile old gentleman dozed.'"

Silence.

"They are *so* not funny," I said.

"Well, they *were* written a long time ago," Paragon replied. "I suppose the sense of humor in those days was significantly different to the sense of humor nowadays. Things evolve. Even jokes. Nothing stays the same for long."

"I can't imagine anyone laughing at that—even back then," I said, taking the dictionary from Vivi and throwing it to the floor.

"Hey! What are you doing?"

"Come on. I'm fed up with listening to you reciting the dictionary and Paragon reciting terrible poetry. Let's go and do something fun."

....

"Are you sure we should bring him here?" Vivi said, a worried look on her face. "Won't there be people?"

"There might," I replied. "But most of the people who come here seem to spend their time down in the office complaining about the place. I don't think they're exactly on the lookout for seven-foot-tall robots dressed in the discarded clothes of an old philosophy professor, do you?"

As we climbed over the broken-down fence, into the field of long-trampled grass, Paragon looked around at the mess.

"Hmm," it said. "Sunny Vale. Did you name this place, Auden?"

"No. Why?"

"Well, the amount of sarcasm needed to come up with a

name like that would fill an entire desalting unit. Wouldn't you agree?"

I grinned at the stupid machine. "I would agree, Paragon. Definitely."

....

"Do you know the rules of hide-and-seek?"

Paragon could barely control the tut that formed somewhere in its amplification unit. "Of course I know how to play hide-and-seek. What sort of high-functioning creature would I be if I didn't understand the rules of hide-and-seek?"

The word *creature* made me wince, but I let it go.

"Great. So . . . we have an extra rule that we also like to use when we play around here."

"What's that?"

Vivi answered. "We try not to be seen by anyone. Anyone at all."

Paragon sort of shrugged. Again, if it had eyebrows, it would probably have raised them. "Are you sure that's not a rule you've only just made up because of the big metal guy you've brought with you today?" I laughed again. Paragon was proving to be very funny. "You sure it's not because you don't want some random person seeing me?"

Vivi was smiling, too. "No, honestly. We always play like that. You see, we shouldn't really be here."

"Ah." Paragon's shoulders swelled like it understood. "Illegal trespassing."

"You don't have some program that prevents you from doing something illegal, do you?" I asked.

Paragon's fingers tapped a rhythm along what would probably have been its lips. It was thinking. "Hmm. Let me think. Is it just a teeny bit wrong?"

"Oh yes," I said. "Really little."

"On a scale of one to ten, just how wrong do you think trespassing on Sunny Vale Caravan Park is?"

"Ooh, about—"

"Three," Vivi interrupted.

"Three?" asked Paragon.

"Not even that," I quickly added. "I'd say probably about a . . . point-five."

"Point-five, eh?" It seriously looked like it was weighing it all up. "Point-five's nothing. Well, practically nothing. Five percent. One in twenty. Hmm . . ." The fingers tapped out their rhythm. "Okay, then."

"Really?"

"Yep."

We all edged our way over to where the long-abandoned caravans started.

"Now, you're not allowed to use any of your tricks to try to find us, okay? No heat sensors or movement sensors or anything like that. No lasers. Nothing. Right?"

"O-kay. So I'm going in blind, so to speak?"

"Yes."

"Should be interesting." Paragon adjusted the collar on

the jacket so that it was sticking up and covering its face. "Deliberately disabling myself to see just how difficult life must be for you humans. Should be quite an insight."

"Don't get too excited, Bot Brain," I said. "It's just a game of hide-and-seek. Nothing more. Now count to a hundred."

"Do you want me to put my hands over my eyes?" Paragon asked, its fingers spread all over its metal face.

"Don't think there's any need, is there? All you need to do is turn off your vision . . . thingy until you get to a hundred, don't you?"

"Oh no." Vivi shook her head half violently. "I think you should put your hands over your eyes. Makes it all more authentic, doesn't it?"

Honestly. I give up sometimes.

Paragon started counting and Vivi and I both sprinted away toward the caravans. As we neared the first of the rotting box-shaped chalets, Vivi peeled away from me and dashed down behind a hefty clump of trash. I pushed on past—I knew exactly where I was headed.

Three aisles into the park—way before the potential of bumping into anyone unfortunate to actually be staying there—was a caravan under which someone had (optimistically) stuck two water barrels alongside one another. A strip of guttering ran across the roof of the caravan—now complete with a twisted, dislodged aerial—and two grubby plastic pipes slid down into the tops of the barrels.

The gap between the two barrels was just wide enough

for a flexible young man—such as *moi!*—to fit into. I had used this particular hiding place a number of times before when playing with Vivi, and with a bit of a squeeze and a tight-hold-of-the-breath, it was possible to slot myself in and be practically unspottable by the outside world. I shuffled myself around and let my back slide down the dusty wall of the caravan and crouched out of sight, trying to keep my breathing as under control as possible.

I squatted there quietly and waited. I listened as the breeze gently brushed across the long, uncut grass and through the straggly hedges.

Suddenly something flashed quickly past the gap—far too quickly to be made out—and I held my breath even tighter. A moment later and—

"Oh!"

It was Vivi's voice, far off.

"Found you!"

Paragon's.

"Now to find Auden."

Whoosh!

The blur flashed past the gap once again.

I fixed myself to the spot. If that was Paragon, he was moving at an incredible rate. Perhaps that was his purpose. Speed. Perhaps he was some sort of messenger drone—carrying important messages from one place to another. Or a news drone, taking back news stories to the etherweb composition centers.

Whooooosh!

I crouched and half squinted up my eyes. The tension was almost unbearable.

Suddenly—

Tap, tap, tap.

Something was tapping on my head. I looked upward and found myself staring straight into the fake, metal eyes of Paragon. It had climbed up onto the roof of the caravan behind me and was leaning over the edge, knocking me on the top of my head with the tip of one of its multi-jointed fingers.

"Hello, Auden. I appear to have found you. Ha!"

I scrambled out from between the barrels.

"Yes, yes. Well done." I dusted my clothes and tried not to look too impressed with the irritating lump of metal above me. "Bit of a risk climbing up there, though. Might get seen. Might get spotted by someone on the other side of the park. A bit reckless, if you ask me."

"Oh, nope. I don't think so." Paragon was now lying down, supporting its "cheek" in the palm of its hand, its elbow digging into the roof. It looked as if it was resting. "I might have disabled my senses for you, but not for the rest of the world. I was still aware of what the rest of the world was up to, you know. I even managed to avoid that funny-looking boy."

"What funny-looking boy?"

"The one with the swollen head."

Suddenly, there was a loud shout from somewhere far off.

"I SAID YOU'RE TRESPASSING! WHAT'RE YOU DOING HERE?"

"What's that?" I asked as Paragon shifted position up on the roof of the caravan to try to see.

The shouting continued. "YOU'RE NOT ALLOWED ON THIS SITE. I COULD GET THE POLICE AND THEY COULD CHARGE YOU WITH TRESPASSING. THEY COULD LOCK YOU UP FOR IT."

"It's the boy," Paragon said, craning its neck. "He's shouting at Vivi."

"What?"

Paragon started to climb down.

"No. Wait. You can't be seen. You need to stay there. Keep your head down."

"But I—"

"No!" I ordered. "Stay there!"

Paragon gave a sort of tut but stayed where it was.

I crept my way around a couple of the caravans, toward the area where the noise was coming from. As I came around a corner, I could see Vivi up against the side of a rickety-looking shed, her entire body shaking, her cheeks shining with tears. In front of her was a dark-haired boy with his back to me. Even though I couldn't see his face, I could sense that he was knotted up with anger.

"YOU'VE GOT NERVE COMING ROUND HERE! ESPESHALLY AFTER WHAT YOUR LITTLE FREAK-SHOW BOYFRIEND DID TO ME THE OTHER DAY." He pointed to his forehead and as he did so, he turned a little to reveal a large, dark bruise that had swollen up on the left-hand side of his head.

Boyle!

"BUT HE'S NOT HERE TO HELP YOU NOW, SO I'M GONNA TEACH YOU THE LESSON HE SHOULDA GOT THE OTHER DAY BUT HE WAS TOO MUCH OF A COWARD TO TAKE."

"Please, Boyle . . ." Vivi pleaded.

"Fabius! Oh, Fa-bi-us!" Suddenly, a woman's singsong voice from somewhere far off seemed to start calling.

"WHA?" Boyle looked confused. "WHAT IS IT NOW?"

"Fabius! Lunch is ready."

Boyle sighed.

"Fa-bi-us."

Something softened in Boyle's tone. "OKAY. COMING, MOTHER! JUST A MINUTE!" he called back, before quickly turning to face Vivi once again, the snarl in his voice reinstated.

"Tell your freak-show boyfriend that I'm going to make life so hard for you both at school next year that you'll do anything to be expelled."

Without warning, Boyle lurched forward and grabbed Vivi by the shoulders before shoving her into the dirt.

Angry, I stomped forward a step or two only to be quickly and silently pulled backward by someone behind me. A cold, metallic hand slipped over my mouth to stop me from shouting, and I twisted my head to find myself staring straight into Paragon's unblinking eyes.

"Oh, and . . . er . . . give your boyfriend this little present from me!" Boyle rushed at Vivi and landed a solid kick right in the middle of her stomach.

I wriggled hard in Paragon's grip, desperate to get out and show this bully that he had no right to hurt my friend like that. But Paragon just held on tightly, refusing to let me go.

"Sorry to leave you like this," Boyle said, sneering at Vivi. "But . . . er . . . lunch is ready. *Adios*, Rookmini."

Boyle turned and strutted away toward the little house on the edge of the site. Paragon kept its arms clasped around me until Boyle had gone inside.

The moment Paragon released me I raced over to Vivi. She was still crying, her hands clutching her stomach.

"Vivi! Are you okay? Vivi?" I picked her up and tried wiping the muck from out of her hair.

"Vivi." Paragon came alongside her and helped her straighten up. "Are you hurt?"

"Why didn't you just let me go?" I shouted at Paragon. "I could have stopped him from hurting her."

Paragon shook its head. "Not always the best idea. Not when you're angry, Auden. You should never make any decisions when you're angry. You might have made things worse."

"You don't understand! You're not human! You don't—"

"Please!"

It was Vivi.

"Please! Don't argue. Not now. Not about this. I'm okay.

I'll be all right." She pulled a lump of dry mud from out of a pocket on her trousers. "I'll live."

....

"Boyle? Hmm. Appropriate name," said Paragon.

We were sitting in the back garden of Unicorn Cottage, Vivi dusting herself off with towels.

"His family must own the caravan park," she said. "He's not a nice person—as you can see. Doesn't like anything that isn't 'normal' in his opinion."

"The concept of 'normal' is, of course, based entirely on the individual's perception," Paragon started wittering on. "What one person sees as 'normal' is considered completely 'abnormal' by others. Thus rendering a generalized concept of 'normality' entirely redundant, i.e., there is no such thing as 'normal.' Or, if you like, on the other hand, everything is 'normal.' "

"Thank you, Einstein," I said, before telling them about my encounter with Boyle, Putter, and Keane just the other day.

"So he said he was going to get me, too, did he?" Vivi looked concerned. "Thanks, Auden. Thanks a lot. He definitely managed to do that."

"Now, now, Vivi," Paragon interrupted. "Let's leave the sarcasm to Auden. As he's so good at it."

I gave a huge sarcastic smirk just to confirm Paragon's point.

"Sorry, Vivi. Boyle is such a coward. Hurting a girl like that. If I hadn't knocked him over the head with my

Snowflake the other day and escaped, he probably wouldn't have been so angry. I'm sorry. It's all my fault."

"No. It's not. He's just a horrible person," said Vivi.

"Yes," Paragon added. "Definitely the sort of person who needs to be taught a lesson." It looked straight at me.

Vivi scowled at Paragon. "What are you saying?"

But Paragon had planted the seed of an idea and my brain was already running away with it, piecing things together and formulating some sort of a plan.

Paragon could be useful.

Vivi shook her head viciously. "No. I don't think I want to be part of anything nasty. It's not right."

"He *did* just kick you in the stomach, Vivi."

"I don't care. I still don't think it's right."

"It doesn't have to be anything nasty," Paragon reassured her, but she still shook her head.

"It's okay, Vivi," I soothed. It was true, she wasn't cut out for revenge. "You don't have to have anything to do with it. In fact, it's best if you don't even know anything about it."

CHAPTER 14

THE TRUTH

The following evening, rather than hide Paragon away in its underground bunker under the shed at the bottom of the garden, I took it all the way back to Sunny Vale. As the light started to dim, we made our way across to one of the long-abandoned caravans with the cracked glass and the soggy walls. I turned the handle on the door and it opened easily. Stepping inside, I was hit by a fog of cold, stale air and dust that had probably not been disturbed for a number of years.

The furniture had been left to rot and, at some point, someone had clearly come in and smashed up everything they could get their hands on. Splintered wood and badly snapped and bent plastic were strewn all over the place. Cushions and bedding had been ripped apart, sending fluff and feathers and hunks of polystyrene across the floor. The little gas cooker had been pulled out from its mooring and now lay blocking the passageway to the equally vandalized bedrooms.

"Hmm," Paragon said. "This is nice."

I turned and looked at its face. "Is that sarcasm?"

"I suppose. Got a good teacher."

I laughed.

"Okay, now, I'll be back before sunrise. You wait here and then we'll put our plan into action. Understand?"

"Yes, boss."

I tugged the top part of Paragon's coat to one side.

"You know what, Paragon," I said before pushing the on/off button.

"What?"

"I think I misjudged you at first. Actually, you're okay. You're all right."

I punched the button and he powered down.

....

In the morning, I scarfed a quinoa bun, patted Sandwich on top of her yawning head, and softly closed the back door behind me. I didn't want to wake Mum up. She would wonder what I was up to. I didn't think she'd look too kindly on me sneaking out first thing to play a trick on a school bully, aided and abetted by a poetry-quoting robot.

Twenty minutes later, I was pulling open the door to the caravan and powering up Paragon.

"Good morning, Auden," it said as the lights stuttered to life. It peered down at its chest and gently tapped the one light that still wasn't working. "Nope. Still nothing. I really don't know what that is, you know. I wish I did, but I don't." Paragon looked up at me. "It still worries me."

"Never mind that now. It may just start itself up at some point. I wouldn't worry. We've got a trick to play. Are you ready?"

"Of course."

"Good."

It was still dark outside, but that was good because I could see so well. Everything was clear to me. Even the smallest of detail. As crisp as it was to a "normal" person in the bright light of day.

We silently worked our way over the park toward Boyle's cottage. There were no lights on in any of the caravans. If there was anyone in any of them, then they were still asleep. Even the birds in the trees hadn't bothered to rouse themselves quite yet, and the early-morning breeze was still trying to summon up its own strength.

When we reached the cottage, Paragon slowly paced right the way around it before coming back to me.

"One adult—female—in one bedroom. One young person—male—in the second bedroom. Both sleeping peacefully."

It reminded me of a fact that I already knew. That Boyle was an only child. No brothers or sisters. A bit like me. Only not as nice. Or clever. Or handsome, for that matter.

We went around to the side of the cottage where Boyle was asleep.

"Okay," Paragon said. "Now what?"

"Can you climb up to his window?"

"Climb? Ha! I'm the king of Climbsville."

Suddenly Paragon leaped onto the wall and scurried up like a spider. Within a second or two it was alongside the Boyles' paint-flaky window.

"Wow! Now do your voice," I whispered.

"Now?"

"Yes. Now." I moved out of the way and hid behind a large, stinky plastic bin.

Paragon levered the window open, pretended to clear its throat, and started to speak.

"FABIUS BOYLE," it rasped in a—to be honest—pretty scary voice. Sort of hissy and low. It almost made *me* shiver. "FABIUS BOYLE!" it continued. "WHERE ARE YOU, FABIUS BOYLE?"

A snorting from above. From inside the small house I could hear Boyle waking up. "What? Eh? What is it?"

"FABIUS BOYLE . . . I AM LOOKING FOR YOU, FABIUS BOYLE."

Boyle seemed to kind of squeak.

"What do you want? Who are you? Mum?!"

"DO NOT CALL FOR YOUR MOTHER, FABIUS BOYLE. SHE CANNOT HELP YOU NOW." Another squeak from above. "YOU MUST FACE ME ALONE."

"I don't understand! Who are you? What have I done?"

"I AM THE PART OF YOUR SOUL THAT FEARS AND HATES." I scrambled out from behind the bin, dusting myself off, and ran out to about twenty feet away from the cottage, where I turned to face Boyle's bedroom window. I could still hear Paragon's and Boyle's voices.

"I AM THE ACCUMULATION OF YEARS OF HATRED AND FEAR. FABIUS BOYLE, YOU HAVE SPENT YOUR CHILDHOOD FILLING OTHERS WITH FEAR. NOW THAT FEAR HAS RETURNED TO WREAK ITS HAVOC UPON *YOU*!"

"But I don't understand!" Boyle's voice was shaking and tearful and I was finding it difficult to keep a straight face.

"TAKE A LOOK OUT OF YOUR WINDOW AND YOU WILL SEE."

Paragon swiftly crawled up the wall to a position directly above the window. A few seconds passed—Boyle clearly debating with himself whether or not he should actually look outside—before the curtains twitched and a petrified face appeared in the open window. When he saw me standing stiffly before him in the darkness of the morning, Boyle almost jumped.

"Dare?!"

"YES," continued Paragon. "I HAVE TAKEN THE FORM OF YOUR MORTAL ENEMY. IT IS TIME TO MEET YOUR FEARS FACE-ON."

"What's going on?"

I stood still, staring hard and impassively at the window as if I were a ghost.

"STEP OUTSIDE, FABIUS BOYLE. . . ."

"No!"

"STEP OUTSIDE AND FACE YOUR FEARS. IT IS TIME."

"No, it isn't!"

"YES, IT IS."

"I'm not going out there!"

"BUT YOU *MUST*, FABIUS BOYLE. YOU *MUST*. FOR IF YOU DO NOT, THERE WILL BE CONSEQUENCES BEFORE THE SUN RISES."

"Huh?"

"YES. CONSEQUENCES!"

I watched as Boyle tried to manage a fit of uncontrollable gulps.

"STEP OUTSIDE, FABIUS BOYLE."

The face left the window and at precisely the same moment, I saw Paragon clambering to a point above the kitchen door.

The door opened reluctantly. Then slowly—so incredibly slowly—Boyle came out onto the top step, tugging the belt of his robe tightly around him.

"What is this?" His voice quavered. A combination of fear and the cold of the very early morning, perhaps? "What's . . . going on? Is . . . is this some kind of joke? Dare? Are you . . . are you having a little . . . little joke? Eh?"

I stood dead still and just stared at Boyle. No reaction on my face. This unsettled him further.

"Am I dreaming? Is that it? Yes . . . I think I must be having . . . a dream."

He came down from the steps and stood on the patch of gravel in front of them.

"That's all this is . . . a strange lit—"

And then Paragon swooped into action.

Leaning out from the stone wall, Paragon grabbed Boyle on each of his shoulders and lifted him clear of the ground.

"Aahhhh—" Boyle screamed, and Paragon quickly repositioned one of its hands so that a couple of fingers were clamped over Boyle's open mouth. Boyle's legs thrashed wildly and uselessly in the air, and his hands reached up to try to release Paragon's grip. But Paragon's grip was so much stronger than Boyle's, and pretty soon the boy found himself tiring and giving himself up to the situation.

I came nearer to see Boyle's eyes staring pleadingly down at me.

"NOW," Paragon continued in his scary voice, "YOU HAVE BULLIED AND FRIGHTENED CHILDREN ALL YOUR LIFE. THE TIME TO STOP HAS ARRIVED. WHEN YOU GO BACK TO YOUR SCHOOL YOU WILL NOT BULLY OR ATTACK A SINGLE PERSON. ALL YOUR TEACHERS AND CLASSMATES WILL NOTICE THE REMARKABLE CHANGE IN YOUR DEMEANOR. ANYWAY, YOU NEVER KNOW, SOME OF THEM MIGHT ACTUALLY LEARN TO *LIKE* YOU AND YOU MIGHT . . . JUST MIGHT . . . FIND YOURSELF WITH A FRIEND—A *REAL* FRIEND—A WHOLE NEW EXPERIENCE FOR YOU, I'M SURE." Paragon gave Boyle a little shake to make sure he was listening. "OF COURSE, IT IS VERY EASY FOR ME TO CHECK THE RECORDS AT YOUR SCHOOL. IT IS A SIMPLE MATTER OF JUST PLUGGING INTO THE SCHOOL'S ETHERWEB-BASED RECORDS SYSTEM AND FINDING WHAT I WANT. AND IF I SEE YOUR NAME CREEPING UP ON REPORTS OF BULLYING AGAIN . . . I SHALL BE PAYING YOU ANOTHER VISIT. DO YOU UNDERSTAND, FABIUS BOYLE?"

Boyle gave a tiny nod within Paragon's large metal hands. The movement was so oddly comical that I couldn't stop myself from grinning. Boyle noticed me smiling and his forehead crumpled into a sort of half frown.

"I AM NOW GOING TO PUT YOU BACK ON THE GROUND. BUT REMEMBER ALL I HAVE SAID."

Boyle didn't nod. He just glared at me as Paragon lowered him gently down. As his feet hit the ground, Paragon released him, and Boyle's head swung upward to see what it was that had just lifted him so easily into the air.

But Paragon had gone.

Boyle straightened himself up and tried to regain his breath.

"What was that?" he murmured, more to himself than to me.

"That was all your years of scaring people rolled into one," I said, still unable to stop myself from smirking. It had been satisfying to see this bully dangling in the air, scared and confused. I know I should have felt guilty for having enjoyed it—but I didn't. Boyle had recently hurt my best friend and it was hard to feel any kind of sympathy.

"What . . . what did you just do to me?" He still looked puzzled, but now there was a slight glint of anger in his eyes. "What just grabbed me? What did you do, Dare? How did you do it?"

"None of that matters," I answered. "All that matters is that you never bully anyone again. Because if you do . . . trust me, you *don't* want to know."

Boyle pulled the top of his robe tighter around his neck. "I don't understand what just happened. And why are you here like this?"

I sighed. "I'm here to teach you a lesson. I'm here to stop a bully. After all—" I paused for a second. "Everyone knows that all bullies are cowards."

"Huh! That's good. Coming from you, of all people."

I took a step closer. "What do you mean?"

"You know all about cowards, I'm sure."

It was my turn to look confused now. I shook my head and wrinkled up my face to make it clear that I didn't know what Boyle was talking about.

"You know. Don't pretend you don't know what I'm getting at."

"I don't." I retrieved my smirk and cranked it up to try to make Boyle feel foolish.

"Yes, you do. You know. Lots of people come here to stay. Lots of people from *London*. My mum talks to them all. They tell her things."

"So?"

Boyle suddenly looked smug. "I'm talking about your dad. Everybody knows about him."

My legs stiffened and I was stuck to the spot. "What do you mean?" My smirk had vanished, dwindled away into nothing.

"He's a coward. Just like you."

"No, he's not. He's away fighting in Europe. He's been away for months."

Boyle laughed. "Yeah. He's been away for months, all right. In prison!"

Blood seemed to rush around my ears, and I found myself unable to hear anything but Boyle's grating voice.

"Found guilty of deserting his post—that's what they say. Left some other soldiers to die. So they sent him to prison. He's not abroad fighting at all. Didn't you know? He's in a military prison. Somewhere in England. For cowardice."

No.

No. It wasn't right.

"You're a liar!"

Boyle laughed again. "Well, why don't you ask your mother? I'm sure she'll tell you the truth if you ask her nicely."

I clenched my fist hard. I wanted to walk the seven or eight paces to Boyle and smash it roughly into the boy's face. Knock him flat on the grass.

But I didn't.

"Fabius! What's going on? What's this noise?" Boyle's mother—bleary-eyed and half-dressed—appeared in the doorway behind him. "What are you doing?"

Boyle ignored her, still spitting his venom out toward me. "Ask your mother. Go on. Get her to tell you the truth for once. I *dare* you!"

I spun on the spot and sprinted away—the blood still racing around my head.

"That's it! Run away!" Boyle shouted behind me. "Be just like your dad!"

....

I kept on running. Over the fields. Along the lanes. My legs pounding away, never slowing. For all I knew, the sun may have been starting to come up. My chest may have been screaming out in pain. The wind may have been cold and penetrating. The birds may have been singing and welcoming in the new day. But I wasn't listening. I didn't care.

All I could think about was my dad.

My dad!

Eventually I rounded the corner and came to the lane on which Unicorn Cottage sat. Without slowing, I ran onto the drive and into the house.

Mum was in the kitchen. When she heard me come in, she quickly turned around and did her scowl face at me.

"Auden! Where have you been? I've been worried about you! I heard the door shut and I came down here and I—"

"Mum! Tell me . . ." I was out of breath. "Tell me . . . about . . . about Dad."

"What?"

"I want to know."

"I don't—"

"I want to know the truth!" I shouted. "About Dad. Tell me the truth."

She didn't have to say anything. The look on her face told me everything I needed to know.

"No!" I cried.

Mum sat down on one of the wooden chairs, her shoulders small and defeated. Like a balloon that's lost all its air.

"I'm sorry, Auden. I didn't know what to say. I didn't know how to tell you. I thought that if we came here we could make a fresh start. Get away from it all. I thought that—"

But I didn't want to hear any more.

I ran back out through the door and into the yard. I ran through the small gap in the hedge and onto the field with the irrigation pyramids. I ran and I ran across the field, my feet pushing hard into the dry crops.

Far off in the distance, I could see a shape. It was a man standing with his arms outstretched, like he was waiting for me. I sprinted faster and faster toward him, the sweat flicking off my brow. As I got nearer, the arms stretched out even more, opening wide for me, and I pounded toward them.

I thought of my father, racing me in the park, pushing me on the swings. The games of football. The bedtime stories and the stupid jokes. The tears came flowing down my hot cheeks and I kept on running. I thought of the songs and the rhymes and the bicycle rides. The words of advice and the tellings-off.

My dad.

My dad, the hero.

I ran and I ran toward the open arms until finally I fell into them and they wrapped themselves tightly around me, holding me close and swaying me softly, gently into comfort. I flung my own arms around the cold body and squeezed as hard as I could, never ever wanting to let go. Never wanting to go back and face this terrible truth.

I just wanted this hurt to go away.

I cried. I cried for so long that my tears felt like grit in my eyes and everything became a grayish smear. I cried until my breaths turned to stutters before finally becoming more even once again.

And all the while, the arms hushed me. Calmed me. Soothed me. Lulled me into feeling like everything would be all right again. Like everything would be okay.

I looked up at the flickering lights on the chest. The wires along the arms. The metal grille where the mouth should have been.

"Shhh," Paragon said, his hand resting on my head. "Shhh, Audendare."

PART FIVE

PURPLE

CHAPTER 15

STARS AND SPARROWS

"I thought it was a bad idea to try to get back at Boyle." Vivi squinted through the telescope that pointed out of her bedroom window, over the quad, and into the night sky.

"I wasn't trying to get back," I replied, a tad annoyed. "I was trying to teach Boyle a lesson. After all, he did hurt you."

"Oh, so you did it all for me, did you?"

"Well . . ." I paused.

"Quickly, quickly." She waved at me and then stood back from the telescope. I bent over and put my eye to the eyepiece. "See that star? The one in the middle?" I thought I did. "That's Antares. It's part of the constellation Scorpius." The shining dot in the center of all the blackness seemed to twinkle. "They call it the 'Rival of Mars.'"

"Why?"

"Because it's a really deep red in color."

I turned and gave her a look. "Well, I couldn't possibly know about that, could I?"

"Oh. No. That's true. Sorry."

I imagined my mother flicking the little elastic band around her wrist.

It was irritating. No, that's far too mild. Sometimes it was just so *bloody annoying* not being able to see color. All the time—every single day—I would miss out on some experience or other—or at least have a very watered-down version of it—just because I couldn't tell one thing from another. It made me sad and it made me mad.

"Forgiven," I sighed eventually. I put my eye back to the telescope and watched the dot sparkle a little more, all the while slowly moving across the lens.

"You know, the best way to look at stars with the naked eye," Vivi rattled on beside me, "is to look just past them. Try and stare straight at them and you miss a lot of the detail. You'll find it difficult to focus. But look a tiny bit away—take your eyes off them—and you can see them much more clearly."

"Hmm."

Vivi and I swapped places again and she gave the two metal sticks attached to the telescope a couple of little turns.

"So? What are you going to do now? About your dad, I mean."

I shrugged. "Not much I *can* do. Mum says we can write letters. He can make a QWERTY call every few months. That's about it."

I went too quiet too quickly and Vivi picked up on it.

"What? What's wrong?"

"Well . . ." I wasn't entirely sure I could bring myself to even form the words. Even after everything, it still felt vaguely treacherous. "The problem is that . . . well . . . I don't know if I can."

"Why not?"

"He left soldiers to die . . . that's what the army says." Whenever I thought about it, it made me feel sick. "I don't know what I'm supposed to think. On one hand, he's my dad. And on the other . . ."

The room suddenly became embarrassingly silent.

Eventually, it was Vivi who broke that silence.

"Well, at least you actually *have* a father. That's one up on me. Even if he *is* in prison."

I didn't say anything.

"Still, you should have listened to me about getting your revenge on Boyle. It didn't do you any good in the end, did it?"

"Yes, yes, Your Royal Highness." I put on a fake posh voice. "I shall certainly be listening to you next time with your wise and thoughtful words. How foolish I have been not to heed your advice. I bow to your greater knowledge." I gave a little curtsy.

Vivi stopped what she was doing and looked at me.

"Why are you always so sarcastic, Auden? I don't understand. Why are you always so sarcastic about *everything*?"

The question caught me off guard.

"I, er . . ."

"I'll tell you what I think, shall I? I think you use sarcasm to protect yourself. I think that you think that you can
hide behind a sarcastic comment and not reveal what you
really feel. Am I right?"

I was shocked. She was absolutely correct. I definitely *did*
use sarcasm like a shield. Without a doubt. Even *I* hadn't
really realized it before she said so, but now that she had it
was obvious.

Of course, I wasn't going to tell *her* that.

"Er, no! I don't think so!" I said in a kind of über-sarcastic
way, and Vivi laughed.

"You know, you really are hopeless, Auden."

I smiled, and stared out the window at the clear starry
sky that hung like a poster above Trinity.

....

Vivi wasn't entirely correct. Getting my revenge on Boyle
wasn't a complete waste of time. Apart from finding out
the truth about my dad, I suddenly saw Paragon in a whole
new light. Perhaps he *was* just a robot filled with circuit
boards and pneumatic pistons but, to me, he had become a
whole lot more. Caring, comforting, consoling. A friend.

After all, he was there for me when my dad wasn't.

....

We all watched the Sifters below, motoring from one large pile of trash to another. They picked out individual items with their pincers, inspected them with their visual sensors, and pulled the salvageable parts off, stacking them onto a trailer before tossing the useless ends into a large rectangular bin.

Me and Vivi and Paragon were sat on top of one of the enormous mountains of discarded trash that dominated the recycling yard. The sun was burning down and I felt so incredibly thirsty.

"We still haven't worked out what *your* job is, Paragon," I said, my mouth dry and clicking. "Perhaps you could do that." I nodded my head toward the Sifters, one of whom was now having difficulty wheeling itself over a long sheet of corrugated metal.

Paragon gave a short laugh. "Nope. I don't believe so. Somehow I don't think that any of those machines down there know anything about the poetry of Christina Rossetti or the paintings of John Constable or the names of all fifty-five of Jason's Argonauts or the Latin name for a three-toed sloth, do you? I mean, why would they?"

"So why do *you* know all this stuff?" I asked. "Have you been designed to replace a teacher? If so, please replace the one we're having next year. He's vile."

Paragon laughed again. "I don't believe I'm a teacher. I don't know why I believe I'm not a teacher. . . . It's just a sensation I have. A gut feeling."

Only days before, comments like that would have made me go purple with rage. A robot, after all, deals in black-and-white and is not allowed to have "gut feelings" about things. Are they? They deal in yes/nos and on/offs. Not in-betweens. Right?

But now . . . I had come to realize that the world is not always the logical place it likes to think it is, and that people are hard to read. Life is not the straightforward, one-after-the-other A, B, C that you imagine when you're young. It's all more complicated than that. More twisted around. Like a ball of string. Or to be more precise, like *lots* of balls of string all tied around each other, impossible to pull apart.

So why not accept that a robot might think? Might feel? Might understand what it was I was going through?

"You're incredibly fast," I said. "Is that the main reason for you? To be fast? To race? To do something quickly?"

Paragon shrugged.

"I don't know, but . . ." He picked up a spherical rubber-ball-like thing from the pile of junk that we sat on. "Watch this. . . ."

He held it between finger and thumb, rolling it slightly as he showed it to us. Suddenly, he clamped his entire hand over the ball, hiding it from view.

"Now," he said, a hint of mischief in his voice, "what have I got in my hand?"

"A ball," Vivi replied.

"Ah-ha. But have I?"

Vivi nodded. "It's a bit like a ball, anyway. Looks like one."

"Yes. Okay. Let's not get too tied up in what the thing is—let's assume it's a ball, shall we? It's close enough. What I'm interested in is . . . do I have it in my hand? Do I *really* have it in my hand?"

The way he said *really* reminded me of me.

"Yes. You do," said Vivi.

"Ah-ha."

Slowly he peeled his fingers open to show that there was nothing in his hand. Vivi gasped and I just smiled.

"Did you just crush it to dust?" I asked.

"Nope."

"Where is it, then?" Vivi puzzled.

"Ah-ha!" Paragon brought up his other hand, which was wide open and empty. Steadily he curled his fingers over into a fist before opening them again.

Sitting in the palm of his hand was the ball.

"Whoa!" It was my turn to sound amazed. "How did you do that? Have you got a secret tunnel running along your arms or something?"

"Prestidigitation," Paragon said.

"Prestid . . . what?"

He gave his fingers another flourish. "Magic!"

"You mean it's a trick?" Vivi said. "Sleight of hand?"

Paragon nodded. "It's a simple thing to learn. Just a series of moves. That's what prestidigitation is. A combination of skills designed to look impressive. Humans have to practice a long time to make them work. Luckily"—he kind of swaggered where he sat—"I come preloaded with all those skills." He reached out and pulled a five thousand pound note out of my left ear. "See."

"I wish you could conjure up some water from somewhere," I said, the back of my throat burning. "I'm so thirsty."

....

As the afternoon dragged on, we made our way slowly back toward Unicorn Cottage. Most of the countryside around Cambridge was deserted and we very rarely saw anybody at all. Whenever we did, Paragon would either hide behind a hedge or simply pull up the collar on the trench coat and tug down the wide-brimmed hat that he had recently started wearing at a jaunty sort of angle before quickly passing them by. Thankfully, today we didn't see anybody. It made things much easier when we didn't.

I'd also stopped checking to see if I was ever being followed. Since the day I'd bumped into Boyle in the streets just outside Trinity, I hadn't noticed anyone trying to track me. Maybe I had been *imagining* that the soldier guy was following me? My silly black-and-white brain just playing tricks on me.

We took a slight detour from the lanes along which we usually walked and crossed over onto Wandlebury. Thousands of years ago, the Wandlebury Ring was a hill fort. The shape of a circle, it meant that the inhabitants could defend themselves easily from attackers down below. Then at some point it had been turned into a park with a massive stable block dominating one end.

"We were always taught at school that there were two gods called Gog and Magog buried somewhere around here," Vivi said as we climbed toward the ditch that ran around the edge of the park. "I don't know why. I can't really remember the rest of the story." She looked a bit disappointed with herself that she couldn't recall the detail. "Remind me to look it up later. . . ." She glanced at Paragon. "When my QWERTY's working again."

As we got nearer the top of the small hill, my foot suddenly lost its grip on some rubble and my left leg slid away from beneath me. My body slumped to the ground and I hit the side of my face on a jagged rock that was sticking out of the earth. Stunned, I just lay there.

"Auden!"

Paragon bounded over and crouched on his knees beside me. His hand reached out and seized me by the shoulder.

"Auden. Are you okay? Here. Let me help you up." He grabbed me under the arms and lifted me with ease back onto my feet again, dusting the mess from my shirt. "There! Oh no, you're hurt." His fingers dabbed at the side of my face and I could see blood dripping off the tips of them. "You've cut your head."

"It's all right," I said, my own fingers feeling the small gash that had sent blood trickling down the side of my cheek. "It's nothing."

"Wait." Paragon bent over and, getting hold of the bottom of the trench coat, ripped a strip of material from it. It was about two inches wide and fifteen inches long. "Come here." He positioned the strip around my head, covering up the fresh hole, and tied it swiftly and securely, the material squashing across the top corner of one eye. "There. That'll keep it clean for now. But when you get home you must wash it out. With water. Okay? You have to clean it up with some of your daily allowance. Yes?"

"I will." I felt a bit odd with the bottom couple of inches of a trench coat wrapped around my head. "It'll be all right, though. It's nothing."

"I know, I know," Paragon said. "You'll live." He patted me on the back. "You okay? Or do you want to go home?"

I pointed upward.

At the top, everything leveled out. The ground was flat and dotted with trees. The grass looked mostly dead. The large stable building was grubby and run-down. Nobody had been up here in a long while.

No humans, anyway.

Because above us, in the trees, birds sang like it was the first light of morning. Sheltered from the noise of the wind, the birdsong echoed from tree to tree, bouncing like a pinball from one tall pine to another.

The three of us stood there and listened as bullfinches, crossbills, sparrows, and siskins (Paragon had spent an entire afternoon teaching us which was which) made their music and sang to one another like a high, spread-out choir.

Suddenly, Paragon threw his hat and his coat onto the ground and took several strides away from us toward the center of the circle. He stopped and held his arms heavenward, his head turning left, then right as he watched the tops of the trees.

And then he started whistling.

High-pitched.

Like a bird.

I looked at Vivi, who did a sort of don't-ask-me face.

A second or two later, something fluttered down from one of the trees and landed on Paragon's right arm. A sparrow. It twitched its head as it tried to make out what sort of strange thing it had just landed on. Paragon watched it as it skipped its way along his arm toward his face.

A moment passed, then another sparrow came to land on the top of Paragon's head, quickly followed by another alongside the first on his right arm. Three birds, all of them singing along with Paragon's whistling.

He slowly turned around to face us.

It was usually impossible to tell whenever Paragon was smiling—his face was immobile after all. The grille for a mouth never moved. The lights in the eyes simply glowed. But I knew that at that moment he was smiling like he'd never smiled before.

"This," he said as quietly as possible so as not to disturb

the birds. "This is a special place." A fourth bird took up its place on Paragon's left arm. "A very special place. If I were to get all rusted up and left to power down here, I don't think I'd mind. I can think of worse places to be."

One of the birds on the right arm hopped over Paragon's head to meet the newcomer on the left arm. Paragon laughed and I found myself joining in.

"What do you think, Vivi? Wouldn't make a very good scarecrow, would I?"

"No. You wouldn't." She grinned. "One of the worst."

A smaller sparrow seemed to join the others. It pecked a little at one of the lights blinking on and off near Paragon's elbow before flying off again.

" 'Hope is the thing with feathers,' " Paragon began.

" 'That perches in the soul . . .' "

"Christina Rossetti?" Vivi asked.

"No. Emily Dickinson," Paragon replied.

"You're quite keen on her, aren't you?" I said, trying to disguise the fact that for some peculiar reason—right at that very moment, and from out of nowhere—I felt like I wanted to cry. Deep down in my chest, the poem or the vision of Paragon and the birds—something, anyway—was making me want to curl up on the ground and cry. I tried to brave it out. "You like her poems, don't you? Always quoting her poems, you are."

Paragon looked hard at me and I knew that he knew. I realized then that he always knew.

"Oh, you know, Auden," he said, the lights on one of his

eyes flickering like a wink. "She's okay. She's all right. Wouldn't you agree?"

....

"So when do you think you'll tell your mother all about me?"

Paragon was staring out my bedroom window watching the irrigation pyramids spitting over the crops.

"I mean, you can't keep me secret forever. All secrets tend to come out in the end no matter how hard you try to cover them."

Sandwich was sitting at the bottom of my bed. She was so used to seeing Paragon around in the day that she didn't pay him any attention anymore. She was cuddled up and purring, and every now and then Paragon would stroke her ears gently and make her purr and dribble even more.

"I don't know," I said, my pencil scratching over the large sketch pad. "I haven't really given it much thought. I just assumed I'd keep you a secret forever and hide you away down under the shed every night." I was trying to capture the exact shape of Paragon's head, but I was finding it difficult. Each time he moved I could see I was doing it wrong. I'd already worked my way through about a third of an eraser in the time I'd been attempting to draw him. "I'm not sure how she'll react to a seven-foot-tall robot who's been living under her lawn. I don't think she'll be all that happy."

"Might be a bit of a shock, I suppose," Paragon noted. "Although I could be useful. Keep the house tidy. Take care of the garden. Cook dinner. That kind of thing. I might be useful, what with your dad being away."

I kept on sketching. Badly.

Paragon turned from the window and looked at me.

"You haven't talked much about it," he said. "Not since you found out."

"Not much to say, is there?" I rubbed one of Paragon's eyes out and blew the crumbs of eraser off the page.

"There's always stuff to say, Auden."

I sighed and put the pad down on the bed, alongside Sandwich.

"I dunno," I said. "It's a bit like everything I've ever known has turned out to be wrong. Like finding out the moon's not real or something. Or that there are more than a hundred and eighty degrees in a triangle. I can't trust all the stuff I have always assumed to be true. I'm not sure I can trust what people tell me."

"Auden." Paragon leaned back against the wall and folded his arms. "I may not be a human being, but I know an awful lot about them and the way they behave. It is true that humans are imperfect creatures. They have cracks in their behavior. But these cracks are—trust me—only tiny. Humans are, in fact, nowhere near as imperfect as they like to believe themselves to be. Oh yes, there are some who are badly damaged. People who lie and hurt and take pleasure in doing so. A bit like your 'friend' Boyle, I suppose. But for the most part, humans are kind and truthful and wise and decent. If you ask someone for help, then chances are, they will help you. And that's always been the case. Ever since the first human crawled out of the swamp and stood on two legs. If it wasn't the case, then the entire human race would have died out thousands of years ago. It is only through support and trust and love that humans have survived."

"What about wars, then?" I asked. "Why do we have wars? Why are thousands and millions of people off fighting right now?"

Paragon shook his head. "I honestly don't know. That's the one aspect of human behavior that I really do not get. Some people say it keeps the world in balance—straightens everything out before the world can evolve even further. Some say it is mankind acting out behavior that was necessary at the beginning of time—when they had to fight for food—and that people have never managed to forget it, despite evolution. But I don't know. War is the one thing that makes no sense to me."

"I wish I could make the war stop," I hissed. "I wish this stupid war had never started. If the war had never started, then my dad would be home right now and he would never have deserted his post and ended up ashamed and in prison." I felt a tear building in the corner of my eye. "We'd be playing football and making model airplanes and things, and everything would be okay."

Paragon rested his hand on my shoulder. "I know it's not the same, Auden. . . . I realize that. . . . But I could play football with you and make model airplanes. If you wanted."

I smiled up at him.

"Like I said, it's not the same thing. I'm not your dad. But if you wanted me to . . . I think I might be quite good at football."

"Thanks, Paragon."

Sandwich got up, arched her back into an enormous stretch, yawned, and jumped down from the bed.

"That's okay," Paragon replied. "I hope Vivi's feeling better."

Vivi had QWERTY'd me earlier that morning to say that she wasn't feeling very well and that she wouldn't be going out today. A bad stomach, which meant that she had to drink more water than normal. That was every parent's nightmare, a child with a bad stomach. They could work their way through their usual weekly allowance of water in just a matter of hours. After that the family would have to scrimp on their usage, or—even worse—illegally buy some of the terrible, dirty Cat's Pee that was available on the black market.

"She'll be okay," I answered, wiping my nose on my sleeve. "I know that Immaculata has a small case of water locked away in a cupboard for emergencies. She'll be working her way through that."

"Good."

"You know what I find most incredible about war?" I jumped awkwardly back on the subject. "You know the strangest thing about it? It's that they have rules about what to do. What's allowed and what's not allowed on the battle-field. At some point in the past, the leaders of all the countries sat around a big table and decided that certain things were forbidden and other things were okay. You would think that in a war, as long as you defeated the other side and killed as many of their soldiers as possible, that that would be all that mattered. But, no. You can only kill people in a certain way."

Paragon watched me as I chattered on.

"So they came up with a big set of rules about how to fight and kill. Ridiculous! A big set of rules called . . . what is it? It's named after a city in Europe somewhere. What is it? The . . . er . . . that's right . . . the Geneva Conventions. They're the set—"

I stopped.

Paragon whirred and straightened up, clanking loudly as he locked himself into the stiff position—arms dangling vertically, head level and staring ahead—like he did on the hilltop a few weeks previously, when he'd heard the word *achromatopsia* for the first time.

He was doing it again.

Suddenly, he spoke, with the same dull, monotonous, robotic voice that he'd used on the hilltop.

"Dr. . . . Milo . . . Treble . . . The . . . Wellspring . . . Science . . . and . . . Innovation . . . Center . . . Dartford . . . Road . . . Huntingdon . . . The . . . Fleming . . . Building . . . Third . . . Floor . . . Room . . . F318. . . ."

Then he stopped talking, moments before his entire body slumped to the floor, hitting the carpet with a solid thump.

"Paragon!" It was my turn to rush to his aid. "What's wrong? What happened?"

"Oh . . ." He pushed himself up and steadied himself against the wall. "I'm okay, Auden. Don't worry about me. Just another of those funny turns. Very peculiar."

I grabbed his arm.

"What was that you said? You said somebody's name. And an address. Who is that?"

Paragon checked himself over. He bent and straightened his limbs and ran his fingers over the lights and switches. Everything appeared to be working as it had before the seizure.

"Milo Treble."

"Who's Milo Treble?" I asked.

"I don't know. But I believe it's somebody who could help me with this." Paragon pointed to the dead light on his chest—the one I'd always previously been so quick to dismiss. "I think he might be able to help me get this working again."

CHAPTER 16
THE 726

Huntingdon, it turned out, was about twenty miles away. To get there we had three possible options. First, we could tell Mum about Paragon and then—after she'd got over the shock of it (which, let's face it, might be weeks)—ask her to drive us there in the Bot Job. That didn't seem like a sensible plan to me. For a start, I couldn't really rely on the Bot Job to even get us the other side of the city. Since Mum had bought the thing it had broken down at least eight times and it was only a matter of time before the wheels fell off completely. No, it was all too much of a risk.

Second, we could walk. Twenty miles was probably nothing to Paragon, who could run so incredibly quickly. But to me and Vivi, twenty miles might as well have been a hundred miles. There was no way we could get there and back in a single day. It was far too far.

In the end, we settled on the third possibility. That was to catch the bus. Two buses, in fact. One into Cambridge, then another from the bus station to Huntingdon itself. It would be another massive risk, but with no other way of getting us all to Huntingdon, it was a risk we would have to take.

So far, Vivi and I had always taken Paragon in the opposite direction to the city. Out into the fields and onto the hills where very few people bothered to go. There, it was easy to keep him out of the way of inquisitive eyes. But by taking him into the city, we would be exposing him to hundreds and hundreds of people.

That meant he needed a better disguise.

"What"—Paragon held the wig between his finger and thumb and stared at it like it might have been a dead rat—"is *that*?"

"A hairpiece." Vivi smiled.

"Am I right in thinking that you want me to put *that* on the top of my head? So that it looks like I have hair?"

I nodded.

Paragon plonked the thing comically on the very top of his shiny metal skull and looked at us. The hair fell down over his eyes and, as he turned his head, the wig slipped a couple of inches so that it covered his left cheek.

"What do you think? Is it my style? Do I carry it off?"

Vivi and I laughed out loud and Paragon gave it a center part, which made it look even more ridiculous.

"I think," Vivi eventually said, "we may need to glue it on."

Vivi had brought a large bag of clothes and accessories from her mother's cast-offs sack. She dug about inside and brought out a pair of sunglasses. "Try these."

"I think"—Paragon snatched the shades from out of Vivi's hand—"that you are only doing this to have a laugh." He positioned them on his nose and tucked the arms behind the small raised bumps on the side of his head where the ears would normally be, just under the wig. "Hey, man!" His voice was deliberately deep and gravelly. "This is *soooo* cool. Wanna go and shoot some pool? I hear there's a real rad band playing down at the Golden Nugget."

Vivi and I struggled to control our laughing again.

Paragon was brilliant at playing the fool. It was like he didn't take himself too seriously. He was happy to sit there and do funny voices and look utterly ridiculous if it meant that we enjoyed it.

He reminded me a little of Dad.

"Perhaps you're a sort of performing robot. Designed to act on the stage," Vivi said.

Paragon stayed in character. "Me? Some kinda common actor? Huh! Are you pulling my string? Are you pushing me under a bus? Whaddya think, like, I'm only good for singing and dancing, huh?"

By the time we'd fully dressed Paragon, my sides were aching and my cheeks were sore from laughing. We both stood back and admired our handiwork.

Vivi had somehow managed to strap a pair of size twelve shoes around Paragon's feet. She'd had to make a slight cut at the back for them to fit, but somehow they stayed on. Over his legs were pulled a pair of canvas chinos—a belt of string around the waist held them in place. A thick woolen sweater covered the chest and arms, and over that Paragon had put on and buttoned up his rather ragged trench coat. Leather gloves disguised the metallic hands. And the wig that Vivi had glued on framed the sides of his head. The sunglasses hid Paragon's eyes and the wide-brimmed hat—positioned at its usual cheeky angle—threw a shadow over much of his face.

The only things that were not completely covered were the mouth and chin.

"What's the point in keeping the rest of him covered up if everyone can see that he's not got a normal mouth?" I asked. "They'll spot that straightaway."

"Hold on." Vivi rummaged about in the bag. "Here." She pulled out a stripy scarf. "Wrap that around the bottom half of your face, Paragon."

He took it off her and twisted it around and around his mouth.

"Any good?"

"Well . . ." I stood there with my arms folded, shaking my head to myself. "They're definitely not going to be looking at you because you look like a robot," I said. "There's no worry about that. But they *will* be looking at you because you look ridiculously overdressed for a hot day like this."

"That's all right," Vivi said. "That doesn't matter. We

can just pretend that he's our uncle or someone and that he's not very well."

"Not very well?" I smiled. "I don't think I'd feel very well dressed like that."

Paragon gave a twirl. "To be honest, I think I look very dapper. Like a proper human being. I don't think anyone will pay me any attention whatsoever. I think I'll fit right in."

············

The bus pulled up in front of us and the doors hissed open.

"I'll buy the tickets," I whispered. "Paragon, just keep quiet."

"Okeydokey."

We stepped onto the bus and I dug some notes out of my pocket. "One adult and two children for the city center, please."

The driver stared openmouthed at Paragon.

"I said one adult and two children, please."

Silence.

"Don't worry. I'm their uncle," Paragon suddenly blurted out from behind the scarf. "And I'm not very well."

The driver's mouth fell even wider.

"Lovely day, isn't it." Paragon adjusted his scarf and looked nervously around. "Lovely bus you have here. Very . . . full of seats."

I slapped some of the money down on the little ledge. The driver jumped and shook himself back to normality.

"Er . . . eight thousand pounds, please," he said, his eyes leaping back and forth between me and Paragon. The driver fed the money into the cash machine and three tickets dropped out. I scooped them up and tugged on Paragon's coat.

As we walked up the aisle, the passengers all watched the strange, tall, overdressed man make his way toward the back of the bus. I shoved Paragon into a window seat and sat down next to him. Vivi sat on the empty seat in front and twisted around to see us. A second or two later the bus started to move.

"I thought I told you not to say anything," I mumbled to Paragon.

"Oh, I know you did. But when he looked at me like that I got a bit jumpity. I think this scarf and the sweater are ever so slightly overheating my decision gate boards. Quite frankly, I don't understand why human beings have to wear so many clothes. It can't do you any good, surely."

"Well, try not to say anything. We don't want to attract too much attention, do we?"

"No. Okay."

As we got nearer the city center, more people got on the bus. An old lady with a knotty wooden walking stick came and sat across the aisle from us, and from the corner of my eye I could see her staring.

"Excuse me," she said.

I tried to ignore her.

"Excuse me."

"Auden." Paragon nudged me with his elbow. "Auden. That old woman wants to talk to you."

"Shhh."

He nudged me again. "Don't be rude. She wants to talk to you."

"Excuse me."

Sighing, I turned around. "Yes?"

"Is your friend all right? He looks a bit hot and bothered to me."

"No. No. He's fine." I smiled.

"I'm their uncle." Paragon pointed to both Vivi and me. "And I'm not very well. Thank you for asking, madam."

"Oh." She sat back in her seat, confused, and deliberately looked out the window for the rest of the journey.

....

The bus station was just as stressful. Too many people in too small a space, most of them wondering what the issue was with the tall man in a hat. Why was he wearing sunglasses inside? Why did he have a big scarf wrapped around his face on a sunny summer's day? And why was his hair looking so lopsided?

"I think the glue's melting off," Vivi said as we scanned the screens for the correct bus number. "I think he's getting all heated up and the glue's gone and melted."

"Oh no. Try not to move your head too quickly or your wig'll come off," I said to Paragon.

"I'll try."

We made our way along to Stand 6 and waited for our bus to come in.

"You going to Huntingdon?"

A man with a fluffy beard and a huge head of hair standing behind us was directing a question at Paragon.

"You waiting for the 726 to Huntingdon?"

"Er . . . yes, I believe I am," Paragon replied.

"Dreadful service, the 726," the man said, seemingly unaware that Paragon was dressed like somebody preparing for the worst winter storm in a hundred years. "Late most of the time. That's if it isn't canceled at all. You going to Huntingdon to see family?"

"Er . . . no. No. Er . . . an old friend."

"Old friend, is it? I have an old friend in Huntingdon. I wonder if it's the same one. Tell me, what's your friend's name?"

Paragon gave a nervous twitch. "Er . . . Milo Treble."

"Who?"

"Milo Treble."

"Never heard of him. No. My friend's name is Rory McDonald. Do you know him?"

"No. I'm afraid not."

"Nice guy, Rory."

Vivi and I were trying not to laugh as we listened in on the conversation.

"Used to run a biscuit factory. That wasn't in Huntingdon, mind. That was in Saffron Waldon. Doesn't do it anymore. Retired, see."

The man peered around us all.

"Where is this darn bus?"

Suddenly Paragon moved just a little too quickly and his hat and wig slid to the floor.

"Oh!" The man with the beard bent over and grabbed hold of the wig before reaching up and slapping it back onto Paragon's bald head. "There you are!" He patted it back into place. "Can't have that coming off now, can we? After all"—he tapped the top of his own head with his finger—"we toupee-wearers must stick together, mustn't we?"

....

The journey to Huntingdon was easier. There were fewer passengers and hardly any of them paid Paragon any attention. The three of us sat on the long seat at the back of the bus—Paragon staring out of the window while Vivi and I talked.

"What was the word that started him off, again?" Vivi asked softly.

"I said something about the Geneva Convention. Straight after that he began spouting off the name and address."

"Why 'Geneva Convention'? I don't understand."

I shook my head.

"The Geneva Convention is to do with war, isn't it? Perhaps this Milo Treble has something to do with the war. Or killing." She suddenly looked nervous. "Do you think we will be able to trust him? I mean, we've not even told our own mothers about Paragon. And now here we are, about to show him to a complete stranger. What if he takes him away from us? What then?"

I didn't want to think about it. It had taken me so long

to come around to accepting Paragon for what he was that I didn't want to lose him now. I'd only just started to get to know him. It would be like some sort of sick joke. First my dad gets taken away, and then Paragon.

It was too horrible to consider.

Still, I had to trust Paragon. There was no other choice.

"Paragon seems to think Treble might help him," I said. "I'm hoping he might know something about the rainbow machine—might be able to tell us where the battery is. I mean, Treble is obviously a scientist. Perhaps he knew Uncle Jonah. There are lots of questions we don't know the answers to. I hope Milo Treble can give us some."

CHAPTER 17

THE WELLSPRING SCIENCE AND INNOVATION CENTER, DARTFORD ROAD, HUNTINGDON

We hopped off the bus on the very outskirts of Huntingdon and walked the mile and a half to the Wellspring Science and Innovation Center. The road was long and sweeping, and clearly underused, judging by the hardy weeds that sprang up along the edges of the curbs. It took us away from the direction of the town and out into even more sparse countryside. After a while, the road opened up and directly ahead of us we saw the buildings.

It was an enormous complex. Tall, boxlike buildings—lots of them—with shiny mirrored windows, sticking out of the ground like the pins on an upturned plug.

"Wow," I found myself saying. "Look at this place."

Around the complex ran a twenty-foot-high fence with barbed wire strung across the top and, even from where we were standing, you could hear the strong buzz of electricity running along its length.

As if to hammer home the fact, a signpost nearby warned in a severe font: KEEP OUT. ELECTRIC FENCE. RISK OF DEATH.

The road led all the way up to a gate where a bored armed guard was prodding some dried-on old chewing gum from the tarmac with the tip of his boot.

"Not exactly the inviting scene I thought it might be," I said. "Do you think they'll even let us in?"

Vivi stepped forward. "We'll never know unless we try. Come on."

The three of us strolled as casually as we could possibly manage toward the gate. The guard—having given up with the chewing gum—glared at us as we approached, his rifle at the ready.

"Halt!" he shouted.

We stopped.

"Who goes there? What do you want?"

"We are here to see Dr. Milo Treble," Vivi called back, her voice strong and confident. If she was as scared as I was, she certainly didn't show it. "Dr. Milo Treble in the Fleming Building."

"Do you have an appointment?" the guard asked.

"No. But we are here on a matter of the utmost importance." Vivi obviously thought that that was a clever thing to say, and she gave me a nod to highlight just how clever she thought it was.

The guard, though, wasn't impressed. "Doesn't make any difference. No appointment means no entry." He waved the rifle toward us. "Now run along or I shall have to shoot you for acting in a threatening way."

We all stood there for a while, astounded at just how abrupt our visit had been.

"Go on." The guard waggled the rifle up and down. "Off you go now."

"Come on," Paragon muttered. "Let's go."

"But—" I began.

"No buts. Let's go."

He turned around and slowly started walking back from where we had just come, his shoulders slumped.

Vivi and I just stared at each other before racing off to catch up with Paragon.

"You can't just leave," I said as I came alongside him. "You said Treble could help you. Why didn't you try harder to get in?"

Paragon said nothing. He just kept on walking.

"I'm sure they'll let us in if we just explain the situation to them," Vivi argued as she skipped to keep up. "Don't you think?"

Paragon marched on, his head bowed.

"I thought you were stronger than that," I growled. "I thought you would at least try. For goodness' sake, I thought you were brave."

Paragon stopped dead.

"Don't worry, Auden," he said. "I haven't given up yet."

He turned and looked back at the guard, who'd gone back to his previous occupation of trying to pry chewing gum off the road with his toe. Suddenly, Paragon started walking away from the road and over the tumps of stringy grass. Vivi and I followed. "You see, we're not going to get in through the *front* door. . . ."

"So we'll get in through the *back* door! Of course." Paragon had not given up after all. He was simply thinking out of the box!

"Or the *side* door at least. Come on."

We trudged over the earth until the guard disappeared from sight and all we could see was the wire fence, buzzing and clicking like a fly trapped in a bathroom. The fence eventually turned back on itself by about ninety degrees and we continued to follow it. A few hundred yards later, Paragon stopped.

"This is probably good enough," he said. He slipped off both of his gloves and handed them to Vivi. "Now, whatever you do, do not touch me while I'm connected. Okay? It could kill you."

We both nodded and automatically took a step back.

Paragon moved closer to the fence and brought up his left hand. It sat just a couple of inches away from the fence.

"Paragon!" Vivi squeaked.

Paragon looked toward Vivi and whispered, "Shhh."

Suddenly, Paragon reached out and grabbed the fence

with his hand, gripping it with his fingers. A couple of sparks flew from the fence and Paragon gave a small judder, making his hat slide off.

"Paragon?" I asked. "Paragon? Are you okay?"

He didn't answer. It was like he was miles away, dreaming of something else, the lights for his eyes stuttering on and off.

"Is he okay?" Vivi looked worried.

Then he started talking.

"Dr. Milo Treble is here today. He electronically signed in at eight thirty-five this morning. There are three armed guards on duty in the complex. The one at the gate and two patrolling the grounds. One of those guards follows a route that passes the Fleming Building every sixteen minutes or so. The last time he passed it was seven minutes ago, meaning we have nine minutes left in which to enter the building."

"We could wait until he's passed again," Vivi said. "That would give us the full sixteen minutes in which to get in."

"Nope," Paragon replied. "That guard is about to take his lunch break in the guards' room, which overlooks the entrance to the Fleming Building. If we wait now, we'll be waiting for well over an hour. During that time, two Scoot drones fly over the area to check the periphery of the site."

"But you can disable drones from a distance, can't you?" I said.

Paragon shook his head. "This is open country. If they fly across from the other side of the park then they might well spot us before they are close enough for me to disable them."

"But how are we going to get in?"

Paragon—still holding on to the fence with his left hand—lifted up his right hand with the index finger extended. Then the weirdest thing happened. The tip of the finger twisted completely back on itself, exposing a tiny pipe. Suddenly a fierce flame about an inch long started burning. Paragon brought it up to the fence and started cutting away at the wires, melting through them like butter.

"Won't they be able to detect that?" I wondered out loud. "They'll know the fence is damaged and send the guards to get us, won't they?"

"Nope. I'm redirecting the flow of the electricity around the gap I'm making. They won't suspect a thing."

If you'd told me a few months earlier that I would find myself standing in the middle of the Cambridgeshire countryside with a friend from school and a robot, cutting our way through an electric fence to break into a science park in order to try to talk to a man none of us had ever met before, I'd've laughed. But, as it was, it seemed perfectly natural for us all to be there.

In fact, it almost felt like fate.

Paragon worked steadily through the wires and, after about four minutes, the last wire was sliced and a wide section of the fence big enough for us to crawl through fell to the ground.

"There." He pulled his left hand away from the fence. "Let's go."

Paragon went first, followed by Vivi and then me.

"The Fleming Building is that way. Now walk normally. Don't attract attention."

I half laughed to myself, thinking of the way the driver of the first bus stared at Paragon. Dressed the way he was it was hard for him *not* to attract attention.

Then, from out of nowhere, a small electric van zoomed past.

Quickly, Paragon turned us around and pointed up at something as if he was an adult showing us something incredible in the sky and we were two little children fascinated by whatever it was. The van went on without stopping and disappeared way in the distance.

"Come on."

We carried on down a long, dull road before turning a corner onto another long, dull road. The whole area seemed like it was deserted. Clearly many of the people who normally worked here were off fighting.

"There it is." Paragon nodded up ahead.

THE ALEXANDER FLEMING BUILDING, read the flowery sign on the lawn directly in front of it.

We sped up and walked up the steps to the vast glass door. I gave the door a push but it didn't budge.

"Look." Vivi pointed.

The door was locked and the large touch-sensitive pad on the wall next to it revealed that it could only be unlocked by somebody with a registered handprint.

"We can't get in," I moaned.

"Paragon. How long have we got?" asked Vivi.

"One minute exactly."

"What are we going to do?"

"Aha! Stand back." Paragon stood in front of the touch-sensitive pad and held up his right hand yet again. This time it was the tip of the smallest finger that flipped backward, revealing a needlelike wire. Paragon felt around the pad before inserting the wire into it. The pad glowed bright and then faded.

"Now, Auden. Put your hand on the pad."

"But it won't recognize my handprint."

"No, it won't. But in the millionth of a second during which it questions your handprint I am going to register you on the system. Essentially, I am going to race their computer. Okay? You ready?"

I positioned myself next to Paragon, my hand flattened and ready to hit the pad.

"Okay. Go."

I put my hand on the screen and less than a second later the glass door whooshed open.

"You did it!"

"Phew! It was close, though. They've got some efficient software here. I only just got there in time. It required me making several thousand nano-bypasses to be able to do it."

"That must have been the quickest race ever," Vivi said with a smile as we rushed into the hallway of the Fleming Building. Outside, we could see the guard coming down the road, swinging his gun as he headed toward his lunch.

CHAPTER 18

MILO TREBLE

The building was utterly silent. It was almost as if it was due to be demolished and everyone had vacated it, leaving it hollow and echoey. As we made our way up the granite stairs, our footsteps bounced around the stairwell like intruders and, in the remainder of the silence, you could hear the usually inaudible whirs and bleeps that came from somewhere within Paragon.

"Where is everybody?" I whispered, though it sounded like a roar in this place.

Paragon shook his head. "The war? Some may be away fighting. Others have probably been conscripted into some other government work. Who knows? There are probably only a handful of scientists working in this complex now."

We worked our way up each flight of stairs without seeing a single person. On the third floor we consulted a sign on the wall and tip-tapped down an endless corridor. The lights were all blazing as if the building was still a normal, up-and-running place of work, and a number of the screens on the walls were still flashing up the occasional message.

REMEMBER—WATER IS PRECIOUS. DON'T WASTE. DON'T SPILL.

CREATIVITY IS THE KEY TO PEACE AND PROGRESS.

WORK SO THAT YOUR CHILDREN MAY HAVE A BETTER, BRIGHTER FUTURE.

The messages gave me the creeps. They seemed to have the smell of brainwashing about them. What exactly was this place?

Paragon suddenly stopped.

"What is it?" I asked.

"Drones."

"Drones? Inside?"

"Yes. They're behind us. Just around the corner. A hundred and twenty-two of them. And they're coming this way."

"A hundred and—"

"Shh!" He pushed Vivi and me against the wall of the corridor, next to a metal filing cabinet. What was happening? How could a hundred and twenty-two drones be coming toward us? There was no noise. Surely we would be able to hear them coming.

I peered around the filing cabinet and something weird began happening. It was like the air at the end of the corridor was starting to shiver. Quiver. A cloud of what seemed like dust hovered and rippled halfway between the floor and the ceiling. Still there was no noise. Then I noticed the cloud was getting bigger. No. It was moving toward us.

"What is it?" Vivi hissed to Paragon, who was standing firmly in the center of the corridor still.

"I . . . can't . . . talk," he mumbled. "Not now. Trying . . . to . . . block all one hundred . . . and twenty-two of them. Difficult." His fists clenched like he was struggling.

"Paragon! Are you all right?"

The cloud got nearer, and then, as it passed into the light streaming in through a window, I could make out what they were.

Butterflies. Tiny, shiny mechanical butterflies.

Butterfly-shaped drones. Each of them only a little bigger than an actual butterfly.

"Almost . . . done. Hard to . . . keep them all . . . blocked together." Paragon looked tense. "Now to . . . reprogram them. . . . All of them. . . . Every . . . single . . . one!"

The fluttering mass of butterfly drones got slowly closer and closer until they were about six feet from Paragon.

"Okay . . ." Paragon gripped his fingers even tighter. "Time for . . . you all . . . to . . . go."

Suddenly, one of the butterflies—a largish one with wide wings and spiraling antennae—peeled off from the group, flickered upward, brushed against the ceiling, and then flew off back in the direction from which it had come. A few seconds later, two others did exactly the same thing. Then, almost as one, the rest of the cloud seemed to pause before turning back on itself, each of the minuscule robotic butterflies fluttering away from us.

"Wow," whispered Vivi. "They're beautiful."

As the last of the cloud disappeared back around the corner, Paragon seemed to relax and loosen his fists.

"Phew! A hundred and twenty-two of them at the same time. That's quite a feat. Really tested my multidimensional tasking ability." He either swaggered with pride or wobbled through exhaustion. It was hard to tell which. "I'm giving my systems a workout today!"

"What sort of drones were they?" I asked. "I've never seen any drones like *that* before."

"Zephyr drones," Paragon replied. "Internal surveillance units. Still at the prototype stage."

"Well," Vivi announced as we started to make our way along the corridor once again, "I think that Zephyrs are now my favorite type of drone. They're *so* much prettier than the Ariels."

....

"Wait!"

"Hmm?"

"Quiet. Can you hear that?"

Vivi and I strained to listen. We strained and then we strained a bit more.

"No. I can't hear anything."

"Me neither."

Paragon took a turn off the main corridor. "It's coming from this direction."

Vivi and I followed close behind. After about a minute, we could both hear what Paragon had been hearing.

Music. Classical music.

"What's that?" Vivi asked.

"It's Rachmaninoff's Piano Concerto Number Two in C Minor, Opus Eighteen. The 1965 recording by Earl Wild." Paragon tossed out the information like it was nothing to him.

We walked toward the music. It got louder and louder as we got nearer and nearer until—

BANG!

A door flew open and slammed into the wall as a man marched into the corridor from the room beyond, his head bent over a sheet of paper. He was so absorbed in reading whatever was on the paper that he didn't even notice us standing about twenty feet from him.

"Rubbish!" he muttered to himself. "Insubstantial light-weight rubbish!" He reached up and opened one of the windows on the corridor before scrunching up the paper and tossing it out.

I looked out the window and watched the paper as it fell and landed on a grass verge covered with thousands of other little balls of scrunched-up paper.

The man closed the window and turned to go back into the room. That was when he saw us.

"Who are you?" he asked in an annoyed sort of voice. "What do you want?"

Vivi stepped forward again. "Dr. Treble?"

He was a man of about forty with long, curly dark hair and a small ring of a beard around his mouth. He wasn't fat, but then again he wasn't slim. He was wearing a T-shirt and jeans that, in my opinion, desperately needed a wash. His eyes looked tired.

"Yes?" he asked suspiciously.

"We're here to talk to you about Jonah Bloom, sir." I took a step nearer. "We're here to ask a few questions, if you don't mind."

The man barked a laugh. "I've already answered all the questions I'm ever going to answer about Bloom. Who are you, anyway? How did you get in here? This is a secure complex."

"My name is Auden Dare, sir. I am Jonah Bloom's nephew."

Treble frowned and looked hard at me. "You're the boy who can't see color."

"Yes."

Treble didn't say anything. He was obviously weighing things up in his mind. "Look, I've nothing more to say about your uncle. I gave a number of statements to the Water Allocation Board. They accepted all my versions of events. If you've any questions, you'd be better off talking to them."

His hand reached for the door handle back into the room from which he'd just stomped. "I'm sorry about Bloom. It's very sad. But, please, I have work to do. Leave the way you came. Good-bye." He turned the handle.

"Wait," Paragon called, and Treble released his grip. "Wait. Dr. Treble. I think there's something you should see."

"Do you now? Well, what exactly is that, may I ask?"

"Me." In one smooth movement Paragon threw off the hat, glasses, and scarf and ripped the coat and sweater from his torso. The light blazing in through the windows reflected brightly off his hard metal body and dazzled Treble momentarily.

Treble stood with his mouth wide open as Paragon approached and stood directly in front of him, towering over the scientist.

The silence that filled the corridor was even more deafening than the silence that was smothering the entrance hall. Nobody said a thing. Not for ages. And then, eventually, Treble broke the silence with a single word.

"Paragon?" he said.

....

We were in Treble's large and wonderful laboratory. There were huge machines that did things that I couldn't understand. There were flames busy bubbling substances that I'd never seen before. There was shelf upon shelf and row upon row of pieces of scientific equipment that I didn't know the names of.

It was like a strange new magical world.

Screens and monitors beeped and fizzed, and weird shapes and equations were scribbled all over a scruffy whiteboard.

And the smell!

Rotting eggs, burned metal, sickly sweet sugary. All mixed together.

Treble pulled the stylus from the screeching record and stood Paragon in front of him.

"My, my . . ." he admired as he closely inspected the intricacies of the robot's limbs and head. "My, my. Magnificent work. Bloom surpassed himself with this. Superb craftsmanship, I must say."

"How did you know Paragon's name?" Vivi asked.

"Eh?" Treble, slightly annoyed to be distracted, turned to look at her. "How did I know its name? Oh, because I named it."

"You named him?"

"Inadvertently, I suppose. Bloom was looking for a name for his next project. He never told me what it was, exactly— said it was going to be something that was going to change the world. Something perfect. So I suggested Paragon. A paragon is something that is considered to be perfect, you see." He went back to his inspection. "And this is it. Bloom's paragon. My, my."

"Him. He," I said.

"Hmm?" Treble half ignored me.

"Paragon is a 'him.' Not an 'it.'"

"It's a humanoid robot," Treble corrected me. "It's

not actually human. Just human *shaped*. It doesn't have internal organs. It's not capable of independent thought. It's an 'it.'"

"Ahem." Paragon coughed. "Should you all be discussing me like I'm not here? Seems like bad manners if you ask me."

I laughed. Vivi laughed. Treble frowned.

"So you were good friends with Dr. Bloom," Vivi said.

"Well . . . er . . . ." Treble hesitated. "Once upon a time." He poked at something near Paragon's ear.

"Ouch!" Paragon jumped. "Do you mind?"

Treble frowned again.

"What does 'once upon a time' mean?" I asked.

"It means what it says. It means we were once friends but then we weren't."

"Why not?"

Treble sighed. "It's all very dull, I'm afraid. You wouldn't be interested."

"Go on. Try me."

"Stretch out your leg," Treble ordered Paragon, who duly obliged. "Fascinating. Absolutely fascinating."

"Dr. Treble."

Treble sighed again. "We had a professional argument. Over an academic prize. The Geneva Prize for Scientific Advancement, if you must know."

Geneva? So that was why Paragon was triggered to

reveal Treble's name and address. It wasn't the phrase "Geneva Convention." Just the word *Geneva*. I looked at Vivi and she looked at me.

"Anyway," Treble continued, "we argued over who was likely to first win the Geneva Prize. Silly, I know. But then scientists can be silly over things like that. Vain. We both set ourselves the challenge of being the first to win it, and we went our separate academic ways." He suddenly sounded sad. "I didn't speak to him at all for the last year of his life."

I peered around the laboratory. "So what are you working on now?"

"A number of things. None of them very successful, I'm afraid." He patted Paragon on the back. "Nothing like this." Treble looked back at us. "What's its cognitive function like?"

"Cognitive what?"

"How he thinks." Vivi put me straight.

"Why don't you ask him yourself?" I said. "He's rather fond of poetry."

"Poetry?"

"Especially Emily Dickinson," Vivi added.

Treble looked confused.

"I can quote you some now, Dr. Treble. If you'd like." Paragon cleared his throat and was about to launch into something or other.

"Er, no," Treble cut him short. "No. Don't."

Paragon appeared deflated.

"What about its mobility?"

"He's very fast," said Vivi. "He's very good at playing hide-and-seek."

Treble raised his eyebrows.

"There *is* something, though, Dr. Treble," Paragon quietly remarked. "This light here . . ." He pointed. "It's not working. And I don't know what it's for or how to get it started. I was wondering if you might be able to help me."

Treble tapped the dead light. "Might it not just have blown?"

"No," Paragon answered. "It's fully functioning. But for some reason it's not reacting to any of my diagnostics."

Treble thought and as he did so he stroked the beard around his chin.

"Okay." He walked away from Paragon toward a computer situated near the back of the laboratory. He clicked a button and a wobbly line suddenly materialized on the screen. "Does it have a coaxial digital data jack?" He aimed the question at Vivi and me.

Paragon answered by walking up to the computer and flipping back yet another of his fingertips. He proffered the finger to Treble, who grinned and attached a lead to it.

"Bloom really did think of everything. Amazing."

Treble plugged the other end of the lead into the computer and began to tap at the old-fashioned keyboard.

"Right . . . Let's see what the problem is. . . ."

A series of shapes started to flit across the monitor.

Three-dimensional shapes. Wiry-looking cubes and cuboids. Spheres and cones. Triangular prisms. Twisting all over the screen. And then more complicated things—shapes for which there are probably no names. After that came a number of two-dimensional tessellations, scrolling from left to right, then top to bottom. I had no idea what any of it meant, but Treble clearly did.

"Dr. Treble?" I ventured as the man's eyes glared at the screen. "I think my uncle was working on a machine to help me see color."

"Hmm?"

"Something he called a 'rainbow machine.' We found it at his house but it's missing its battery. I wondered if you knew anything about it? Did my uncle tell you anything about it?"

"Erm . . ." He was still focusing on the images in front of him. "No. Sorry. Don't know anything about that." My heart dropped like a stone again.

"Did you try passing the secondary load over the central auxillary system?" Treble asked Paragon.

"Of course." Paragon sounded a bit put out. "It was one of the first things I tried. I've attempted all the possible permutations of power-to-resistance ratio, but nothing seems to work."

"Inverted the amplitude substructures?"

"Yep. Many times."

"Hmm." Treble looked stumped. "Are you sure the bulb hasn't just blown?"

Paragon gave a sigh. "I'm sure."

Treble tapped at the keyboard a bit more and the whole screen went ziggy-zaggy.

"What about . . . what about undermining the whole motor system and backtracking the primary load within the pseudoparameters? Momentarily, of course."

Paragon tilted his head at a curious angle. "Why would I try that? I wouldn't want to risk losing all motor function, now, would I?"

The whole conversation flew over my and Vivi's heads like a Scoot drone. "No, but . . . if you do it for less than a billionth of a second, there should be no serious comeback. Everything should just work as normal." He hovered a finger over one of the keys on the keyboard. "I can do it for you if you'd like."

"Er, no. I'm not so sure that's a good idea, after all—"

"Too late." Treble hit the button with a loud tap.

"No! . . . Oh." Paragon looked at his arms and his hands. "Oh. It's okay. I still have mobility. Ha!"

A second or two passed before—

"Look!" Vivi pointed. The light on Paragon's chest had started flashing. Constantly. About once a second.

"Oh! Thank you, Dr. Treble." Paragon rushed up to Treble and held out his hand. "Thank you so much."

Treble looked at Paragon's hand like it was something alien before slowly—and perhaps slightly reluctantly—taking it and shaking it.

"That's . . . okay . . . Paragon."

"So," I said, the disappointment still showing in my voice, "now that you've got it going, what does it do?"

Paragon stood perfectly still like he was giving the matter some serious thought.

"I . . . don't know."

"What?"

"I have no idea what it is."

"Hold on," I huffed. "You've been worried about the light not working. And now that you've got it working, you don't know what it does?"

Paragon thought again. "Nope. No idea."

"Unbelievable!"

Treble was still staring at the monitor. "Wait a minute. There are still some other functions that have lain dormant since your initial power-up. I can see something here."

"What do you mean?" Vivi asked.

Paragon had a puzzled look. "Other functions? That can't be. Everything in my database is now accounted for. There *is* nothing else."

"Not according to this, it isn't." Treble jabbed his finger at the screen.

"But I don't understand."

"Let me see if I can get it to . . ." The sentence faded away to nothing as Treble focused back on the images flashing over the monitor, his fingers dancing over the keyboard.

"There must be a mistake," Paragon argued. "I've fully exhausted every possible operation of my being. There is nothing more that I can do."

"Yes, there is." Treble didn't even look up. "Hold out your arms."

"I'm sorry?"

"I said hold out your arms. Straight in front of you."

Vivi and I watched, perplexed, as Paragon leveled his arms so that they were horizontal.

"Now. Watch." Treble slapped another key.

As he did so, something moved on the back of each of Paragon's forearms. Two rectangular plates of metal lifted away from each arm by about a centimeter or two, then curled around both sides of the forearms.

"What's going on?" I thought out loud.

Then, slowly, a long, thin, dark metal pipe raised itself up from inside until it was looking like it was sitting along the length of each arm. There was a click as the two pipes locked into position.

"What are they?" I asked.

Treble swiveled in his chair. "Machine guns."

....

"There were rumors. About Jonah Bloom. You see, the scientific world is actually a rather small, close-knit one. Everyone has a fair idea of what everyone else is doing. So even though he and I hadn't talked for a year, through colleagues and other members of scientific establishments, I was still vaguely aware of what he was up to. Sandwich?"

Treble dug some sandwiches from out of his plastic lunchbox and handed them around. They were made with real bread. That told me Treble was clearly well paid.

"And the first rumor was that he was doing some work for the Water Allocation Board. No one knew what, precisely, but something. Something big. The second rumor said that he had fallen out with them and was refusing to complete the project. On ethical grounds. Quite soon after that second rumor bounced around the scientific establishment, Bloom was found dead."

"Yes," I said quickly. "I think he was murdered."

Treble's eyebrows arched.

I told him about the way Unicorn Cottage and Uncle Jonah's rooms had been trashed. I told him about the threatening letter we'd found in a file. The clues that both Vivi and I had been left in order to find Paragon. All the tiny little pieces of evidence to suggest that Jonah Bloom had not died a natural death.

Treble put his own sandwich down on the desk. "It's exactly what I've been thinking ever since he was found. Of course, I couldn't prove anything. I doubt anyone can—not even you, Auden. But it seems rather more than a coincidence that Bloom dies soon after walking out on a top-secret scientific project."

"What about the police?" Vivi leaned across the desk. "Didn't you tell them that you thought Dr. Bloom was murdered? Wouldn't they find out the truth?"

Treble gave an awkward shrug. "The police investigation

found nothing untoward. What could I do? Anyway, the police and Water Allocation Board are too closely interlinked to be completely fair and unbiased. They are basically in each other's pockets. They're the same thing."

We sat in silence for a while as we digested the information.

Was the Water Allocation Board responsible for killing my uncle?

"Soon after Bloom was found dead," Treble eventually continued, "the WAB paid me a visit. The first of several, actually. Questioned me—well, interrogated me, to be more accurate. Asked me if I knew anything about Bloom's current work. Had I had any contact with him recently? That sort of thing." He picked up another small sandwich and shoved it whole into his mouth. After he had swallowed it, he went on. "They also asked if the word *Paragon* meant anything to me. Obviously I feigned complete ignorance. I think they bought it. And to be honest, apart from giving him his name, I knew nothing whatsoever about Paragon. Until now, that is."

We all looked over to Paragon. He was sitting some distance away from us, on a stool, bent over and staring at the floor. Since the guns had been revealed, he had been in a kind of depressed stupor.

I got up and went over to him.

"Paragon?"

"Hey, Audendare." He looked up at me but the glow in his eyes seemed a little dimmer than usual.

I knelt beside him and put my hand on his shoulder. He'd been there for me when I needed him, when I found out my dad wasn't a soldier but a prisoner. He'd supported me and comforted me and told me everything was going to be okay.

Now I was going to do the same for him.

"How are you feeling?" I asked.

"Oh. Not so good."

I put my arms around him and held him tight.

"You know, I don't understand," he said, his hand patting my arm. "All this knowledge I have. All the poetry and language and art and nature. Why do I have it? Why have I been given it? It doesn't make sense."

"I don't know."

He gave a bitter laugh. "Weird, isn't it? All these weeks, you and Vivi have been wondering what exactly my role is. We've exhausted most things. Doctor. Teacher. Farmer." He shook his head. "And then it turns out I'm nothing more than a killing machine."

He squeezed my arm, his hand soft and careful. Gentle. It was not the touch of a killing machine.

"I see how you felt now. Finding out about your father," he said. "Coming across a truth that hurts. Everything dropping beneath you. The whole world just falling away. Like a big hole that you hadn't even noticed was there. A pain you just weren't expecting."

"What does any of it matter?" I said, trying to sound cheery, but with tears in my eyes. "It doesn't make any difference. I mean, my dad's still my dad. And you're still you. Just because you were designed in a particular way, doesn't mean you have to *be* that way. You're better than that. You've risen above it. You're Paragon. You're *my* Paragon. And I love you."

PART SIX

YELLOW

CHAPTER 19
THE WATER ALLOCATION BOARD

The loud bang awoke me. Without thinking I threw the covers off my bed and stood up. *What was that?*

Voices. Growly voices. And footsteps. Heavy boots pounding up the stairs.

Something wasn't right.

I pushed the window open and leaned out of it. Suddenly, my bedroom door flew open so I leaped out, grabbing hold of the tree branch and dropping down onto the trampoline before bouncing hard onto the ground, my bare feet scratching on the dry earth.

"He's got out of the window!"

"He's in the garden!"

Loud, angry voices from above me.

I didn't know what to do, so I sprinted toward the hole in

the hedge. If I could get through the hole and across the field I might be able to hide away and assess what was going on.

Mum!

I couldn't just leave her in the house. Whatever was going on, I couldn't just desert her. I had to go back.

That was when one of them tackled me to the ground. They thumped roughly into my shoulders and dragged me down.

"I've got him!" he called to the others. "I've got the boy."

My face was buried in the dirt and I couldn't see. The man pulled my arms behind my back and tied something around my wrists so I couldn't move them. Then he picked me up by my pajamas, stood me on my feet, and turned me around.

The man had tough features and cold eyes. His chin was covered in a thin, scratchy layer of stubble. And he wore the dark uniform and protective helmet of the Water Allocation Board. Over his chest, crossing from top right to bottom left, was a belt of bullets, and on his hip, strapped away within a leather case, was a revolver.

"Come on. Move!"

He gave me a harsh shove and forced me back toward the house.

··············

The house was full of them. Dozens of them. They were kicking things over and pulling pictures from the walls. I could hear a loud ripping noise coming from the sitting room as one of the soldiers sliced a big hole in the sofa.

The man who had tackled me kept jabbing me in the back as we made our way past the men, through the house to the kitchen.

"Keep moving."

"Here he is!" It was a smooth, educated, well-spoken voice that greeted me as the soldier gave a final shove and closed the kitchen door behind me.

My mother was sitting at the table, a nervous, confused look on her face. Next to the back door, another of the soldiers was standing at attention, his watchful eyes pinning both me and Mum down. He looked familiar somehow.

But it wasn't him I was interested in.

In front of the sink—the window behind him—was a man dressed in the uniform of a Water Allocation Board officer. He was older than the other soldiers. More lined around the eyes. His slick hair looked grayish and a substantial grayish mustache dominated his top lip.

"Good of you to join us, Auden. Please"—he indicated a chair—"sit."

I sat on the chair next to my mother and felt her arms pulling me nearer.

"Now." He turned to the sink. "I hope you don't mind, but I'm feeling rather thirsty." He took a glass and turned on the tap, filling it to the very top. He spun back to face us and took a long sip from the tumbler. I noticed that he'd left the tap running behind him.

"That's better."

"Who are you?" I said. "What do you want?"

"Now, the second of those questions I believe you already know the answer to. So let me answer the first." His movements and his speech reminded me of a snake. "I am General Heracles Woolf of the Second Infantry Division of the WAB. British Aquarian Protection Cross (First Class). Distinction in the Field of Utilities Medal, awarded with honors." He gave an almost sarcastic little bow, and I hated him straightaway.

"Please." My mother's voice quivered. "What do you want from us?"

"Why don't you ask your son that?" Woolf remarked bitterly. "I'm sure he can tell you. After all, he's been a very busy boy."

I didn't understand. Why were they here now? Why hadn't they come earlier to try to find Paragon? What had changed?

And then it dawned on me.

Treble.

Treble had contacted them and told them where Paragon was. He'd probably made a deal with the WAB, asking for some involvement in developing Paragon so that he could try to win the Geneva Prize. Vivi was right when she said that we might not be able to trust him. His academic vanity had got the better of him and he had betrayed us all. Including my uncle.

At that moment I hated him more than I hated General Woolf.

"Now, Auden." Woolf took another sip. "There are a

thousand questions that I need to ask you. And, in due course, I will ask you every single one of them. But, at this moment in time, I only *really* need the answer to one." He stared straight at me. "Where is it?"

I tried to look away. "I don't know what you mean."

Woolf shook his head. "Come on, Auden. Credit us with some intelligence. We know it's around here somewhere."

I looked down at the floor and ignored him.

"Oh," he said. "Look." He turned back to the sink, where the tap was still trickling out water. "Silly me. I left your tap running." He twisted the tap and the water suddenly started to gush out even faster, making the warning gauge flash. "Look at me wasting your allowance like this. How remiss of me. Be a shame if I were to use up your entire weekly allowance by being careless like this, wouldn't it?"

He turned the tap off, folded his arms, and looked directly at me again.

"Where is it?"

My mother swiveled her head toward me. "What is he talking about, Auden? What have you done?"

My chest felt tight. The soldiers were all over the house and garden. It was only a matter of time before they pulled up the floor in the shed and found Paragon's little hiding place, surely.

"Just so you are aware," Woolf said, and scooped Sandwich up from the floor and started stroking her. "There is another team of WAB infantry currently tearing apart Miss Rookmini's rooms at Trinity College." He held

Sandwich close to his face and snuggled her close to his chest. "I do love cats. Such independent creatures. Always on their own. Never trusting of anyone. Perfect."

I watched as Sandwich wriggled in the general's tight grip and I found myself thinking of Vivi and Immaculata. Their warm, cozy rooms being ripped to shreds like they didn't matter. It didn't seem fair. How could this be happening? Vivi and Immaculata didn't deserve this.

I suddenly felt sick.

"Okay," I said.

"What?"

"You want to know where he is?" I could barely bring myself to look at Woolf. "Then I'll show you."

....

Two of the soldiers ripped the floorboards out of the shed, tossing them into the garden like they didn't care where they landed.

"The boy's right," one of them called over to General Woolf. "There's a space beneath the shed."

"Go down. See what's there. But be careful. It might be booby-trapped."

Woolf was standing next to me and Mum—both of us still handcuffed—on the hopeless lawn in front of the shed. We watched as the soldiers busied themselves, stripping apart everything they could get their hands on. At one point I saw a particularly dozy-looking soldier clamber under the overhanging trees and fiddle about with the rainbow machine that I'd shoved under there all those weeks ago. He obviously didn't think it worth investigating because he quickly left it to go and find something more interesting to meddle with instead.

"I hope for your sake you've been telling us the truth," Woolf half growled as we watched the last of the boards being thrown out onto the lawn. "I'm not exactly known for my patience."

I didn't say anything. I simply kept staring at the scene that was playing out in front of us.

A minute or so later, a soldier came out from the shed and held up his thumb. "We've found it. It's here."

Woolf breathed a heavy sigh of relief. "Good. Get it out."

The soldier nodded and went back into the shed.

"Corporal."

"Yessir." The soldier who'd been standing at attention in the kitchen stepped up next to Woolf, his eyes keen and alert, and I suddenly remembered where I'd seen him before. He was the man in the cap who'd tried to follow me that afternoon from Trinity.

"Put these two in the van. Take the mother to one of the holding cells in the city center and the boy to the temporary camp." Woolf nudged his head toward me. "We'll interrogate him properly there."

"Yessir."

The soldier grabbed Mum and me by the shoulders and marched us around the side of the house to where a military van was sitting. He opened the rear door and we both climbed in before the door slammed shut again behind us.

The engine started and, just before we started to move off, I peered out the little window.

Three soldiers were carrying Paragon's body out of the shed. They hadn't switched him on, so he looked limp—like he was dead. The only thing that showed he wasn't dead was the recently restarted, constantly pulsing light that sat in the middle of his chest.

It flickered and beat just like a heart.

....

"What's happening, Auden?"

"It's all right, Mum."

"I don't understand what's going on." She looked lost, like she was trapped in a weird dream and didn't know what was going to happen next.

"Please, Mum. It's all going to be all right." It was like I was the adult and she was the child. Roles were reversed. I was the one who knew all the answers and she was struggling to try to find them. I didn't like that feeling one bit.

"What were they looking for in the shed?"

"Just . . . something . . ."

"Something?"

I took a deep breath. I couldn't put this off any longer.

"Look, Mum. There are some things you need to know."

So I told her everything. The clues within the Snowflake letters. The key within the attic. The messed-up rooms of Uncle Jonah. Six Six and Vivi. The metal chamber under the shed. The invisible ink. The Pisces constellation. The discovery of Paragon. The note to Uncle Jonah from the WAB.

The corporal following me from Trinity. Teaching Fabius Boyle a lesson. Finding out about Dad. The journey to Milo Treble. The machine guns hidden within Paragon's arms. During that journey from Unicorn Cottage to the WAB military camp, I gave her all the details and she sucked them up without saying a single word.

And, to be honest, it felt good to tell her. All these weeks I had held on to the secret—well, I suppose Vivi and I had held on to the secret—and it was only when I had let the secret out that I realized just how heavy it had been to carry.

Secrets are like weights. They are chains tied about your legs. If they don't slow you down, they will trip you up.

So at that moment, I knew exactly how my mother must have felt holding on to the secret about my dad. It must have been so difficult and draining for her trying to keep up the pretense. Protecting me. It must have made her very sad.

I moved closer to her along the bench and she kissed me on the forehead.

....

The makeshift camp had been erected virtually overnight on a disused field that I knew quite well. Temporary buildings made of slatted wood sat alongside large, almost circus-size tents and long metal constructions that looked like adapted freight containers. Some of the site had not yet been completed, so a crane was lifting sections of buildings into position and swarms of soldiers were carrying supplies into and out of the camp.

The whole place looked busy.

Was this all because of us?

The corporal who'd driven us threw open the door and barked orders to get out. Mum and I stood up to go.

"Not you!" He stabbed a finger toward Mum. "Sit down. Just him."

"What?"

"You heard."

"No!" Mum reached over and threw her arms around me. "No! I want him to stay with me!" Her face was suddenly soaked with tears.

"Mum!" I pushed myself into her embrace and realized that my face was wet, too.

"No!" The corporal climbed into the van and peeled us apart as easily as the skin from a banana. "You're going somewhere else." He shoved her, hard, back into the van, then pulled me out and slammed the door closed.

"Mum!"

"Get on!" He banged the back of the truck and it revved its engine before slowly moving off.

The man grabbed me by the collar and marched me over to an open-sided tent where an officer wearing glasses was ticking items off lists. He looked over the rim of his glasses as we approached.

"Dare?" he asked the corporal behind us.

"Yessir."

"QWERTY, please."

The corporal yanked my QWERTY off before tossing it onto the table.

"Container B2. Make sure you remove the restraints."
He stared at my pajamas. "And give him some clothes."

"Yessir."

We walked over the churned-up field, past a kitchen where the smell of porridge was thick as a cloud. We stumbled past men laying out long, thick, snaking trails of electrical cable and others with large plastic watercoolers strapped to their backs.

Outside one of the more substantial and solid-looking wooden buildings, I saw a man dressed differently from everyone else. He wore a long, white jacket and the sort of thin hat that you sometimes see doctors wearing. He was smoking a cigarette and, when he finished, he tossed the end of it away before going back inside. Instinctively, I knew that that was where they were going to take Paragon. The man was a scientist. There would be others, too. Was Treble among them? Was he inside that building right now? Was he preparing to cut up Paragon? They would open him up and look inside and plug him into machines. They would check to see if he was operating correctly. They would replace the parts that were wearing out.

They would wipe his memory.

Soon Paragon wouldn't even recognize or remember me. All the things we'd done together would be gone forever—erased in the blink of an LED eye.

We arrived at one of the adapted freight containers—a heavy corrugated metal box with a barred window cut into it. The corporal tapped on the number pad, which gave out several different-pitched bleeps, and the door swung open.

Glancing back over my shoulder, I could see another small truck. Out came Vivi, looking as scared and as dazed as I had been. She, too, was marched toward the officer with the glasses in the open tent.

"Vivi!" I called. She looked over.

"Shut up," the corporal said, and pushed me into the cell, the door banging shut behind me.

....

The only light in the cell came through the window—no electric light had been strung into position—so the whole place was dim and dusky. Of course, that wasn't a problem for me. With my condition, I could still see everything as clear as a glass of water.

In the corner was a bed, and on top of the bed were some itchy-feeling sheets and blankets and a pillow that looked as though half the stuffing had fallen out. A wobbly table was pushed against the wall, and a hard wooden chair was rammed under it. The bucket that was tucked into another corner was something I didn't want to think too much about—the smell that came from it wasn't very pleasant.

I moved the table to the window and climbed up. From that position I could just about see what was going on in the camp. Trucks came and went and, by my estimates, there must have been somewhere between a hundred and two hundred WAB soldiers in the compound.

Not long after I was put in there, another soldier came

with a bowl of porridge and some clothes for me to change into. The porridge tasted awful and the clothes were dull and stale and at least one size too big for me.

It was just before lunchtime that I was taken away for interrogation.

In one of the wooden buildings, General Heracles Woolf was sitting behind a desk, some sheets of paper spread out across it. I was made to sit in a chair facing him. There was nothing and nobody else in the room.

"Auden." He didn't even look up from the papers. "I understand you have difficulty seeing color."

"No. I don't have *difficulty* seeing color," I responded in a sour tone. "I can't see color *at all*."

"Mmm." It was as if he didn't pick up on the bitterness in my voice. Either that or he just batted it away like it was nothing but a fly. "So you see everything in black-and-white. That's interesting. A little like the way your uncle always saw things in black-and-white."

He stood up and strolled slowly around to the front of his desk.

"What do you mean?"

"Auden . . . some people have a very simplified view of the world. There's left and there's right. There's right and there's wrong. There's black and there's white." He leaned back onto the desk. "The problem is that life is much more complicated than that. It's not so clear-cut. In between black and white there are a million different colors."

I frowned.

"Your uncle couldn't see the true worth in what he was doing for us. He thought there were good guys and there were bad guys and, like I said, life isn't always as simple as that. He got scared. He began to question which side he was on."

"And what was he doing for you, exactly? Designing a machine that could kill hundreds of people?"

Woolf gave a sickly smile under his gray mustache. "We are living in difficult times. Our coastlines are constantly under threat from our enemies. The desalting units are precious to this country. Without them we are as dry and as dead as many other previously great nations. And I don't know if you've noticed but most of our fighting-age population are abroad right now helping countries less fortunate than ourselves." His fingers came up and stroked his mustache. "We cannot leave the protection of the desalting units to old men. We need something better than that. That was the purpose of Project Rainbow."

Project Rainbow? Project Rainbow. I didn't understand. So Project Rainbow wasn't about helping me to see color, after all? It wasn't anything to do with a rainbow machine? It was about having robot soldiers protecting the desalting units? I tried to straighten out the ideas running through my mind.

Woolf continued. "The machine called Paragon that Jonah Bloom created was originally designed to protect the coastline. That was the brief that the WAB gave your uncle. The problem was that your uncle—only seeing things in black-and-white, like you do—didn't exactly take to the idea of a mindless machine that would do whatever it was told. He wanted to create something that could actually make decisions. Decide for itself. He filled it full of useless information and gave it the ability to think." He snorted. "I mean, what is the point of an android—whose primary functions are to defend and to kill—what is the point of it being able to tell you the Latin name of a shrub or some such thing? Pointless."

Aaron's Rod. *Verbascum thapsus*. I don't know why I thought of it, but at that moment it flashed through my head.

"So . . . soon after we'd asked for Bloom to revise his approach, he quickly destroyed his blueprints and hid the Paragon machine from us."

Then another of those funny sort of clicks happened in my mind. The letter from the WAB. The initials at the bottom. An *H* followed by a *M* or a *W*. No, definitely a *W*. Without a doubt a *W*.

Heracles Woolf.

"And that was when you killed him."

Woolf glared at me through half-shut eyes.

"Dr. Bloom had a congenital heart condition that not even he knew about. It was just unfortunate that it decided to make itself apparent at that particular time."

"You killed him!"

Woolf said nothing.

Instead, he got up from the desk and walked to the window.

"We tried to find the machine. He'd hidden it and we tried to find it."

"Ha!" I laughed. "You didn't try very hard, did you? He was buried under the garden all along."

"According to our experts, Bloom had placed a signal-smothering device of his own design within the code boxes down there. Ingenious. It meant that our sadly outdated equipment could never pick up on the fact that there was an entire room beneath the lawn." He watched as someone walked past the window. "Nevertheless, heads will roll for that. Heads will roll. And one of them won't be mine, I can tell you." Woolf gave a small sigh. "It's a pity, really. Bloom was highly talented. If only he'd understood his position in the whole setup, he would have proved exceedingly useful to us. Such a shame."

"Well, at least you've got Milo Treble on your side," I barked. "I bet he likes to follow your orders and do as he's told."

Woolf looked confused. "Treble? It's true that he's next on our list for questioning but . . . to be honest, Treble has always been obstructive and difficult when it comes to doing any sort of work for the government. More so than Bloom, even." His eyes honed in on mine. "What makes you think that Treble is 'on our side,' as you put it?"

It was my turn to be confused. "But . . . didn't he inform you? About Paragon? After yesterday?"

Woolf gave one of his acid little laughs. "Inform? Treble would refuse to even tell us his own shoe size. No, we managed to find the machine because the tracker started to work again."

The tracker?

"Bloom obviously disabled it and that left us blind. But yesterday, when it began again, we followed the signal from Treble's office all the way back to your horrible little cottage."

The light on Paragon's chest! Stupidly, we had fixed the one bit of Paragon that we really shouldn't have fixed. By getting it to work again, we'd attracted the attention of the people that Uncle Jonah was trying to avoid in the first place!

I felt sick again.

"Now, enough of this." He walked back behind the desk and sat down. "There are some questions that I need to ask you."

He then went on to ask me lots and lots of questions to do with finding Paragon and all the things he'd done since we discovered him. Why didn't we tell our mothers about him? Why didn't we tell *anyone* about him? How did I know how to start him up? What sort of information had he divulged to us? Had he revealed the guns on his arms to us? Had he used those guns for any reason? Had anyone else ever seen him?

I answered most of them as truthfully as I dared, only holding back and leaving out details on a few of the questions. There was very little point in lying now. It had all fallen in on us and the WAB seemed to know most things anyway.

After what felt like hours, I asked a question back.

"What are you going to do with Paragon now?"

Woolf finished scribbling the answer to his previous question on one of the sheets of paper.

"Why?"

"I'm interested."

Woolf put the pen down and looked up.

"Because your uncle destroyed the blueprints for the Paragon machine, we've no idea how it was constructed. So . . ." He sat back in the chair and crossed his arms. "In order to be able to build others, we need to rip it all apart."

"You mean kill him?"

He sighed. "Like I said, we need to rip it all apart."

CHAPTER 20
THE BRILLIANT VIVI ROOKMINI

As the afternoon wore on, I found myself lying on my bed staring over at the barred window. From that angle I could watch the clouds in the sky and it reminded me of the skyspace that had been built into Vivi's bedroom ceiling.

It seemed like a thousand years since I first followed the clouds "scudding" (that was the word she used) across the sky. Hopeless, wispy clouds that carried so very little rain.

Vivi.

I hoped that she was okay. That she wasn't too scared. None of this was her fault. It was only because she knew Uncle Jonah that she had found herself caught up in all this mess. It had nothing to do with her. Not really. But she was being punished for it all the same.

I thought about Mum, too, taken away to a cell of her own, worrying herself half to death about me.

And I thought about my dad. Was this how he felt every day? Stuck in a room with nothing to do except stare at the sky and think about other people doing the same? Was this the way he was living his life right now?

At about six o'clock, a soldier brought me my supper—a plateful of warmed-up frozen vegetables with a splodge of reconstituted potato and barely a sliver of roast beef. I gobbled it up hungrily and went back to my bed.

At around seven, a loud bell rang in the camp and suddenly there was a huge collective muttering and a clatter of boots outside. After a couple of minutes, the camp was the quietest it had been all day.

I climbed onto the table and peered out through the bars. Far off, in the distance, everybody was lining up for dinner alongside one of the big tents. I stayed there and watched the queue of hungry soldiers shift slowly along.

"Auden!"

There was a whisper just below the window.

"Auden! You there?"

"Vivi?" I stood on tiptoe and looked down. Vivi was standing flat against the freight container, her head looking upward to see if she could see me. "What are you doing here?"

Vivi smiled. "I've come to break you out."

"I don't understand. How have you got out of your cell?"

"I'll explain later. But first I have to find a list of all

the codes." She looked around the camp. "I think I saw the soldier who brought in my supper carrying a board with codes on it into that building there." She pointed at one of the makeshift wooden structures nearby. "Give me a minute."

She crept quietly away and I watched as she softly pushed open a door and went in. A couple of minutes later she came back out, a sheet of paper flapping in her hand.

"Got it!" She waved the paper triumphantly. "Go to the door. I'll let you out."

My heart jumped about a thousand feet in the air.

I climbed down from the table and waited by the door. Outside, Vivi punched the code into the keypad and it bleeped accordingly. There was a click and the door unlocked itself. I pushed it open and stepped outside.

"Have I ever told you how brilliant you are, Vivi?"

"Not often enough."

The camp looked almost deserted. Most of the soldiers and officers and scientists were busy feeding their faces in the canteen, and there were only one or two unlucky soldiers patrolling the compound.

"Where's your mum?" I asked. "Did they bring her here? They took mine away somewhere else."

"Mine, too," Vivi replied, her head darting left and right. "I don't know where. We can't worry about them now. Come on."

I followed her. Moving around in between the buildings reminded me of something. It quickly dawned on me that it was like playing hide-and-seek at the Sunny Vale Caravan Park—admittedly on a larger and rather more frightening scale. Instead of residents and Fabius Boyle, the game was to avoid armed infantrymen.

"What about Paragon?" I asked. "We need to save him."

She looked around. "Have they brought him here?"

"There's a large wooden building. Possibly the biggest building. I saw it when I came in. I think that might be where they were going to take him."

We slipped down past a couple of tents toward the wooden structure. And froze. It just so happened that this particular place had a guard on duty right outside. We ducked down and hid behind one of the tents.

"What are we going to do?" Vivi asked. "We can't get past him."

I didn't answer. There had to be a way.

Quietly, I tiptoed around the other side of the tent and peered carefully around the corner. One of the large water-coolers had been placed against the side of the tent and was in the direct view of the soldier on the door. I went back and told Vivi.

"So? How does that help us?"

I thought a little more.

"Well, we could use it as a distraction."

"How can we use a watercooler as a distraction?"

I held the flap of the tent open and waved her inside. We could see the outline of the watercooler against the canvas.

"Let's knock it over," I said.

"What?"

"We need to do it with one big push or else the guard'll see us and we'll get caught. If we can do it in one go, he won't notice us and he'll just think it's some sort of accident."

She had a look on her face that showed she thought I was mad.

"Then what?"

"Then . . . we'll see."

She shook her head. "Not the greatest plan I've ever heard. In fact, hardly a plan at all. But . . . time's running out and we need to do something. You're sure he's in there?"

I nodded. "Why keep a guard on the door?"

"True."

We positioned ourselves near to where the watercooler stood. Neither of us knew exactly how heavy a watercooler was, so the amount of strength required was going to have to be a bit of a guess.

"Just give it everything you've got," I whispered. "On the count of three. One. Two. Three!"

We both ran hard into the side of the tent, knocking the watercooler—which wasn't as heavy as either of us had imagined—out of its mooring and onto the earth beyond. It hit the ground with a thud and a slosh.

Vivi and I quickly slipped out of the tent and, peering round the corner again, watched the guard at the door.

He was staring at the cooler, his face shaped like a big question mark. Then he looked around and saw that there were no other guards nearby to put the cooler back into its position. You could almost see the debate he was having in his mind being played out over his features. Should he leave his post and put it back? Or should he stay where he was and watch as precious water leaked slowly out of a couple of cracks and seeped wastefully into the ground?

The soldier licked his lips.

Then left his post.

He disappeared from our view, and as we heard him lower his gun to the ground to get hold of the cooler, we made our break. Running on the softest and most soundless parts of our feet, we covered the twenty meters in seconds— Vivi in front, me just behind.

At the door, Vivi twisted the handle without making a noise and pulled the door open just enough for us both to slip in. With the tiniest of clicks, the door locked itself closed behind us.

....

The room was filled with equipment and, if I'd paid it much attention, I would have thought that it resembled Milo Treble's laboratory. But I didn't pay it much attention. Because strapped onto a table in the center of the room was the only thing that I wanted to focus on.

Paragon.

Wires were attached to his arms and legs and wound their way into monitors and computers. The screens flickered and danced and bleeped and buzzed even though he was lying perfectly still. He was in standby mode and the only part of him that looked alive was the flashing tracker light that fluttered like a heartbeat.

But he was intact.

They hadn't started ripping him apart quite yet.

"What are they doing to him?" Vivi looked at all the wires.

"This is nothing," I warned. "Give them a day or two and there wouldn't be anything of him left. He'd be gone forever."

We both stood there for a minute or two, imagining this machine so full of soul, so full of life, being decimated.

"We need to get him away from here," I said, leaning over and flicking the on switch. "Quickly."

Paragon whizzed and whirred back to life, his limbs lifting themselves slightly from the table; his head twisted left, then right.

"Where . . . where am I?"

"Paragon?" A wave of panic washed over me. Had they already cleared his memory? Would he look at me like he'd never seen me before?

"Hey, Audendare! Vivirookmini! What's going on?" He seemed fine. Then a moment of recognition. "Oh. That's right. Now I remember." His head tilted at a sort of concerned angle. "Are you both okay?"

"You need to keep the noise down," I hissed. I could hear the guard taking up his position right outside the door again.

"Oh. Okay." Paragon turned his head to face me. "Auden. There's something I need to tell you. Something important."

"Not now," I replied. "First we need to get you out of here."

"What are we going to do about these?" Vivi was holding up one of the wires that fed into Paragon's legs.

"Don't worry too much about those." Paragon sat up and ripped all of the wires out of himself, tossing them aside. "They aren't important."

Paragon stood up and made a movement that looked as if he was stretching after a heavy night's sleep.

"That's better. What's the plan?"

We were trapped in a building with one door, directly outside of which stood an armed guard.

"Er . . . I dunno," I said. "I was rather hoping you might come up with something."

Paragon looked around the room. "O . . . kay." He was staring at a large pane of glass at the rear of the room that looked out onto another temporary wooden structure. "If we can't use the door, we'll have to make another one."

Paragon went toward the window and pushed a table of equipment aside to get to it. He tapped the glass with his knuckles.

"Not especially thick . . . so . . ."

Suddenly his thumb on his right hand bent all the way back, exposing something small, sharp, and shiny.

Then out of the palm on his left hand sprang a rubbery

pad. He pushed the pad onto the window and then started scraping the glass with the sharp implement.

"High-grade industrial diamond." Paragon looked at us over his shoulder. "Will cut through glass like a chainsaw through a bucket of jelly."

I laughed at the imagery.

Vivi and I watched as Paragon scraped a deep groove upward, then across, then down, and then back to where he started. Once the ends were joined, he slotted his thumb back into position.

"Now, just a little push . . ."

He pushed with his left hand and . . .

Clink.

. . . the large rectangular piece of glass came easily out of the window.

Paragon carefully pulled the glass through the hole he had made and leaned it up against the wall.

"There! That's how we get out. Now, let's go."

He bent over to pick up Vivi.

"Wait!" I cried.

"What is it?"

"That!" I pointed at the flashing light on Paragon's chest.

"What about it?"

"It's a tracking device. It's how they found you in the first place."

Paragon looked down at the light. "A tracking device?" He sounded sad. "Is that what it is? But I thought—"

"Yes," I said almost as sadly. "I know. It's what we all thought when it started beating."

We stood there silently for a few seconds watching the light on Paragon's chest pulse.

"I thought it was a heart." Paragon touched the light with the gentlest tips of his fingers. "Or at least . . . sort of a heart. A representation of a heart."

Vivi stepped forward and touched him on his arm. "No. I'm afraid it's not. It was just a way of keeping track of you. I'm sorry."

I looked back over my shoulder and saw the outline of the soldier on duty. Time was running out.

"Look. Can you disable it?" I asked.

Paragon shook his head and sighed. "Nope. It runs on a system that I can't override. Only a human can switch it on or off."

"But you can't escape with it active. They'll find you in minutes."

"Let *me* try." Vivi was holding one of the discarded wires.

"You can't do it!" I said.

"Auden," Vivi said with a huge sigh, "some of us actually pay attention to things. When Dr. Treble managed to get the light working yesterday, I was watching everything he did. It wasn't that complicated. I'm sure I can turn it off again."

"You think?" I realized as I said it that it sounded as though I didn't trust her.

Vivi shook her head. "Honestly, Auden."

"Vivi," Paragon interrupted. "I have perfect faith in you. Absolute one-hundred-percent perfect faith. As does Auden." He took the wire from her and plugged it back onto the tip of his finger. "So . . . let's do it."

Vivi stuck the other end into a computer. All the while we were aware that dinner might soon be over and that the scientists would be back to finish whatever job they had started with Paragon.

We needed to be quick.

Vivi sat on a chair in front of the computer and tapped away. Lots of strange shapes flashed up and scrolled across the screen. Her fingers danced like lightning—I'd never seen anyone type so fast in my life.

Then she paused.

"Right. . . . I think this is the correct thing to do. If not, I might be isolating the tracking device and making it impossible to be turned off. It's one or the other."

"Vivi"—Paragon brought his head down close to Vivi's—"go for it."

Her fingers continued to blur over the keyboard.

"Ready?"

"Yep."

"Okay. . . ."

She hit a button and . . .

The light on Paragon's chest flickered faster for a second or two and then . . .

It stopped.

"It's stopped," I said.

We nearly cheered but just about managed to prevent ourselves, remembering the guard outside.

Paragon grabbed Vivi's shoulders. "Have I ever told you how brilliant you are, Vivi?"

"How did you get out of the cell, anyway?" I asked. "You didn't say."

"By singing."

It was my turn to look confused now.

"The lock," she explained. "It was activated by the keypad tones." I recalled the different-pitched beeps as the soldier punched the code in. "When the guard brought my supper to me, I listened and tried to remember the notes. Then, after he'd gone, I put my head close to the door and sung them back. Took me some time to get them exactly right—I'm not the greatest singer in the world—but I got there in the end." She seemed pretty pleased with herself.

"Genius!" I grinned.

"Absolute brainbox!" Paragon added, and both Vivi and I laughed at his choice of words.

"You know," Vivi whispered, "I really do think we ought to get out of here."

"Yes. You're right." Paragon went back to the large rectangular hole in the rear window. "Come on. I'll lift you both through."

He picked up Vivi and eased her gently through the gap before picking me up and feeding me through. Then he climbed as silently as he could manage out into the early-evening light.

"Follow me." We made our way around a couple of the flapping tents and the wooden buildings, ducking and hiding from the occasional daydreaming guard. We dashed across a thirty- or forty-meter unoccupied space to the broken-down barbed-wire fence, crawling underneath into the field beyond.

Once through, we squatted down to plan our next move.

"So," I said. "We're out. Now what?"

"We can't go home," Vivi replied. "They'll be waiting for us there."

The evening was particularly clear, and already the temperature was beginning to drop. Within an hour or two it would be unbearably cold outdoors. We needed to find somewhere indoors to hide away.

"I know where we can go," Paragon said.

"Where?"

He ignored the question. "The thing is we need to move quite quickly. Any minute now suppertime will be over and people are going to realize we're gone. Then they'll be after us."

"We need to start running, then."

"Ah yes. The problem is neither you nor Vivi can run very fast. If we go at *your* speed, we're going to get caught within minutes."

"But . . ." Vivi was thinking. "If we go at *your* speed . . ."

Suddenly, Paragon scooped us both up, one in each arm, so that we were sitting on his forearms.

"Exactly. Now," he said, standing up, "bear in mind

that this is something I've never done before. Well, to be honest, you've never done it, either. It's a new experience for all of us. Hold on as tight as you possibly can. And don't panic."

"Wait!" I shouted. "You're going to run with us in your arms?"

"Yep. That's the idea."

Vivi's eyes were wide with fear. Like me, she'd seen how fast Paragon could run.

"Oh my . . ."

"Don't worry, Vivi," Paragon reassured her. "I'm not going to let you fall."

"Yes. Don't worry, Vivi." I smiled, hardly able to hold my excitement. "This'll be fun."

....

It *was* fun. After we got over the initial lurch of the stomach as Paragon set off, that is. He didn't seem to slowly build to his top speed like most runners—he just started incredibly fast and stayed incredibly fast. The air whipped over our faces and flicked our hair backward.

Vivi had her eyes shut tight and her arm clung around Paragon's neck. I gripped on to his shoulder, but watched as the landscape flashed by.

We got across the field in a matter of seconds, and, as we neared the hedge, Paragon showed no sign of slowing. If anything, he sped up slightly.

"What are you—" I started to ask but didn't have time

to finish, because just nine or ten feet away from the hedge, Paragon jumped.

Vivi squeaked. So did I.

We sailed through the air and over the hedge.

Thump.

He landed with a jolt the other side and carried on running like nothing had happened. Within seconds, the hedge on the other side of the field approached.

"Oh no!" Vivi cried, and buried her face into Paragon's neck.

"Oh yes!" I screamed as Paragon soared over that one, too, landing as surefootedly.

A couple of hedges later and even Vivi was half giggling as Paragon jumped them with ease.

Paragon turned onto a long lane that we had all used several times, then took a quick left onto a rougher dirt track. One more skip over a hedge and Paragon came to a standstill.

"Here we are."

I looked about and recognized the less salubrious edge of the Sunny Vale Caravan Park. We had only been running for about three minutes, but I estimated that Paragon had covered about six or seven miles in that time. If my math was any good, that meant he'd been racing along close to 130 miles an hour. That was the fastest I'd ever moved in my whole life!

Paragon lowered us both to the ground.

"I do *not* want to do that again!" Vivi said, eventually prying her arms from Paragon's neck. "That was scary."

"No, it wasn't," I said, staring madly into Paragon's eyes. "It was great!"

Paragon gave us both a friendly pat on the head and we walked toward the deserted caravan.

CHAPTER 21
THE TRUTH ABOUT THE TRUTH

It was the same caravan in which I'd left Paragon the night before the Boyle disaster. The mess was still there and Paragon had to help Vivi climb over the dislodged oven. Clearly, no one had bothered to come out and clean the place since our last visit.

Paragon gave the door to the main bedroom a shove and we went in.

Thankfully, the bedroom was in a much better state than the rest of the caravan. There was no bed, admittedly, but the mattress on the floor looked clean and comforting. Stacked to one side of it were a couple of pillows and some woolly-looking blankets. They were covered in dust but a quick shake outside soon fixed that.

"I wonder if they know we're gone yet," Vivi said, pulling the flowery curtains closed.

"Probably." Paragon tried slapping some life into one of the flat pillows.

"What will they do?" I asked.

"Well, first they'll check the camp. They won't believe that two children and a robot could get very far, I'm sure. They will underestimate us. Foolishly. The first fifteen or twenty minutes after discovering our disappearance will consist of checking out all the buildings and vehicles around the camp. After that, they will widen the search to the surrounding areas and the routes toward your homes. By the time they've exhausted that, it'll be dark."

"They'll search for us through the night, though, won't they?" I said. "They won't stop until they find us."

Paragon nodded. "Yes. They'll keep searching. Nighttime makes things difficult, though."

"But if they've got heat-sensing equipment, they may well be able to detect us in here."

"Don't worry about that," Paragon said as he squatted down on the floor next to the mattress and wrapped his arms around his knees. "Dr. Bloom provided me with a piece of software to take care of such things. I can disguise the heat from your bodies. They'll never pick up on it."

"Good."

I took one of the blankets and pulled it around myself, sitting down on the mattress with a pillow between my back and the flimsy wall of the caravan. Vivi did the same.

"What are we going to do?" Vivi mumbled. "We can't go home. We can't go anywhere."

I didn't say anything.

Vivi looked distressed. "They're going to catch us in the end, aren't they? They're going to catch us and take us away from our mothers."

Paragon reached over and gave her shoulder a soft pat. "Shhh, Vivirookmini."

"I don't care what we do," I said. "We can't let them get their hands on Paragon. They can't rip him apart and turn him into a killer. That's not what he is. We have to keep him away from them. Even if it means we have to keep running for the rest of our lives. I'm not letting them take him away from me."

We sat in silence for a while, the light through the curtains dimming by the minute.

"There's something I need to tell you, Auden." Paragon's lights flickered and glowed in the small dusty room. "Something I found out."

"What's that?"

Paragon shifted his position slightly. "When the Water Allocation Board scientists had me strapped to their computers and were busy assessing me, I managed to access the army's military records database." He picked a thread of cotton off his metal kneecap and dropped it onto the floor.

"Yes?"

"Once I'd breached the protective software I . . ." He paused. "I accessed your father's military records."

I caught my breath. Did I want to hear the rest of this?

"As you know, Leo Dare is currently in a military prison for having deserted his post."

Why was Paragon telling me this? I knew all this. Telling me again wasn't going to help the situation. Wasn't going to pull my father back from the shame and embarrassment of his predicament. Reminding me of what happened wasn't going to turn back the clock.

Nothing was going to be able to make this better.

Paragon continued. "But do you know *why* he deserted his post?"

I shook my head. Of course I didn't. Why would I? Why would I want to think about it any more than I had to?

"The reason he deserted his post was because, if he hadn't, three children would have died."

"What?"

Paragon's eyes glowed brighter than I had ever seen them glow before.

"I don't understand. What three children?"

"Sit back," Paragon ordered, "and I'll tell you the whole story."

....

"Your father's battalion was making its way through a small town just outside of Liberec in the Czech Republic when they came under enemy fire. The trucks they were traveling in were hit hard by antitank missiles fired from sniper zones. They tried to escape, but as the trucks zoomed out onto a side street, one of them clipped a car that was passing. The car flipped over onto its roof and burst into flames.

"The captain of the battalion ordered his men to continue their retreat. So truck after truck passed the burning car without stopping.

"But the driver of the last vehicle *didn't* pass by. Against orders he pulled over, took one of the army-issue fire extinguishers, and quickly got the fire under control.

"Inside the car were a thirty-two-year-old mother and her three young children—aged four, seven, and ten. The mother was dead. But the children were still alive. Despite still being shot at, the driver managed to drag each of the children away from the car and to a place of safety nearby. They were then taken to a military hospital.

"However, despite having saved three lives, the army immediately court-martialed the soldier for deserting his post. It was claimed that some of the army deaths could have been avoided had he continued driving past the burning car.

"The thing is," Paragon suddenly began whispering, "while I was strapped to the computers back there, I examined all of the footage that was captured on that day. And what the army court said is nonsense. All the evidence suggests that the deaths of the soldiers—four of them— happened *before* the trucks had even hit the car.

"You see, the only conclusion I can come to is that the army wants soldiers who do as they are told. Not soldiers who can think for themselves. As far as they're concerned a soldier who can step out of role even for a second is a dangerous thing. It's something they find difficult to handle. They can't control them. And so, for that, they have to be punished."

I found my fingers clutching the blanket far too tightly. "That driver," I said, eventually loosening my grip. "That was my dad, wasn't it?"

Paragon nodded.

"So you see, Auden, your father is hardly a criminal. In fact, he is even more of a hero than you thought."

I felt tears beginning to build in my eyes. "But I . . . I thought he was a coward. They said he was . . . a . . . coward." The tears began to roll. I felt like a traitor. "And I believed them."

Paragon shuffled in between Vivi and me and put his arms around us. "I don't think you did believe them, really. I think that deep down—somewhere inside your spirit or soul or whatever you might want to call it—deep down, you knew the truth. You knew that the person you called 'Dad' was certainly not a coward."

He stroked my cheek and wiped the tears away.

"There are things we just know. Instinct, I suppose some people call it. Now, instinct may or may not be a real thing. Perhaps it is just the accumulation of data and a refinement of our judgment. But there are just some things that you seem to automatically know."

Paragon gave a sort of awkward cough. "I realize I am a robot and that my experience of these things is pretty small, but I'll try to use an analogy that even I feel comfortable with.

"Consider the order of things. We always say 'Left. Right.' The 'Left' comes before the 'Right.' Does anyone ever say 'Right. Left.'? I doubt it. Or on a form, you will see the options 'Yes/No.' It is never 'No/Yes.' Similarly, 'Up/Down' and 'On/Off.' We have come to understand the order of things and it almost feels like instinct. So if you were to see 'No/Yes' written somewhere, you would think it strange.

"That's what happened when that terrible Boyle child told you your father was in prison. It struck you as wrong. Everything you had come to know about your father suggested he wouldn't leave his post. He wouldn't run away. It was against all you knew. And that's why you struggled with it so much. Because you knew it couldn't be right.

"So, yes. Deep down I think you realized it couldn't be true. You knew your father wasn't a coward.

"After all, who could know a father better than his own son?"

We fell silent.

Dig deep, Auden. Dig deep.

Outside we could hear the distant *woompf, woompf, woompf*

of a helicopter's blades. It got louder and louder until it sounded almost overhead, and a strong beam of light flashed left, then right, over the top of the caravan. Paragon pulled us both closer and within a few seconds the sound slowly faded away and the light disappeared.

We didn't move or say anything for a while.

"Was that them?" Vivi whispered.

Paragon nodded. "Don't worry. They won't find us. I guarantee it."

A little later, after Vivi had managed to drift off to sleep, I propped myself up on my elbows and looked at Paragon, who was still sitting, watching over us.

"The problem is that *I* know my father's not a coward, and *you* know it. But the army doesn't care. He's going to be in prison forever. They're never going to let him out."

"Ah . . ." Paragon began and I could sense that he was about to say something designed to make me feel better. "Well. After I checked out your father's military record and the footage of the incident, I made a copy of it all."

"You stole it?"

"That's . . . one way of putting it. I made a copy and sent it to the International Court of Human Rights."

"What?" I sat up.

"I also posted it to a number of charitable bodies. And, to be on the safe side, I sent it to a few news organizations— some of the bigger ones." If he could have smiled at me, then I'm sure that at that point, he would have done so. "So, all the information is out there, and one of those things at least will make an issue or a story out of your father. I am sure."

I reached over, took his hand, and squeezed it.

"Thank you."

Paragon squeezed back, and we sat that way until my eyelids began to droop and the comforting fog of sleep eased over me.

CHAPTER 22
EVERYTHING

When I woke up the next morning, Paragon was gone. I shook Vivi, who was still fast asleep, and she opened her bleary eyes and rubbed her hand across her face and looked around the room.

"Where is he?" She barely formed the words on her tired lips.

"I don't know," I replied anxiously. "What if he's gone back on his own? To save us! He might think that by—"

Suddenly the door to the bedroom sprang open and Paragon came in carrying something.

"Here!" He tossed a couple of cereal bars and two slightly bruised apples at each of us. "Breakfast."

I sighed, relieved. "Where did you get these from?" I asked, ripping open the packaging with my teeth.

"Don't ask," he said, and set two bottles of mineral water on the floor in front of us. "Let's just say that some of the holidaymakers staying here might find themselves having to eat out this morning."

We tucked in, Paragon watching us and scooping up any mess we left and putting it into a neat pile in the corner of the room.

After we had eaten, I pulled the curtain back a little and looked up at the sky. The clouds were the thin and wispy type. High up and barely there, like a thin streak across the sky. I thought hard, back to the time Vivi had told me the names of the clouds. It seemed like a hundred years ago now. So much had happened since. *What was it?* I thought.

Then I remembered.

"Cirrus," I said.

"What?" Paragon asked, quickly standing up. "What did you say?"

"Cirrus," I repeated.

Suddenly Paragon started his stiffening and straightening, his arms locked at his side. His eyes fixed directly ahead.

"It's happening again!" Vivi shouted.

Within a second or two, Paragon's body began to relax. It was then that the idea struck me.

"Cumulus!" I called, and Paragon's body jerked back into position again.

"Stratus!" Vivi joined in, and Paragon seemed to shudder where he stood.

A moment or so later, Paragon collapsed in a heap on the floor.

"Paragon. Paragon." I came alongside him and pulled at his arms. "Get up, Paragon."

Vivi went to the other side and we started to lift him up. He was so heavy that neither of us could move him at all.

Suddenly the lights on his eyes flickered and his head twisted one way and then the other.

"I . . ." he began to speak. "I know *everything* now."

....

We were all too aware that we might be spotted. Crossing the fields that led away from Sunny Vale, all it would have taken would have been a passing WAB unit or a high-flying Scoot drone and we'd have been done for. Seized and locked away.

But there was nothing.

Perhaps they were too busy still searching the areas just outside of the camp to come this far out. Perhaps they were waiting for some backup before starting the search in earnest. Perhaps we'd just got lucky.

"Where are we going?" I asked.

"There." Paragon pointed to a telegraph pole slap-bang in the middle of the next field.

"Why?"

"I need to make a phone call."

Vivi and I looked at each other again. It was barely eight

o'clock in the morning and already it was turning into a strange day.

When we finally arrived at the base of the pole, Paragon told us to wait there and then began climbing to the top of it.

"What *is* he up to?" I asked as I watched Paragon reach out and grab hold of one of the wires.

"There's no point asking me," said Vivi. "I know about as little as you do."

At the top of the telegraph pole, Paragon sounded as if he was talking to himself. A couple of minutes later he jumped down from the pole, landing with a thump just a few feet from us.

"Who was that you were talking to?"

"Dr. Treble."

"Why were you talking to him?" I was confused.

"There's something he needs to see."

"What?"

Paragon tilted his head. "You'll see yourself soon enough. Now, we've got a busy morning ahead of us. Vivi?"

"Yes?"

"I told Dr. Treble that you would meet him near the Wandlebury Ring."

"Eh?" Vivi looked nervous.

"It's okay. I'll take you there myself." Paragon bent over and picked up Vivi.

"Oh no. Not this again," she muttered to herself.

"Hold on." I took a step forward. "What about me?"

Paragon turned to face me. "I'll be back for you in a minute. Well, seven minutes and fortyish seconds as an estimate." He positioned Vivi on his arm and she gripped on tight. "Then you and I are going back home."

With that they were off, Vivi's shriek disappearing into the distance along with them.

CHAPTER 23
RETURN TO UNICORN COTTAGE

Seven minutes and fortyish seconds later, Paragon pulled up like a sports car beside me.

"What do you mean, 'We're going back home'?" I frowned at him.

He looked a bit puzzled. "I mean, we're going home."

"What? To Unicorn Cottage?"

"Yep."

"Are you mad? There'll be millions of Water Allocation Board soldiers there. They'll be pulling the house to pieces. They'll capture us."

"Millions is a bit of an overestimate, don't you think? At the most there will be about forty of them."

"Forty?!" I cried. "How are we meant to get into the

house if there are about forty soldiers—*armed* soldiers—waiting for us there? Anyway, *why* are we going back?"

"Because there is something there that we need to get."

"What?"

"Something your uncle built. Perhaps you've seen it. It's about this high"—he held the palm of his hand flat about three feet off the ground—"this long"—about four feet—"and this wide"—two feet. "It's on wheels and has a sort of cover over it."

I thought. "Wait. You mean the rainbow machine?"

"The rainbow machine?" He gave a small laugh. "Yes. I suppose you're right. Do you know where your uncle kept it?"

"It was in the shed. Above you. But we took it out from there. Just before we discovered you."

"Where is it now?"

"I pushed it against the fence. Under an overhanging tree." I thought of the previous day, when one of the soldiers started to inspect it but quickly got bored and shoved it back. "I think it's still there."

"Good."

"But why are we going back to get the rainbow machine?"

"You'll see," he said, picking me up and preparing to run off again.

....

While Paragon was running, I could see military trucks in the distance, scouring the roads and lanes for any sign of us. At one point, Paragon had to quickly change course when we saw a troop of soldiers spread out across a succulent field, slowly picking their way over it, hoping to stumble over some clue as to what direction we had originally gone.

Not long after, we came out onto the field behind Unicorn Cottage. The pyramid-shaped irrigation towers were spraying their five-minute daily allocation of water over the crops, and as we rushed past them we got beautifully and hilariously soaked. Diving into the small crop of trees that backed up to the garden, we fell onto the earth and laughed.

"I hope I don't start rusting," Paragon joked.

After we had recovered ourselves, we peered through a gap in the fence. I couldn't see anything, and then I realized why. The rainbow machine was in the way.

It was literally inches away from us. The problem was that it might as well have been a million miles away. I could hear a pair of soldiers talking at the other end of the garden. Getting it out was going to be impossible.

"How are we going to get to it?" I whispered.

"Ah-ha!" Paragon held up his hand, and a fingertip flipped back to reveal the tip of a screwdriver.

"Is there anything you haven't got hidden away in your fingers?" I asked.

"Lots of things," he said as he inserted the head into one of the screws in the fence. "But I won't start listing them now."

The screwdriver tool was almost silent. It turned

counterclockwise and twisted the screw out with absolute ease. After it finally came free, Paragon removed another one and another. It reminded me of the time I unscrewed all the floorboards in the shed not ten feet away from where we were now squatting. When the last of the screws in the one piece of fencing was removed, I took hold of the wood and laid it gently on the ground nearby.

Board after board came away until we had a space big enough through which to pass the rainbow machine. The problem was going to be the beams of wood that ran horizontally along the top and bottom of the fence. We were going to have to somehow lift the rainbow machine through them.

"Don't worry." Paragon leaned forward and grabbed both sides of the machine. "I can get it myself." He pulled and, with enormous strength, gently brought the thing through the fence and into the field beside us.

Suddenly, the overhanging branches of the tree parted and a soldier's face appeared, staring right at us. He opened his mouth to shout something but Paragon hurriedly clasped his hand over the mouth, climbed through what was left of the fence, and disappeared.

Twenty seconds later he returned.

"What have you done with him?" I asked.

"Locked him in my little room under the shed. It's quite cozy, you know. Someone will find him eventually." He grabbed hold of the handle at one end of the machine and turned it around. "Come on. We'd better go before any more of them spot us."

············

It was much slower going. Paragon could push the rainbow machine faster than I ever could, but compared to the racing speeds of earlier, it felt sluggish. The problem was that the wheels on the machine were not designed to go over rough ground.

"It's no use," Paragon finally admitted. "We're going to have to use the roads."

"But they'll see us," I protested.

"If we stick to crossing fields, they're going to see us anyway. At least on the roads we might have a chance."

Paragon wheeled the machine down through a gate and onto a small lane.

"Now, jump on," he ordered.

"What? On you?"

"Nope. On that." He nodded toward the rainbow machine.

I climbed onto the top of the machine and gripped tightly onto the tarpaulin.

"Here goes."

Paragon started racing again—still slower than normal, but at least we felt like we were making progress. He steered the thing around bends and over bumps like a Formula One driver and I held on for all I was worth.

But then I heard the roar of an engine.

Behind was a large truck. And it was gaining on us.

Paragon sped up but the truck still got closer. I looked back and could see the eyes of the driver glaring down on us.

Suddenly there was a loud bang and a spark flew off the back of Paragon.

They were shooting!

Paragon moved even quicker, the wheels of the rainbow machine spinning uncontrollably beneath me.

Then, without warning, Paragon practically spun on the spot and veered off onto a smaller dirt track to the left. It wound its way up a small hill, and I recognized it as the hill Vivi and I climbed with Paragon the day after we discovered him. The hill where the word *achromatopsia* opened up a load of information within his memory bank.

"Hold on tight!" Paragon shouted at me.

I looked behind and saw that the truck was too big to make its way along the dirt track. Soldiers were jumping out of the back and running toward us, their rifles at the ready.

"I said hold on!" Paragon half yelled, so I dug my nails even harder into the tarpaulin. A second later I realized why.

Paragon twisted off the track and headed toward the stile over which we had all climbed weeks before. Only, this time we weren't going to climb over it. Oh, no. This time, Paragon was going to smash right through it.

"Hold on!"

I shut my eyes.

The rainbow machine hit the rotting wooden structure

with such speed that it splintered apart. Unfortunately, I hadn't been gripping tightly enough, because as it hit, I bounced off the top of the rainbow machine and bumped onto the grass before rolling a fair distance down the incline.

"Auden!" I heard Paragon's voice somewhere above me.

Bang! Bang!

Gunshots. Followed by the *ping, ping* of bullets hitting metal.

As I sat up, two arms grabbed me and lifted me clear off the ground.

"Come on, let's go."

It was Paragon. He carried me with his back to the firing soldiers and plonked me roughly on top of the rainbow machine.

"Stay where you are!" a voice screamed. "Do not move."

Paragon ignored the voice and began to push the machine along once again.

"I said stay where you are! Or we'll shoot the boy!"

Paragon stopped and lowered the trolley. Then he turned around.

"Paragon? What are you doing?" I asked.

Paragon raised both of his arms. The panels on the forearms slid apart and the barrels of the guns came into view. He pointed them toward the soldier who had just spoken.

"Paragon! No! Don't! Don't do it! That's not who you are! Please. Don't shoot them."

The soldier, realizing that no bullet seemed to harm Paragon, backed away slightly, lowering his gun.

Paragon took a step toward him.

"No! Don't!" I screamed. "Don't hurt them!"

He stood still, his guns still trained on the man.

"Please."

Nobody moved or said anything. The only sounds came from the wind and the squeal of traffic miles away.

"Go back," Paragon said to the men after a while. "Take your guns and let us be. We have important work to attend to."

The gun barrels on his arms retreated back inside and Paragon turned and continued to push the rainbow machine slowly along the path that wound its way around the bottom of the hill.

There were no more gunshots.

WHITE

THE POWER SOURCE

"This whole area is swarming with Water Allocation Board soldiers," Treble said as we approached him and Vivi. "I've never seen so many of them in my life. They must really want to get hold of you, Paragon."

"Oh, they do, Dr. Treble. They do."

Treble stepped forward. "They came for me last night. Luckily I managed to escape out the back door without any of them spotting me. I don't think they're the brightest of organizations, you know."

Paragon laughed. He was still pushing the rainbow machine as I walked alongside. After racing around so much over the last two days, it was a huge relief to just walk.

"Have you had an accident?" Vivi asked, staring at the massive rip in one of my trouser legs. It must have happened when I rolled off the top of the machine, only everything was so intense and scary at that point that I didn't notice it. Now that Vivi had pointed it out to me, I wondered how I could miss such a thing.

"Yes" was all I said.

"I hope you haven't been waiting too long." Paragon started to push the rainbow machine along the path that led to the top of Wandlebury.

"Not at all." Treble sounded surprisingly jolly considering there were men with guns trying to hunt us out at that very moment. "Vivi and I have been having a rather interesting discussion about planetary formation, haven't we?"

"Yes, we have."

It was weird. They both sounded so similar.

"It seems we have the same ideas about the Big Bang."

We made our way up toward where the trees started, Paragon pushing the rainbow machine, the rest of us close behind.

"Tell me, Paragon." Treble looked quite excitable. "Is it true? Do you think it will work?"

"Yes," Paragon answered without hesitation. "It will work."

"How do you know?"

"Because Dr. Bloom programmed me to know."

"Oh." Treble stopped for a second, unsure how to take in that information.

Why were they all so keen on the rainbow machine all

of a sudden? What was so impressive? What was so important about it that we were all risking our lives?

We entered the wood that ran along the brow of the hill.

"I wish Bloom had told me all about this. I wish he'd told *anybody* about this," Treble muttered. "Why didn't he just tell people what he'd done?"

Paragon didn't even turn around to look at Treble. "Because he didn't get the chance to, I suppose. He left the instruction buried within me because he knew he was at risk. I think he wanted to run it through more tests—to be certain—before going public with it."

I suddenly found myself wishing Milo Treble wasn't there. He was chattering on and taking away from the fact that this whole adventure should only have been about Paragon, Vivi, and me. No one else. Why was he involving himself now? Or, to be more accurate, why was Paragon involving *him*?

As if in answer to my question, Paragon spoke. "I think it's right that you are here to see this, Dr. Treble. We need a recognized member of the scientific community to bear witness to what will happen here today." Treble seemed to swagger. "Someone with the the respect of the wider scientific world. Someone they can trust."

"Well . . . er . . . I . . . I guess . . ." Treble could hardly disguise his slightly swollen-headed pride.

Paragon looked back at me.

That made me feel better.

"Wait!" It was Vivi's voice. She was staring back down the hill, her arm outstretched, pointing.

Water Allocation Board trucks. Dozens of them. On the roads below.

"They've found us!"

Paragon lowered the rainbow machine and stared down the hill. He then turned and stared up the hill to where we were headed.

"Too soon. They're here too soon." He sounded disappointed. "By my rough calculations, a few minutes later and we would have had enough time to get it done."

"Get what done?" I asked, but nobody answered me.

"You need a distraction," Vivi said. "Something to buy you more time."

"But what?"

Vivi took a few steps away from us.

"I'll run out into the open and go down the opposite side of the hill. I'll make sure they spot me. I'll lead them on a goose chase."

"Vivi—" Paragon began to protest.

"No. It's best."

Treble interrupted. "Paragon, it is *vital* that you do what needs to be done." He walked toward Vivi and turned back to Paragon. "I'll go with her. Tell me, you know *exactly* what to do?"

"Yes, but I need someone to stay with me." Paragon turned to me. "Auden, will you help me do it?"

"I don't know what it is that—"

"Will you help me?" he asked again. "I can't do it on my own."

"Yes." I came alongside him and rested my hand on his arm. "Of course I will. I'll do anything to help you. You know that."

Treble pulled his coat tighter around his shoulders. "Good. Then Vivi and I will distract them. Get yourselves into position and start the thing up." They twisted away and started to run off.

"Vivi!" Paragon shouted after her.

Vivi stopped and looked back.

"Thank you." Paragon waved. "You are without the smallest shadow of a doubt the bravest and cleverest girl who ever lived."

Vivi smiled before rushing off with Treble out beyond the trees.

Paragon pushed the rainbow machine up along the gravelly path that twisted its way toward the top.

All of a sudden, my stomach dropped. Something flashed into my mind, something that should have flashed into it earlier.

"There's no battery for it!" I cried. "We looked—Vivi and me—but we couldn't find the battery that fits it. Without it, the machine won't work."

Paragon didn't even pause. "Don't worry. *I've* got it."

An eruption of shouting came from the bottom of the hill. I peered through the trees. Soldiers who had leaped from the trucks had spotted Vivi and Treble running around the side of the hill. One of them squatted and took aim with his gun.

"Vivi!" I gasped.

"No shooting! Your orders are to take the children alive," barked another distant voice. I shifted my position and could see General Woolf climbing out of a military car. "Give chase. And find that robot."

"Come on, Auden. We need to get going." Paragon was ahead of me, but I couldn't take my eyes off the scene down below. Because out of Woolf's car came two more figures. Handcuffed and guarded.

Mum and Immaculata.

"Mum!"

"Auden! We don't have time!" Paragon called. "Please!"

I shook the image of my mother in handcuffs from my head and ran up to Paragon.

"They've brought Mum here," I said. "Why?"

"To trap you. They're hoping you'll rush back into her arms. It wouldn't surprise me if they gave her a loudspeaker and got her to plead with you to give yourself up."

As if on cue, Woolf's voice boomed through a megaphone.

"Auden Dare. This is General Woolf of the Second Infantry Division of the Water Allocation Board. You'll recall we met yesterday. I have somebody here who wants to talk some sense into you."

A pause as he handed the megaphone over to Mum.

"Auden?" Mum's voice was quaky. "Auden? If you're out there . . . please . . ."

I stopped where I was. Paragon stopped, too, and watched me.

"Mum."

"Auden." Paragon looked straight at me. His voice was quiet. "I need you to help me. Without you, I just can't do it."

I stood still and listened to Mum.

"Auden?" Mum continued. "If you can hear me . . . please . . . DO WHATEVER YOU NEED TO DO. DON'T COME BACK UNTIL YOU'VE DONE IT. I LOVE YOU. DO WHATEVER—"

Her voice disappeared as Woolf snatched the megaphone from her.

"Auden Dare! Give yourself up now. Return the robot to us. It is the property of the Water Allocation Board. Return it to us now and we will dismiss any charges. I repeat, return the robot to us NOW!"

I looked at Paragon, my heart pumping louder and stronger and more determined than ever. My mother wasn't broken by these people, so why should I be?

"Come on, Paragon. I don't know what it is we're doing . . . but let's do it."

Paragon probably smiled.

. . . .

The top of the Wandlebury Ring was hidden away from the breeze. We came out from the thick edging of trees and onto the deserted clearing.

"This will do," Paragon announced, dumping the rainbow machine down about twenty feet in from the path. He spun around and looked at the whole area. "You know, I'd almost forgotten what a beautiful place this is." He stared up at the birds that were swooping across the wide-open sky.

"Paragon," I said, aware of our lack of time, "what do we do?"

"First let's take the cover off."

"Okay."

We both knelt down either side and unclipped the tarpaulin. Paragon took it up and threw it roughly onto the ground nearby.

"Now what?"

Paragon walked around the machine until he was standing directly in front of me and put his hands on my shoulders.

"Audendare," he said, sort of sighing. "Auden Dare."

"What?"

" 'I have no life but this,

"To lead it here;

"Nor any death, but lest

"Dispelled from there;

"Nor tie to earths to come,

"Nor action new,

"Except through this extent,

"The realm of you.' "

"Don't tell me," I said, and grinned. "Emily Dickinson."

"Yep." Paragon laughed.

We both said nothing for a few seconds.

"What's happening?" I eventually asked.

Paragon seemed to pull himself together again.

"What's happening is that we both have an incredibly important job to do." He jumped around to the side of the machine and flipped up the compartment where the battery should have been. "In fact, *you* have the most important job of all."

"Do I?"

"Yes, you do. You see, you have to turn the machine on."

"Me? Why me?"

Paragon looked at me with his eyes in a dim glow. "Because it takes thirty seconds for the battery to be fully engaged. By that time I will have run down."

I shook my head. "What do you mean?"

Suddenly something happened to Paragon that I'd never seen before. The whole of his chest whirred and whizzed and opened up, peeling away from the center to his sides. Inside I could see a boxlike shape, lights flickering and dancing across it.

"The power source," I whispered.

"Yes," Paragon said softly. "We have to remove it from me and transfer it to the machine. When that happens I have residue power for approximately twenty-three seconds—not enough time to switch the machine on."

"But . . ." I was confused. "But we can put it back in you again, can't we? Someone can make another battery that we can give to you?"

Paragon said nothing.

"Please, Paragon." I strode back toward him. "We can put the battery back in your chest afterward, can't we?"

"No."

"What?"

"I said no."

"I don't understand."

Paragon reached up and rested his right hand on the side of my cheek.

"Auden. When Dr. Bloom designed me, he deliberately created a glitch."

"What glitch?"

"He built me so that, should my battery ever be removed, my entire system would shut down and all initialization programs would be obliterated."

"What does that mean?"

"It means I stop working." He lowered his hand. "Forever."

"No," I protested. "That's impossible. Someone can get you started again. Milo Treble, he can—"

"No. It won't work. You see, Dr. Bloom knew just how potentially dangerous I was. He knew that in the wrong hands—or even the right ones—I would be far too much of a risk."

I threw my arms around Paragon's metal body and rested my head against the blinking power source. "That's just stupid. You're not dangerous."

He held me tight and we both just stood there, swaying slightly in the warming air of late summer.

Below us, hundreds of men with guns were trying to find us. But for those few moments, neither of us cared. We were oblivious to all the danger around us.

Just a boy and a robot.

The clearing was silent and we held on to each other like we were both falling to Earth.

"Anyway," Paragon whispered into my hair, "all these weeks we've been wondering about my role. And now, this is it." I looked up into his eyes. "This is what I was designed for. To be here—right now—with you on top of this hill."

"But . . . rainbows? Why rainbows?"

"Oh, this machine doesn't make rainbows," he replied. "It's much more important than that."

"But I don't want you to go!"

"Aud—"

"I won't do it! I won't let you go. I'm not going to turn the machine on. And if I won't turn the machine on there's no point in you taking the battery out. You'll have to just be you forever."

"But when the Water Allocation Board gets hold of me—which it will—it won't let me be me forever. It'll have me stripped apart and reprogrammed within hours. I won't be Paragon then. I'll be something else. Something that won't even recognize you."

"Can't you just hide away? We could hide you—"

"It's no good. They'll still find me." He glanced around. "Please, Audendare. We don't have time for this."

"But—"

"You just have to trust me. You *do* trust me, don't you?"

"Of course. I trust you with my life. I've *always* trusted you."

"Then you must trust me on *this*. More than anything else. Believe me, this is the right thing to do."

"But—"

"Audendare." He pulled me away and looked me directly in the face. I suddenly realized that it was wet and sore with tears. "You have a hero for a father, and a mother who breaks the world in two to keep you healthy and happy. You have Sandwich to leap on your head and wake you up in the mornings. And you have the greatest friend in the universe in Vivi Rookmini." He tilted his head. "You don't really need me."

"Yes, I do! You've been there for me. You took care of me when I was at my lowest. You cared for me. You made me feel better about everything. I love you, Paragon."

"You're right, Audendare." He leaned in closer and hugged me again. "I *have* cared for you. I *do* care for you. In fact, I will *always* care for you. Just because I am not there doesn't mean that I stop caring for you."

"Then why do you have to go?"

"Because . . ." he started. "Because there are greater things than a silly old robot who can do magic tricks. There is hunger and war and disease and pain. There are people and their lives." He patted my back. "I may be full of use-less bits of old information, but there is one thing that I really, honestly, truly know. And that is that if you get a chance to do something good, then you should do it. Regardless of yourself." His hand rested on the back of my head again.

"I still don't want you to go," I mumbled.

"Well . . . I'm afraid it's tough!" he joked. "You're going to have to manage without me."

"Yeah. Like I can manage without you!"

Paragon nodded. "Sarcasm, Audendare?"

"No," I replied truthfully. "No, it's not."

Far off in the distance I could hear the shouting of soldiers.

"You know . . ." Paragon's voice became gentle again. "You've had a lot to cope with in your life. Your achro-matopsia. Your father going off to war. But you're still here. None of those things have actually stopped you. They might have tripped you up sometimes—like those sticky little moments of sarcasm—but, in fact, they haven't really stood in your way. The trick to life"—he did another of his cheeky winks—"is to struggle on and knock all the terrible stuff aside. Recognize the difficulties for what they are, and press on regardless. It's actually something you do rather well."

I said nothing. I just held on to this tall, wonderful, brilliant, and beautiful creature that had made me view everything from a different angle. It felt wrong to think that soon he would no longer be here. He felt so alive.

But I finally understood.

Paragon was doing precisely what he had been created to do. I still didn't know what it was, exactly, but getting the machine here and turning it on was what he had been—secretly—designed to do.

I had to stop being so selfish.

Paragon twitched a little. His head cocked at a strange angle like he was listening to something.

"They're getting nearer. We need to get on with it. Now."

We pulled apart and stood next to the machine.

"Okay, now," Paragon started. "It takes thirty seconds for the power source to fully engage. Once that's done you need to hit the on button. Don't hit the off button, whatever you do, because like me, Dr. Bloom designed it with a glitch. Hit the off button with the battery in place and you'll ruin the machine."

I looked at the front of the machine where the two large square buttons were located. It said nothing on either of them.

"Which one's on?"

"The green one."

I smiled and thought of Mum.

"The green one? Haven't you forgotten something, Paragon?"

"What? That you have achromatopsia and can't see color? No. Not at all."

"So how am I meant to know which one's green?"

"Oh, you'll know," Paragon said. "You see, there are some things that you just automatically know."

What did he mean?

Before I had time to argue with him, Paragon jumped onto another subject.

"One more thing, Audendare. When I do finally . . . come to a complete standstill, I want to be left here. Don't let them take me away—it won't do them any good anyway. Please. Tell them that I want to be left in this incredible place. It's the only thing I ask."

I couldn't believe what I was hearing. It was hard to take it all in. Within minutes Paragon was going to be out of my life—out of everybody's life—forever. How was I meant to deal with this? How was I meant to function knowing that pretty soon the most incredible person—yes, *person*—I had ever met was going to be . . . well . . . dead?

The truth was that I *didn't* know how to deal with it. It had never happened to me before. So I pushed on and tried to remain me.

Auden Dare, aged eleven.

"I promise I'll make them keep you here," I said, trying to keep my voice level. "I'll make sure, Paragon."

"Good." He nodded. "Thank you."

The sound of the soldiers got nearer.

"Quick," I said, taking control.

Paragon stood next to the machine.

"Remember," he whispered. "Thirty seconds, then hit

the on button. The entire process takes about two minutes after that. Whatever you do, do not let any of them turn the machine off for at least those two minutes. Once they see what's happening, I doubt you'll have any more problems from them. They'll be too amazed."

"Right."

"Okay, Audendare." Paragon kind of braced himself. "Let's do it."

The power source in Paragon's chest cavity slid out automatically a few inches. Paragon grasped either side of it and pulled it out and away from his body. He bent over the machine and gently slotted it into place. A soft push down and—

Click.

—it was in position.

"Okay. Thirty seconds. Then hit the button."

Paragon backed away from the machine.

"Well, this is it. Thank you, Audendare," he said as he moved slowly back. "Thank you for everything."

"Paragon!" I cried. "Paragon!" I couldn't move. I stood there and watched him ease away from me. "I'll never forget you, Paragon! I'll . . ." My voice was breaking up. "I'll always . . . dream about you."

"Good," he said. "Then it'll be my job to make sure you sleep peacefully."

With that, he turned slightly and raised his arms up into the air.

And then he started whistling.

High-pitched.

Like a bird.

Within seconds the first sparrow came and landed on his arm.

Through the fog of my tears I found myself laughing.

"Hello, little one," Paragon said, and then laughed himself.

He whistled again and two more sparrows came and landed on his arms.

" 'Hope is the thing with feathers,' " Paragon began.

" 'That perches in the soul.' "

"I love you, Paragon," I whispered under my breath.

His head turned slightly toward me. "I love you, too, Aud—"

And suddenly the light in his eyes died and he was gone.

....

Far over on the other side of the clearing something moved. I wiped the tears from my own eyes and tried to focus.

It was a soldier. Then another. Then a whole load more.

I had to do it quickly. Soon they would see that Paragon had stopped moving and they would rush me.

I squatted down by the buttons and stared at them.

There are some things that you just automatically know. That's what he said. What did he mean?

The adrenaline pumped through my body. I had no time to grieve for Paragon. I had to finish what he'd started. I owed it to him.

There are some things that you just automatically know.

I thought hard. The line sounded familiar. Paragon had said that before. But when? When?

Then it came to me.

It was when he was explaining my sense of disappointment with my father.

Consider the order of things, Paragon had said. *We always say "Left. Right." The "Left" comes before the "Right." Or on a form, you will see the options "Yes/No." It is never "No/Yes." Similarly, "Up/Down" and "On/Off."*

That was it!

ON/OFF. LEFT/RIGHT.

The green button was the one on the left. It wouldn't make any sense for it to be the one on the right.

I punched the button solidly and the machine began to make a sort of fizzing noise. The noise got louder and louder until I couldn't hide behind the machine anymore. I took a couple of steps back from it and watched as something started to swirl out of the funnel toward the front of the machine. It swirled up and up, getting bigger all the time. It reminded me of something.

A tornado.

I had seen old films of tornadoes racing across the flatlands of the USA. Huge, destructive, and dangerous. Ripping up houses and tossing cars aside like they were nothing but paper.

But this tornadolike thing was more controlled. Less scary. It kept itself centered around the funnel and tiny flecks of sparkles glinted in the sunlight as it spun around.

Up and up it went, widening at the top as it rose.

It grew beyond the tips of the trees and stretched out into the sky.

The birds that perched on Paragon got scared and flew off. All except one that dived into Paragon's chest and took shelter.

Suddenly there was the hurried stamp of boots and I turned to see three soldiers racing toward me.

There was no way I was going to let them turn this machine off. Two minutes, Paragon had said, and for that entire two minutes I was prepared to fight. I put myself between the men and the machine and clenched my fists, ready to defend Paragon's legacy.

It would have looked pretty strange to onlookers. Three massive, heavily muscled, fully grown men armed with guns hurtling toward an eleven-year-old boy with a tear in his trouser leg, but I didn't care. I was prepared to do all I could to make this thing happen.

"No!" a voice from the main cluster of soldiers screamed. "Stand down! Everyone . . . stand down."

I looked beyond the three soldiers and could make out the outline of General Woolf. His eyes were fixed on the swirling shape that was reaching up into the sky above.

"I repeat! All men stand down!"

The soldiers stopped about fifteen feet away from me, noticing the tornado for the very first time.

Everyone was watching it.

It whirled upward until it virtually filled the sky about the Wandlebury Ring.

And then it started to pull the clouds in.

All the passing scraps of cloud were pulled toward the vast top of the tornado, dragged like a piece of soap toward a plughole. They came together and stuck to each other, forming an even bigger cloud.

Within seconds the cloud that was being created covered the sky above us, and as more and more small clouds were sucked in, it started to turn dark. Thick, powerful, and black. I had never seen a cloud like it before.

Tap.

I looked over to Paragon's arm. A droplet of water ran down the side of his forearm and dripped onto the dry ground.

Tap. Tap.

Two more blobs of water appeared on the top of the machine.

Tap. Tap. Tap. Tap. Tap.

Rain!

It was starting to rain!

I ran around to the front of the machine and looked at the chalk marks that Vivi and I had spotted all those weeks ago. A bead of water streaked through the middle of the letters, but I could still clearly see them.

Ra
Machi

It wasn't a rainbow machine at all. It was a *rain* machine. Uncle Jonah had created a rain machine!

Suddenly the cloud struggled to hold on to its weight and the rain came down in a torrential downpour. I had never known rain like it. It flattened the pathetic tufts of grass and soaked through my clothes in what felt like nanoseconds. The whole clearing was a hazy blur of rain.

I turned toward the dozens and dozens of soldiers that had started to make their way toward me. Some of them had thrown their weapons to the ground and were dancing in the cloudburst. Others had dug their water canisters out and were holding them up to the sky, hoping to refill them.

In the middle of the soldiers I could see General Woolf, holding his head up to the rain and feeling it running down over his face.

And next to him—each of them handcuffed—stood Mum, then Treble, Immaculata, and Vivi. All of them drenched to the skin.

I smiled at Vivi and she gave an awkward handcuffed wave back.

Woolf noticed and barked an order at a soldier who quickly removed the cuffs from all four of them. Woolf turned to me and nodded—a nod of appreciation and of understanding—before putting his face back up to the sky.

I held my hands out in front of me, the water collecting in my palms, my fingers cold and white.

Dr. Jonah Bloom—Uncle Jonah—*my* uncle—had made something that was going to change the world. A machine that could make rain.

He had also made something that had changed *me*.

I looked at Paragon, silent and still, his arms in the air like he was feeling the rain for the very first time.

EPILOGUE

THE RAINBOW

It took another year for the wars to stop. The world seems to work so slowly sometimes. Nothing important is ever rushed. So by the time the rain machine was accepted by the authorities, followed by the months and months of mass production and distribution, some of the more remote parts of the world were not getting water until about a year and a half after the incidents on the Wandlebury Ring.

Eventually, though, the machines were everywhere. From the tops of mountains to dry, flat plains. From tiny, isolated farming villages to the centers of sprawling, bustling cities.

"Phenomenal," Treble had said after being involved with the initial inspections of the machine. "Silver oxide particles and an intense negative ion generator coupled with what

I've termed the Cumulative Cumulus Device." He shuffled. "As difficult as it is to admit, I have to say that Bloom was an *utter* genius."

That was confirmed the following year when Uncle Jonah posthumously won the Geneva Prize for Scientific Advancement.

....

After it had all happened, Dr. Milo Treble started spending an awful lot of time around at Vivi and Immaculata's rooms in Trinity.

"He keeps bringing Mum flowers," Vivi said, giving her head a little shake. "The thing is, she's started making dresses for herself. And she washes her hair more." Vivi fiddled with the ponytail in her own dark hair. "If you ask me, it's weird."

We made our way up the stone steps and Vivi pushed the big wooden door open.

"Ah, Auden."

It was Treble.

He was sitting on the sofa alongside Immaculata, Migishoo perched on the mantelpiece.

"Dr. Treble. Mrs. Rookmini." I nodded.

"Hello, Auden." Immaculata smiled.

"Am I pleased to see you," Treble said, and leaped up off the sofa. "I've got something that I want to show you."

He dug into the back pocket of his jeans and fished out a little wooden box.

"Here."

I took it from him.

"What is it?"

"Open it and see."

I clicked the tiny latch on the box and flicked it open. Inside was a curved piece of plastic a few centimeters long.

I still didn't know what it was.

"I call it the Optiborg. It's my latest invention and—with a bit of skill and luck—my entry for next year's Geneva Prize."

"What does it do?"

"Clip it behind your right ear and see."

I took the thing from out of the box and pushed it behind my ear.

"Now. Look at . . ." He leaned over and picked up an apple from a bowl on Immaculata's sewing table. "This."

I looked at the apple. Suddenly a really high-pitched noise screeched into my head.

"Ow!"

"That's a red apple." He put the apple back onto the table and picked up a pear. "Now look at this."

I stared and the Optiborg screeched again, this time with a slightly lower note.

"That's a green pear." He tossed the pear back into the bowl and picked up another apple. "Right. You ready, Auden? Tell me what color *this* apple is."

I looked at the apple. The thing behind my ear squealed, again with a lower note.

"Green," I said.

"Correct!" Treble laughed, picking up the first apple

again. "You can tell the difference. Green apple." He held it up and the sound was low. "Red apple." He held *that* one up and the sound was high. "Green, red, green, red."

"That's . . . that's . . ." I didn't know what to say.

"*Genius* I think is the word you are looking for!" Treble cried. "Try a different color. Here—" He picked up a piece of fabric from the table. "This is blue."

I stared at the fabric and an even lower note sounded.

"And this . . ." Treble was excited by his own invention. "This is also blue but . . . tell me . . . is it a lighter blue or a darker blue than the first piece?" He lifted another section of cloth. The Optiborg whined with a slightly higher note.

"Lighter," I said. "It's lighter."

"Ha!" Treble jumped up in delight.

"This is incredible." I moved around listening to the different pitches of the objects in the room. "Absolutely incredible."

"With practice," Treble chattered on as Immaculata went and prepared some sandwiches in the sectioned-off kitchen. "By experimenting, anybody with achromatopsia would be able to distinguish the subtleties of color within a matter of weeks."

"It's amazing," I said, pulling the Optiborg from behind my ear. "You deserve to win the Geneva Prize with it." I held it out to Treble, who shook his head.

"No, Auden. It's yours."

"Mine?"

"To keep. Don't worry, I've made a couple of them."

"Really?" I didn't know what to say. "Thank you."

"Don't thank me." He suddenly looked sad. "You know, I wasn't the greatest of friends to your uncle in the months before he died. There were so many things I should have done and said, but I didn't because of my stupid professional pride. If I hadn't been so self-absorbed . . . well . . . I might not have been able to prevent Jonah Bloom's death, but I'd certainly feel a lot better about things knowing that he'd died as a friend."

And in that moment I could see all the pain that had burrowed away at him. All the wondering "what if" and "why." Here was somebody else for whom life had changed due to Uncle Jonah's death.

"I think he would be pleased," I said, clutching the Optiborg. "I think it would have made him happy to know that you were trying to help me." I smiled. "Thank you, Dr. Treble."

Treble seemed to straighten up, and his shoulders puffed.

"That's quite all right, Auden. My pleasure. Unfortunately, it is absolutely impossible for you to ever *see* color. But at least now you can *hear* it."

....

"It is said that the stars are different colors."

Vivi was on her bed staring through the skyspace at the clear night sky. I was back on the floor, turning the Optiborg over in my fingers. It was a tiny thing, yet so powerful.

"Hmm? What did you say?"

Vivi sighed. "Do you ever *listen*, Auden?"

"To you? Only when I'm forced to."

She threw a pillow down and hit me directly in the face.

"Hey!" I laughed.

"Then listen!" She pretended to be annoyed. "I said that people think the stars are different colors. That they're not all silvery—they just appear that way. They might actually be blue or green or red."

I sat up.

"We could find out," I said.

"How?"

I wiggled the Optiborg around in the air. "With this."

Vivi scrambled from her bed and quickly popped the lens cover off the telescope. Her excitement had a similar feel to Treble's excitement as he showed me the Optiborg for the first time.

"Come on. Let's see."

I slipped the small device behind my ear and waited for Vivi to point the telescope in the right direction and twiddle with the focusing.

"There!" She stood back and I stooped to look.

What I heard made my breath stop.

It was like an orchestra in my head. Big booming bass notes resounded and fell beneath midrange melodies that swept up and down like violins. Piccolo-type squeaks and the pulsing notes of flutes rolled in and out of the beautiful, elegant noise that the heavens above were making.

"Wow" was all I could say.

I stayed there for what seemed like ages, just staring and listening.

When I did eventually pull myself away from the telescope, Vivi raised her eyebrows at me. "Well?"

"It's . . . unbelievable."

"You're crying," she said.

....

The rain eased off as the Bot Job shuddered to a stop just outside the prison gates.

"Any chance it'll ever start up again and get us home?" I asked as we both got out of the car.

"This car is held together with nothing more than wishful thinking," Mum replied. "So just keep your fingers crossed and, perhaps, pray a bit."

We went over the road and waited directly opposite the gates.

"What's the time?" Mum asked nervously.

I glanced at my QWERTY. "Couple of minutes to ten."

"Nearly ten," she told herself, pulling her coat tighter. "Oh, look." She pointed to somewhere above the tall, solid stone Victorian walls of the prison. "A rainbow."

I looked up. I could see the dull, gray arc in the sky, slightly darker at the bottom than at the top.

It was tempting to reach into my jacket pocket to pull out the Optiborg. But I didn't. Not today. Today there was something I wanted to see so much more than a rainbow.

"He's coming!" Mum reached over and grasped my arm.

The smaller door, built into the massive arch-shaped metal one, swung open and out stepped a blond-haired man carrying a rucksack—a man who had recently been granted a pardon by the government, no less. He reached back and shook the hand of someone inside.

" 'Hope is the thing with feathers,' " I sang to myself.

"What's that?" Mum asked, never taking her eyes off the man at the door.

"Emily Dickinson," I answered.

"A new friend of yours?"

I smiled. "You could say that, yeah."

The door to the prison closed as my dad—my hero dad—turned toward us and sprinted across the road, his strong, warm arms outstretched.

....

Vivi and I visited Paragon regularly. We would walk out from the city into the green fields and make our way to Wandlebury, where we would follow the winding path up to the Wandlebury Ring.

When the authorities threatened to take Paragon away, I shouted and screamed and made a magnificent fuss. Dr. Treble pulled strings within the scientific community, and Mum and Immaculata went to the newspapers. Even General Woolf himself made the case for Paragon staying where he was as a monument to the bravery of children. So, after a while, the Water Allocation Board relented.

"Hello, Paragon," I would say when I stepped out of the

clearing. Of course, he wouldn't answer. He would remain in exactly the same position as ever—arms held out to the sky, his face turned to where I once stood, the grass now thick and luscious at his feet.

And I couldn't ever touch him. To protect Paragon, the WAB had placed an electric fence around him with razor wire at the top. Which sounds like a bad thing, but it wasn't really. It meant that the family of sparrows that had nested within his chest were safe and free to feel warm and wanted.

Paragon would have been delighted.

Sometimes I would stand roughly where I stood the moment the lights in his eyes died, and it would seem like he was looking straight at me. Other times Vivi and I would run around, or kick a ball, or sketch the trees, or read some thick, tedious book that Vivi found fascinating. And it would be like he was there. Watching over us.

Protecting us.

At night I would sleep deeply with Sandwich on my bed. Soundly and peacefully like Paragon promised. Safe and warm like the sparrows undoubtedly were. And I know that they say nobody ever dreams in color, but sometimes—just sometimes—I swear I do.

Thank you for reading this Feiwel and Friends book.

The Friends who made

THE EXTRAORDINARY COLORS OF AUDEN DARE

possible are:

JEAN FEIWEL, Publisher

LIZ SZABLA, Associate Publisher

RICH DEAS, Senior Creative Director

HOLLY WEST, Editor

ANNA ROBERTO, Editor

CHRISTINE BARCELLONA, Editor

KAT BRZOZOWSKI, Editor

ALEXEI ESIKOFF, Senior Managing Editor

KIM WAYMER, Senior Production Manager

ANNA POON, Assistant Editor

EMILY SETTLE, Assistant Editor

REBECCA SYRACUSE, Associate Designer

ILANA WORRELL, Production Editor

Follow us on Facebook or visit us online at mackids.com.
OUR BOOKS ARE FRIENDS FOR LIFE.